THE MARSHAL AND THE MADWOMAN

By the Same Author

The Marshal and the Murderer
Death in Autumn
Death in Springtime
Death of a Dutchman
Death of an Englishman

THE MARSHAL AND THE MADWOMAN

MAGDALEN NABB

A Marshal Guarnaccia Mystery

CHARLES SCRIBNER'S SONS

New York

For the Master of Equilibrium who did so much to to maintain mine whilst this work was in progress.

Charles Scribner's Sons
Macmillan Publishing Company
866 Third Avenue, New York, NY 10022

Library of Congress Cataloging-in-Publication Data

Nabb, Magdalen, 1947–
The marshal and the madwoman / Magdalen Nabb.—1st American ed.
p. cm.
ISBN 0-684-18984-4
I. Title.
PR6064.A18M29 1988 88-9636
823'.914—dc19 CIP

First American Edition

Printed in the United States of America

CHAPTER 1

In spite of themselves they paused at the edge of the stone kerb. There wasn't a car in sight, not even the distant sound of an engine, but the gesture was automatic, so much so that they even hesitated before stepping into the empty narrow road, disorientated by having nothing to battle against. If they had wanted to they could have walked down the centre of it, but the overpowering heat of Florence in August kept them close to the buildings within the strip of shade offered by the eaves high above.

'Taken all in all,' Marshal Guarnaccia said, once they'd strolled across, 'there's a lot to be said for it. I'm glad we decided as we did.'

The Marshal and his wife had taken their holidays in July, travelling down to their home town in the province of Syracuse with their two little boys and afterwards leaving the boys there with the Marshal's sister for the month of August when he had to be back in charge of his station in the Pitti Palace. Now it was early afternoon, siesta-time, and at this hour more than any other they sometimes felt like the only two people left in the city.

'It'll be cooler if we cut through here.'

They entered a gloomy alleyway so narrow that the sun never penetrated it. Their footsteps echoed.

'If only there were a few more shops open . . .' the Marshal's wife murmured.

'We've managed all right up to now.'

'*I've* managed, you mean. Yesterday I had to walk right across the city to find a butcher's and they say it's bound to get worse after the fifteenth when the few people who've stayed open until now are sure to shut.'

'We'll eat out more often, like we did today. I enjoyed it.'

'Today's your day off. We can't go round looking for an open restaurant when you're on duty.'

'That's true.'

'Apart from the expense. Mark my words, the only places that will stay open are those after the tourist trade. Bad food at top prices. No, no. We'll manage. They say the paper's going to list the shops that are open in each Quarter. Besides, I've still some preserves left. It's not as though we have to eat meat every day. People managed during the war.'

'Aren't you exaggerating a bit?'

'It's no joke to trail round the streets when it's a hundred and odd in the shade looking for an open shop—not to mention carrying the stuff home from miles away.'

'If you'd learn to drive—'

'We've been through all that. The traffic in this city's a one-way nightmare, and as for the ring roads! I'd die of fright at my age.'

'Not now, though.'

'What do you mean, not now?'

'The traffic. There isn't any.'

'That's true . . .'

They came out, blinking, into a main street where a blast of heat enveloped them and put a stop to their conversation. They'd reached the top of the sloping forecourt in front of the Pitti Palace and were turning left to go through the big iron gates before she said again, 'It's true. I hadn't thought . . .'

Their own little Fiat was parked alongside the squad car and van.

'Even so, at my age . . . And who'd teach me? These schools cost a fortune.'

'Salva!'

'Mm.'

'Say something—or do something!'

The Marshal blinked and looked about him from behind his sunglasses.

'Just take your time,' he suggested after waiting a bit.

'And don't keep saying take your time—can you imagine what it would be like on a normal day with a queue a mile long behind me, hooting, and the traffic policeman marching up to me blowing his whistle? The entire city would have been choked to a standstill by this time and everybody blaming me. If only it weren't so hot! I'm melting into the seat. I told you we should have waited until it got cooler.'

'It gets dark,' the Marshal said reasonably, 'before it gets cool.'

'I'm not driving in the dark, and that's that.'

'No.'

'Now, I'm in gear. Am I? I am. Clutch—no, handbrake. I should have looked in the mirror but—it's going—no. Salva, for God's sake!'

'Have a bit of patience.'

'Patience! Anybody would lose patience with you, sitting there like a great lump of stone with your hands planted on your knees. You might be watching television. How can you teach me to drive if you don't speak? I've been stalling at this junction for the last half hour—it's going!'

'I think you'd better stop.'

'And go through all that again? I shan't stop again until we get home if I can help it.'

'Well . . . Via Romana's one way. Stop and back up. You were supposed to turn right.'

'What? Why didn't you say? The brake . . . If I'd hit anything—you'll have us both killed.'

'Just back up a bit.'

'I would if I could find . . . There's a car coming towards me! Salva!'

'He'll wait.'

'We'll be killed. This is not reverse. If anything happens to us, the children—Now he's backing up and I don't blame him. If you'd help me instead of sitting there—there we are. Now, how do I steer backwards? I wish I'd never got into this. You're impossible! If anybody sees us I'll die of shame. Now I can go down here—or can I? The indicator, I didn't remember the—Well, it's too late now. You might have said something. He's following me. Why is he following me? Do you think he's annoyed?'

'I expect this is the way he wants to go.'

'Well, I'm not going any faster. Should I?'

'Do as you like.'

'And don't tell me to take my time. It's true what they say, that husbands shouldn't teach their wives to drive. They haven't the same patience a stranger would have. They always lose their tempers. He's still behind me.'

'Don't worry.'

'Don't worry? This was all your idea, remember that. Learning to drive is for young people. A woman of my age with children to think about can't—Salva, look at all those people in the road! What am I going to do? I'll have to stop —I'm stopping. I can't park, you know, you'll have to do it if they don't move. Isn't that one of your squad cars? Where are you going? Don't leave me here!'

'Wait for me.'

The Marshal got out, extricating his big body from the small Fiat with difficulty. They were at a crossroads and the tail end of a car jutting out from the narrow road to the right was indeed one of the squad cars from his Station. The Marshal pushed his way through the noisy crowd and tapped at the driver's window. His young brigadier, Lorenzini, was inside, talking into the radio. When he looked up and saw the Marshal's big eyes staring in at him from behind sunglasses he wound down the window.

'How did you get here so quickly? I was just calling in.'

'What's going on?'

'Nothing serious, just two neighbours quarrelling.'

'But the whole street's out here!'

'I know. Bruno's trying to quieten things down.'

'I didn't think there were this many people left in Florence.'

'Just as well there's no traffic. I don't think Bruno's getting very far. He's too young to have much authority, and anyway, they don't care much for police interference in this area.'

'Why call us in, then?'

'They didn't. We were just passing on patrol and found the street blocked.'

The Marshal straightened up. 'Leave them to it, it'll soon blow over.'

Lorenzini poked his head out. The noise level was rising and young Bruno was invisible among the jostling crowd.

'It's a bit difficult. It'll look bad now if we don't clear the street—and then that woman's stark naked which is what's causing more than half the trouble . . .'

'What?'

'She's not all there.' Lorenzini tapped his head.

'Where is she?'

'Up there.'

'Good grief . . .' The Marshal pushed his way forward towards a building fronted by scaffolding, the lower part of which was screened by green netting.

'Let me through.'

No one took much notice, neither stepping back for him nor preventing him from pushing past them. He wasn't in uniform and none of them knew or cared who he was since he wasn't one of them. He couldn't see Bruno and he noticed that the women were doing most of the shouting. A group of men in shirtsleeves stood around the door of the house under scaffolding and one of them was hammering on it with his fists.

'You fuck off!' screamed a hysterical voice from above. 'Leave me alone!'

'You should be ashamed of yourself using language like

that!' bellowed a stocky little woman who was digging her elbow into the Marshal's stomach, 'and cover yourself up, for goodness' sake!'

The Marshal was staring up with the rest of them. The window of the second-floor flat, though not large, reached down to floor level with a small railing along the bottom of it. The woman standing up there, obviously the one Lorenzini said wasn't right in the head, was waving a defiant pink fist, sometimes at the crowd below, but mostly at the window opposite which, in such a narrow street, was only a few feet away. She wasn't entirely naked since she had some sort of house frock or overall on, but it was unfastened and swung back so that her fat pink body was displayed as unconsciously as if she had been a two-year-old in a tantrum.

'Pack it in, Clementina! Close your shutters and let's have some peace round here.'

The crazy woman did at one point reach out for the peeling brown shutters and slam them towards herself, only to throw them open again so as to launch another volley of abuse.

It was impossible to tell what the quarrel was about, and the woman opposite, whose voice was even more raucous than the crazy woman's, was only partially visible since her window was smaller. Perhaps she was deliberately remaining hidden, because a good many of the people below were getting more furious with her than with her opponent.

'You're making her worse, leave her alone!'

A dark head poked out over the sill and the Marshal saw a glint of spectacles and a face red with anger.

'She should be locked up—I've put up with more than I can stand! And whoever's ringing at my door can stop it because I'm not opening up!'

The Marshal twisted round and tried to push across to the door opposite to see if it might be young Bruno who was ringing her bell, but his way was blocked by the broad back of a man taller than himself. He heard a furious voice say, 'Who the hell called the Carabinieri?'

'God knows . . .'

Another concerted appeal was made to the madwoman to cover herself up and produced another stream of foul language which had the same air of innocent defiance as the woman's childlike nakedness.

Although the pushing and shouting was getting worse and the heat was obviously contributing to everybody's irritation, the Marshal knew that there was no real danger, recognizing that the whole thing was a ritualized regular occurrence and would end when everybody got bored with it. Unfortunately, a man's voice in front of him then shouted up to the bespectacled woman, telling her to let the poor mad creature be and not to be such a bitch.

Then another voice said, 'That's my wife you're calling a bitch.' And when the Marshal turned round to see who it was somebody hit him in the eye.

'Cold water's the only thing, just hold it there. You'll have a nice black eye, though. I'll make you a coffee.'

The Marshal's rescuer was the huge man who had blocked his view and who turned out to be the proprietor of the bar on the corner across the square from the house where the trouble had been. He'd brought the still dazed Marshal inside and sat him down at a brown formica table to get his wits back. The Marshal said nothing but held the cold compress to one of his large, rather bulging eyes which was swelling perceptibly. It was lucky the blow had knocked off his sunglasses rather than breaking them or things would have been much worse.

Everyone else was outside where a few more tables were arranged in the road. They were celebrating the end of the quarrel or consoling themselves for the end of that day's entertainment, but their conversation was drowned by the noise of the television that was switched on in the bar, though nobody was watching it. The few people other than the Marshal who had taken refuge from the heat were playing pinball. The air was thick with their cigarette smoke.

'Here's your coffee. How are you feeling now?'

'I'll be all right.'

'How did you come to be mixed up in it? You don't live round here.'

The Marshal told him who he was.

'Sorry. Well, you're not in uniform so . . . I can't imagine who called you in.'

'Nobody did. My lads were just passing.'

'They'd have done better to carry on.'

'The road was blocked.'

'That's right. Well, these things happen. No harm done—sorry, I shouldn't have said that. It's a pity you got bumped into like that. It was an accident, of course.'

'Of course.' There didn't seem to be much point in pursuing the matter since he hadn't seen where the fist came from and it was meant for someone else, anyway.

A cackle of female laughter broke into the men's conversation outside. All the other women had disappeared indoors but the crazy woman, having got herself dressed but still wearing bedroom slippers, had come down to the bar and was being teased by the men outside.

'Give us a kiss, come on!'

'You keep your hands to yourself.' For some reason she was carrying a sweeping brush and she raised it threateningly.

'Go on, give us a kiss.'

The big barman had sat himself down beside the Marshal.

'She's not all there,' he explained. 'Poor soul. They go too far tormenting her but the trouble is she eggs them on. She likes the attention.'

'What was the fight about?'

'Pigeons, same as usual.'

'Pigeons?'

'She feeds them. Right there at the corner under Maria Pia's window and they leave their droppings all over her little balcony and her plants and her washing. There are hundreds of them.'

'And is that all?'

'More or less, only one thing led to another. It was Maria Pia's turn to give Clementina some dinner and she'd given her a bowl of minestrone. Then, when they started quarrelling over the pigeon business, Clementina threw the bowl out of the window and smashed it—oh Lord, somebody's blocked the No. 15 bus again.'

A horn was sounding repeatedly out in the road.

'It must take years off a man's life driving a bus in this city,' commented the barman, 'what with narrow streets and people parking in the middle of them, though there's little enough traffic today, I'd have thought—where are you going?'

The Marshal had jumped to his feet with surprising agility for one so heavy and the cold compress had fallen to the floor.

'My wife . . .'

She was in tears. He drove the car home himself, so she was able to give her full attention to telling him what she thought of him. By the time they were half way home she'd finished and fell silent, except for an occasional sniff followed by an application of the handkerchief. As they came up Via Romana, where every shutter was down and the street deserted, he risked opening his mouth:

'The shops were all open back there, did you notice?'

The hot weather continued unbroken, despite the weather forecasters who predicted a storm. There were storms all right, but only in the north, and for three nights in a row, the Marshal and his wife, watching the news over their supper, saw waterlogged fields, and cities brought to a standstill by the downpour with deep water swirling around abandoned cars. In Florence, not a cloud appeared in the sky. The hot air got heavier and steamier as though the sun itself were sweating at its efforts, and the heat shimmering from the stones of all the great palaces combined with the sweltering glare to distort the vision of anyone foolish enough to go out without sunglasses. The Marshal, whose eyes were allergic to sunlight—it made them stream with tears—never went out without dark glasses. He rarely went out at all, but stayed put in his office at the Pitti Palace Carabinieri Station dealing with dull paperwork, drinking too much mineral water which only made him sweat more, and changing his khaki uniform two or three times a day.

On August 14th, the eve of the national holiday of the Assumption, the temperature rose even higher. The news no longer showed floods in the north but overcrowded beaches and aerial views of the sea's edge thickly dotted with heads. The ferries, as usual, had gone on strike at the busiest period and distraught families were interviewed sweating in their cars as they queued for hours, or even days, under the burning sun, their children quarrelling and whining in the back seat.

'What's the use of turning back now?' shouted one red-faced driver into the microphone. 'We've booked a hotel for two weeks in Sardinia. Fifteen hours we've been sitting here, and if you want to know what I think of the strikers they're—' The interview was cut short before the word could go out on the air, and they were shown a deserted square in the centre of Rome. A lone car crossed it and stopped for the cameras.

'How do you survive in Rome in August?'

'With difficulty, but I'm managing fairly well. The wife and kids are in the mountains so I've only myself to think about. I can usually find a restaurant open if I drive round for a bit.'

'Tomorrow's the fifteenth. Will you find one open then?'

'I doubt it, but I've filled the house with tinned stuff from the supermarket.'

'You sound as if you're enjoying yourself.'

'Well, look around you! Some days I drive all over the city at top speed and park in five or six places just for the hell of it. After struggling with the traffic in this city all year, this is a real holiday.'

The Marshal was reminded of his first years in Florence when his wife had been obliged to stay down south with the boys because his old mother was too sick to be left or moved. It might be fun to be a grass widower for a month but not for years.

Even the film that came on after the news took up the same theme, as a famous comedian played the part of a husband left alone in the deserted city with dust sheets on the furniture and a stock of tins in the larder. Like the man on the news, he was having a glorious time on his own and soon fell in love with a pretty young tourist who was just longing to learn Italian. Each time the man's wife telephoned from the mountains he would put on a tragic face and moan, with a sob in his voice, 'If you knew how lonely it gets, sitting in an empty flat night after night, you wouldn't leave me like this . . .' Then the sorrowful look would melt into a grin as he rushed from room to room, spraying himself with perfume, smoothing the bed and waiting for the doorbell to ring.

The Marshal and his wife had seen the film more than once since it was shown practically every summer, but they watched it, even so, because they liked the comedian. When the film finished and the adverts came on, the Marshal's wife went in the kitchen to finish washing up, leaving him in the darkened living-room where the only light, apart from a small table lamp, came from the flickering images. When the telephone rang, it was she who went to switch the light on in the hall and answer it, her felt slippers making only the faintest swish on the polished marble floor. He went on looking at the television, slightly disturbed by the crack of bright light from the door into the hall and hoping it wasn't the lads on duty ringing through to his quarters because something had happened.

But when he heard her say, 'You'll have to speak up . . . that's better . . . How are they?' his shoulders settled back imperceptibly against the settee. Without bothering to listen further, he knew that it was his sister reporting on the boys as she did about once a week, telephoning at night because it was cheaper.

The late news came on and the Marshal reflected, as he was shown the crowded beach scene yet again, that the criminal population was off at the seaside along with the rest, and that working in August in the city had the advantage, in his job, of there not being anything much to do. He hardly need have worried about that call being for him. He hadn't been called out at night since the end of June, and that had turned out to be a false alarm.

Nevertheless, the telephone and the light had dispelled his somnolent tranquillity, so he heaved himself up and went to switch on the mosquito-killer in the bedroom.

'Salva!'

'What is it?'

'While you're in there, switch the mosquito-killer on.'

'I did.'

He appeared in the kitchen. 'What are you making?'

'Camomile tea. I've got a bit of a headache, it'll help me to sleep. Did you switch the machine on?'

'Mm.'

'If you wait until we go to bed there's always one manages to get me before it dies.'

'What did Nunziata say?'

'The boys are all right. I only hope they're behaving. It's far too tiring for her.'

'Did she say so?'

'Of course she didn't say so, but I know what a handful

they can be and she's had none of her own so she isn't used to it. Do you want anything?'

'No. I bet she's enjoying herself. Are you coming to bed?'

'In a few minutes. When the machine's had time to work. I'll drink this first.'

When she came through to the bedroom the air was heavily perfumed by the mosquito-killer and he was already in bed, yawning and rubbing a big hand over his face.

'I'm tired, I must say.'

'It's this heat, it's wearying. I'm sure that's what's giving me these headaches.'

'At least that call wasn't for me. I thought for a minute it was the duty room.'

'At this time of night?' She had been married fifteen years, but so much of their time had been spent apart that although she was accustomed to the simpler facts of army life like uniforms and living in barracks, his occasional irritation with his captain and incessant worry about the National Service kids, anything that disturbed their daily routine like unexpected calls at night or his involvement in some serious criminal case caused her both surprise and alarm.

So it was fortunate for her that when a call did come for the Marshal at almost three in the morning, the boy on duty did not think fit to disturb him and redirected the call to Headquarters in Borgo Ognissanti on the other side of the river. The two of them slept through the hot night, only stirring in discomfort now and then when even the thin white sheet seemed an unbearable weight.

Would it have made any difference if the boy on duty had woken him? It was a question the Marshal was to ask himself more than once in the ensuing days. His feeling was that it probably wouldn't have made any difference at all. He wouldn't have got out of bed and gone round there. He'd have reacted just as the boy had. And, to give the lad his due, he had called Headquarters himself and got a patrol car to take a look. They'd reported everything quiet. So no one was to blame. Nevertheless, if the Marshal kept on repeating to the lad, 'Don't worry, you did your duty and you couldn't have known . . .' perhaps he was really saying it to himself.

At any rate, nobody knew that anything was really amiss until the following evening, and so the Marshal got a good night's sleep and woke up in a cheerful mood to the sound of church bells. In the kitchen, the window was open, the coffee was bubbling up and there was a warm smell of brioches with jam baked in them, his favourite.

'How did you manage that? Don't tell me there's a baker open this morning?'

'I bought them yesterday and kept them in a damp cloth. Five minutes in the oven and they might be freshly baked. I thought we might as well have a treat for the holiday, even if you are working.'

'There won't be much work to do.'

He was to remember that remark later, and the sweet, almost cloying scent of the brioches which was to cling on throughout the case because of the amount of time he was to spend in the bar where he had sat with a compress on his eye yesterday. In the meantime, he enjoyed a leisurely breakfast in the kitchen, appreciating the light from the open window. The windows were still open in the sitting-room, too, and the sunshine filtered in through white muslin curtains. Even so, the rectangles of light on the floor beneath were already warm. By ten o'clock the shutters would have to be closed against the heat and the house would be in darkness for the rest of the day.

'Are we having something special for lunch, too?'

'Roast rabbit.'

He wouldn't have minded settling down in an armchair with an extra cup of coffee, perhaps because those warm patches of sunlight and the church bells ringing all over the city made such a relaxed Sunday atmosphere. But he looked at his watch and went back in the bedroom to get his uniform jacket.

When he went through to his office, it was Di Nuccio, on day duty, who greeted him with a cheery good morning. The night duty boys had gone off to sleep and the morning passed like any other, except that there was even less to do than usual. He read the night report which mentioned a call about a disturbance which had been referred to Borgo Ognissanti and resulted in a false alarm.

By midday, although he'd taken off his jacket before sitting down at his desk, the sweat was making his uniform stick to his body and he was glad enough to leave the remains of the dull paperwork that never seemed to diminish much, though he'd done little else recently, and go to look in on the boys in the duty room. Only Di Nuccio was there. He had his sleeves rolled up but he, too, had a large patch of sweat under each arm and a bigger patch between the shoulder-blades.

'You by yourself?'

'The lad's gone up to start the lunch.'

One of the boys on duty was responsible for shopping and cooking for the others. A constant complaint of the regulars about National Service boys was that, having never left their mothers before, they couldn't cook. Sodden spaghetti with sour, burnt tomato sauce could create an inordinate amount of ill-feeling in barracks, especially of an evening when the lads had nothing better to look forward to than a good plate of pasta in front of the TV in their little kitchen-cum-common-room. In this case, though, the problem boy was a newly enlisted regular. His first efforts had resulted in a sort of soup made of pasta disintegrated in its water and a sinister-looking brownish sauce obtained by burning the contents of a tin of peeled tomatoes. They'd had to throw away the pan. The Marshal, who had been obliged to survive on his own cooking for many years, took the boy aside and suggested he read the time indicated on the spaghetti packet, adding some encouraging if vague remarks about giving the sauce some flavour. The next day, the leathery yellow strands wouldn't bend round their forks and the sour brown sauce had the charred remains of a dozen cloves of garlic floating in it. So when Di Nuccio commented, 'Thank God he's on nights after today,' there was no need to ask why.

'He'll learn,' was the Marshal's only comment. 'Everything quiet?'

'As the grave.'

'I'm off, then.'

A rich smell of rabbit gravy scented with rosemary met his nostrils as he let himself into his quarters and he couldn't help feeling guilty at the thought of the boys upstairs.

'That you?'

'Mm.'

The bedroom shutters were closed. He switched on the light and undressed. What he needed was a cold shower, but even the cold water was tepid at that time of year. He felt rather better for it, even so, and when he pottered across to the living-room, the sight of their two places laid, in honour of the holiday, on a fresh white lacy cloth in the soft light filtering through the slightly opened shutters was enough to dispel the boredom of the morning and induce cheerfulness and a good appetite.

'Salva, fill the water jug, will you?'

He went into the kitchen and opened the fridge.

'What about a drop of this rosé with the rabbit? I'd rather not drink red in this heat.'

'Open it, if you like. I won't have any.'

'You haven't got another headache?'

'No, it tends to come on in the afternoon but you know wine makes me sleepy at lunch-time.'

'There's nothing to stop you having a nap.'

'You know I feel worse afterwards.'

'Well, it seems a shame not to . . . it's lovely and cool . . .'

He opened the bottle and took it through with the jug of water. It felt more like a Sunday than ever. The bells had stopped ringing so perhaps it was just the smell of the roast . . . Then he realized that it was the lacy cloth which normally appeared only on Sundays.

The rabbit, with a creamy purée, was so good that he couldn't resist a second helping.

'It's a long time since we had rabbit,' he murmured by way of an excuse, since he was and always had been overweight.

'I thought you'd be pleased. But you didn't bother to ask me where I got it.'

'Should I have? Did you have to go far?'

'No, that's just it! I got it in San Frediano where you got your black eye. You were right about the shops being open so I went back there. And what's more, apart from today, of course, they're staying open for the rest of August except the chemist's. The greengrocer's shutting in September to have his shop done up and the butcher had his holidays in July like us. He says he prefers it, it's so much less crowded at the seaside. He has a little boy, younger than our two, and his wife helps him in the shop.'

'You seem to know everything about them.'

'It's the sort of district where people like to chat. Some of them are a bit rough, but still . . . The couple who have the grocer's shop said they usually shut the last two weeks of August but they're having to have the façade of the building re-done and it'll cost a fortune—it's their own, they live in the flat above the shop—so they can't afford to go away this year.'

'You have been chatting!'

'Well, why not? When the boys are at home it's different, but now I've so little to do. I admit I enjoyed it, it reminded me of being down at home where I knew everybody . . .'

'I wasn't criticizing.' It was true that she must sometimes feel a bit lonely. Living in barracks in a city not your own wasn't the ideal way to make friends, and for years she had been used to the constant company of his sister, Nunziata. 'I'm glad you found somewhere nice to shop. Why didn't you mention it before?'

'I thought you were annoyed about your eye and . . . the whole business. You never mentioned it again, so I didn't.'

The truth was that he'd thought she was annoyed, and even now neither of them went so far as to bring up the subject of what had been her first and last driving lesson.

'Anyway, now that your eye's so much better . . . and seeing as you enjoyed the rabbit . . . It's a very good butcher's. I might even carry on going there.'

'What about that crazy woman? Does she go there, too?'

'She spends practically the whole morning in there, but very little money. She must be poor. It's a poor district, anyway, but she must be really hard up, I think. Most days she just sits there on the only chair talking to whoever comes in, or swearing at them. I must say, her language . . . But some days she buys herself a sausage or a hamburger or even a little slice of steak. Whatever she buys he seems always to charge her a thousand lire and then she'll often ask him for an egg, just like a child asking for a sweet.'

'And does he give it to her?'

'Wrapped in a bit of newspaper. I've seen her in the grocer's, too, buying one slice of mortadella as thin as tissue paper and a little end piece off a loaf, hardly enough for a mouse. She always has the same frock on, as well, and I wonder when she washes it because she doesn't seem to be at all dirty. Would you like a peach?'

'I don't know . . . Yes.'

'Or water melon, there's some in the fridge from yesterday.'

'No, a peach.'

'The funniest thing about her is that she spends all her time cleaning.'

'So do lots of women.'

'Wait! Not cleaning her house, I don't mean that. No, she cleans the whole world, or her own little world anyway. She sweeps the entire street—it's a square really, you know, though it only looks like a widening in the road—and I've seen her down on her knees picking up scraps of paper one by one and then mopping the pavement and even any cars that are parked there with a bit of rag. She even empties the rubbish bin attached to the bus stop and puts a clean plastic bag inside it.'

'Saving the street cleaners a job.'

'Exactly! And woe betide anybody she catches dropping rubbish or a burnt match. She goes for them with her sweeping brush. I'm afraid the men who are always hanging about outside the bar there torment her dreadfully. They throw stuff on the pavement behind her as she goes along just to tease her and see how far she'll go. It's a shame.'

'I saw that. If I remember rightly, there were pretending to make up to her, as well.'

'Yes, and she takes it all seriously, but she gets quite violent with them for scattering paper as they do. But then, she's not in her right mind, poor creature, it's the men who are to blame. Grown men behaving like little boys. Not that the children don't do their share of tormenting her, but what can you expect when the adults set an example like that? It's a funny corner of the world altogether, though I certainly can't complain about the way I've been treated in the shops. I'd better get the coffee on . . .'

The Marshal settled in an armchair, feeling replete. Something was missing, though . . .

'Teresa! Where's the paper?'

'There is no paper today.'

'Of course. I forgot.'

'You'll catch the news on the first channel.'

He turned it on and sat down again. But the news didn't hold his attention. He stared at a foreign dignitary getting out of a large car and wondered if his wife were as settled in Florence as she'd always claimed to be. It disturbed people, moving like that, the children, too. But that was army life for you. There was nothing much he could do. Even so, once he was back in uniform and ready to leave, he looked into the kitchen and said, 'I suppose everything's shut this evening, cinemas, too?'

'I should think so. Why? Did you want to go to the cinema?'

It was unusual enough to surprise her.

'No, no . . . I just thought we could do something or other, gò out somewhere. It is supposed to be a holiday.'

'Well, we can always go round the block.'

They called it 'going round the block'. An habitual walk, crossing the river at the Ponte Vecchio, walking up the embankment under the iron lamps as far as the next bridge, back over the river, pausing on their way back to sit for a while in a tiny garden outside the Evangelical church to chat or look across the water at the crenellated tower of the Palazzo Vecchio. The floodlit palaces and the strings of lights, the warm dark sky and the big August moon were such a theatrical spectacle that they never tired of looking at it and preferred it to any film. What's more, if they felt like it they could talk while they were looking. It was one of his wife, Teresa's, constant complaints that he had no sense of place. He was apt, according to her, to come out with some loud, irrelevant aside in the cinema that set everybody hissing, and to sit like a lump of lead, his thoughts miles away, when he should have been making conversation at some family gathering.

It was one of *his* constant complaints that she always exaggerated.

However, tonight they could go 'round the block' and stop near the Ponte Vecchio for an ice-cream. An ice-cream parlour must surely be open, even today, with all the tourists about in the centre.

He was never to find out. The call came at supper-time,

before he'd even had a chance to change. At first he had difficulty understanding, the voice was so quiet, almost casual in tone, so that the urgency didn't get across right away.

'I asked for you personally and though I know I must be disturbing your meal I thought it best. We've met, but you maybe don't remember.'

'Who's speaking?'

'Gianfranco.'

'Gianfranco? But I don't know anyone—'

'Gianfranco Cini,' the voice rolled quietly on, 'but most people know me just as Franco. Don't you remember getting a black eye and coming into my bar—'

'Ah, of course.' Now he could place the voice, as placid and solid as the big barman himself. 'I remember—'

'Anyway, if you could come round or send somebody. She's been dead for a while, I think, and I don't know whether we did right or wrong breaking in. Anyway, what's done is done and we weren't to know. For all we knew, we could have been in time, what do you think?'

What was he supposed to think? He had no idea what the man was rambling on about in tones as mild as if he'd been remarking on the weather.

'Did you say somebody was dead?' Perhaps he'd heard wrongly.

'She's dead all right, there's no doubt about that. Pippo's no doctor, of course, but even so . . . We've called the Misericordia but I said to Pippo, in a case like this they might not want to just take her away, there'll be formalities. To tell you the truth, in spite of the way things look—and I don't suppose there can be any doubt—it gave me a funny feeling thinking about her calling you last night, you know what I mean?'

'Calling me? I—' But there was no hope of getting a word in. The quiet voice rolled on.

'It's probably just one of those things but it gave me a

queer feeling, even so. In any case, I thought you should be informed. I've seen to everything else . . .'

In the end, the Marshal virtually hung up on him, having failed to interrupt the flow even by saying, 'I'll be round there in five minutes.'

'Where are you going?' His wife came out of the kitchen as he was putting his jacket back on.

'I've been called out.'

'Whatever for?'

'I haven't the faintest idea.'

It was as quick to walk there but on second thoughts he drove in case there was anything further to be done. Further to what, he didn't know. What could the man have meant by talking of a call to him last night? He'd taken no call. Even then, he didn't remember at once the call that had been passed on to Headquarters, perhaps because nothing had come of it. There was no point in worrying about the problem now, anyway, since he'd find out everything when he got there. The only clear fact that had emerged from all the barman's ramblings was that she was dead.

Only much later did he realize that he didn't ask himself, or, for that matter, the barman, who the dead woman was. It was as if everything that had happened in the last few days had been a preparation for this, as if he'd been expecting to hear that a madwoman, whose name he couldn't even remember, was now dead.

CHAPTER 2

It was the scene from the week before re-enacted with the same characters, the same crowd collected under the windows of the corner house staring up, and himself pushing his way through. There were subtle differences. The lighting, at sunset, was more subdued and so was the noise the crowd was making. This time he was in uniform, too, so the crowd parted to let him through. When he looked up at the madwoman's window, in place of the plump bare torso there was a thin man in a white shirt. From the sea of murmuring around him, the Marshal heard a woman's raucous voice call out:

'Pippo! Open up, the Marshal's here.'

The man in the white shirt looked down and then disappeared. The Marshal pushed on towards the street door which opened with a click as he reached it. The stairs were very steep and gloomy, lit only by a very weak bare light-bulb at each turn. A pretty, plump-cheeked young woman was standing in her doorway on the first-floor landing, and from behind her came a warmer light and a good smell of supper cooking. She withdrew very quickly when she saw the Marshal but, nevertheless, as the door was closing he heard her murmur faintly, 'Good evening.'

He only nodded in the direction of the now closed door since he needed all his breath for the stairs as he trudged upwards, hat in hand.

Pippo, the thin man in the white shirt, was waiting on the top landing. Before the Marshal had reached him he began:

'It was Franco called you. I thought I'd better stay here with her.' He was a gangling fellow with a big nose and grey eyes that darted about, missing nothing.

The breathless Marshal made no comment but followed him past the peeling black door into a dingy little flat.

'She's in here.'

A kitchen with barely enough room for an old-fashioned sink, an ancient gas cooker and a small table with a plastic cloth on it. A window, no more than a foot square, was wide open on a jumble of red tiles against the sunset and a bit of flowered curtaining was drawn across a small alcove to the left of the cooker. All this the Marshal took in without entering the room since his way was blocked by a body lying just inside the door. After a moment he stepped over it to get in. Pippo stayed where he was outside the doorway.

'Who put this on her? You?' The head was covered with a faded tea-towel so that only a tuft of grey hair showed.

'It was all I could find.'

The Marshal removed it and looked at the face which was twisted up as if to look back at him. The eyes were slightly open and the mouth pulled to one side where there was a dark stain on the cheek. He frowned and bent over the body. It was lying on its side, half covered with the flowered overall, naked down the front, and he saw now that it hung open like that because there were no buttons on it. He remembered the plump nude figure, bursting with life and vibrant with anger, shaking a fat little fist at the neighbours. Now the fat arms were oddly stretched out behind as if their movement had swept the flowered overall back. The knees were bent and showed the same wine-dark stain as the right cheek. Each of the flaccid breasts carried a similar mark.

The Marshal straightened up and passed a big hand over his face with a sigh. The wail of a siren wound down in the street outside.

'Where did you find her?'

'I hope I didn't do wrong . . .' The doorbell rang. 'That's the Misericordia . . .'

'All right. Let them in.'

Pippo went to press the button at the top of the stairs and came back.

'So where did you find her? She wasn't lying here.'

'She might have been alive. How was I to know?'

'Where?'

'With her head in the gas oven. That was why—'

'The gas oven?'

Four black-robed brothers of the Misericordia appeared behind Pippo.

'Can you wait a minute?' The Marshal looked at the cooker and the open window, then turned and looked at the wine-dark stains on the pale flesh again. Then he made a sign to the waiting brothers. When they'd gone he said to Pippo, 'You'd better come in here.' And seeing the man's reluctance to step across the upturned face, he replaced the tea-towel.

'I don't like . . . It was different, you know, at first, thinking she might still be alive.

'Sit down.' There was only one rickety formica chair. 'You'll feel better in a minute.'

Pippo was looking so white that the Marshal was afraid he might faint or vomit. 'Do you want a glass of water?'

'No, no, nothing. I couldn't fancy . . .' As if everything in the room were contaminated with death.

'Tell me what happened, right from the beginning.'

'I wouldn't have come up here, I can tell you, if Franco hadn't said—'

'Never mind Franco for the moment.' Was this barman some sort of tribal chief round here that he seemed to make all the decisions? 'Just tell me, as simply as you can, the facts in the order that they happened. Nobody's saying you did wrong; I just need to know the full story.'

Though nobody knew better than the Marshal that the one thing nobody ever did was to tell the full story about anything.

'If it hadn't been that today's a holiday somebody would have been on to it sooner, but a lot of people were out at lunch-time, visiting relatives and what have you, and of course Franco only opened for an hour or two this morning, otherwise . . .'

The Marshal perched himself on a corner of the table, hoping it would bear his weight. This was going to be a long job and it was evidently pointless trying to get this man to stick to the facts as interruptions generally tend to make people ramble even further from the point, intent as they always are on justifying themselves rather than giving a lucid account.

'Anyway, nobody thought anything of it. The shops being closed and nothing doing in the square, it didn't seem odd that she didn't show herself all day because she never starts cleaning until towards evening. It takes her that way. She . . .' He glanced at the body. 'It's a rum business and no mistake. I'm not feeling too chipper, to tell you the truth. Where was I?'

'She didn't show herself all day.'

'No, well . . . We were out, too, as it happens, at my sister-in-law's. We must have got back about seven. The first thing the wife thought of when we got in was Clementina's supper.'

'Clementina? Is that—?'

'Clementina, yes! That's what we're on about, isn't it?'

'I'm sorry, I didn't remember her name. Go on.'

'We've always given her a bit of something—not that we're the only ones. We all do our bit round here. I'm not saying we're paragons of virtue. We're rough and ready, you know what I mean, but we look after our neighbours and I'm not boasting when I say my wife does more than most and I've never discouraged her.'

On and on he went until the Marshal would willingly have canonized the whole family on the spot if only he'd get to the point. And all the time Pippo was talking he kept his eyes fixed on the table or on his hands, every now and then darting a sharp glance at the Marshal's face, though not directly in his eyes, to see how it was all going down.

The Marshal's face, as always, was expressionless. His big, slightly bulging eyes missed nothing and betrayed nothing.

'A bit of minestrone and some bread—she buys herself a bit of bread every day but when it's a holiday and two days' bread to buy together she always ends up without. Not that it's much, a bit of soup and bread—though there was a peach in the basket, too, now I think, I remember the wife saying—but somebody getting on in years doesn't want heavy food. So anyway, when it was ready she called across from the window but there was no answer.'

Light dawned. The trouble about people who wanted to hide something was that they weren't necessarily hiding the thing you were looking for, and that always confused the issue. The reams of self-praise, the virtuous citizen's speech and those nervous glances at the Marshal's face all added up to the fact that the big fight last week had been between Clementina and Pippo's wife. In other words, Pippo had given the Marshal his black eye! Would they get on any faster if the Marshal told him that he knew and wouldn't dream of doing anything about it now? Not on your life! They'd be another half-hour with all the whys and wherefores of the pigeon problem. All he said was, 'Was the window open when your wife called out?'

'Wide open. And the shutters. And you see how small this flat is. Even if she'd been asleep she'd have heard.'

From what the Marshal remembered of the wife's raucous voice, this was certainly true.

'What did you think when she didn't answer?'

'I thought right away I'd better go and call Franco.'

Of course! Not the Carabinieri or an ambulance or any other authority but Franco, who was evidently going to be a force to be reckoned with in this business, placid and kindly-looking though he was.

'Franco came out with me and we stood under the window calling up. A few others came out and joined in but we couldn't make her hear—well, of course not, but we weren't to know. Our first thought was that she might be a bit under the weather after last night. You know how it is?'

'No. What happened last night?'

'The party. We had this supper out in the square. Franco organized it. The idea was that as everybody except us was away at the seaside we should do something to enjoy ourselves for the fifteenth. We decided on doing it on the evening of the fourteenth, Franco did, so we could all sleep it off this morning. Some people have got tomorrow off as well, I have myself, but not everybody, so that's what we did. Everybody paid so much a week for four weeks and last night we had a real slap-up do. Four courses. A lovely table set—candles and everything. Mimmo played the accordion and we danced a bit after. Clementina danced. She had the time of her life—' He stopped, remembering, and shot another glance at the lifeless Clementina.

'She . . . she had a drop too much and her face was red . . . we even managed to get her to lay off cleaning for a bit.' He had dropped his voice as though afraid she might defend herself against such slander. 'We got her dancing. The lads were reckoning to fight over her—all in good fun, you know, no harm meant.'

'Didn't it sometimes go a bit too far?'

'No, no, I wouldn't say that.'

'Franco says so,' the Marshal said, quick to take advantage.

'He does? Well, if anything, the youngsters get carried away at times, but they weren't at the supper, they have better things to do at their age than eat with the old folks. They didn't come roaring back on their mopeds until after midnight. They might have teased her a bit but nothing more than usual. I mean, for her to have called you in the middle of the night like that . . .'

Again this call business that the famous Franco had mentioned on the phone. For the moment he kept quiet about his ignorance of this call. Better check up on it with his boys first.

'Go on with what happened this evening. You thought she must have had a hangover, is that it?'

'Something like that. Or even a stomach upset. She did herself well last night and she's not used to eating so much.

Anyway, seeing as the window was open and the scaffolding there . . .'

'You climbed in.'

'Did I do wrong? What if she'd needed help? Franco said—'

'No, no. You did quite right, I'm sure.'

'Franco would have done it himself but he's on the heavy side and though I say it myself, I'm pretty fit. I can still kick a ball around. In fact—'

'So you climbed up here. Tell me exactly what you saw.'

'I looked in the living-room and then the bedroom—the bedroom door was open—and then—'

'When you looked in the bedroom was the bed made?'

'No, it was rumpled.'

'Did you touch it?'

'No, I didn't even go in, seeing as she wasn't there.'

That, at least, was something.

'Would she leave her bed unmade all day, do you think?'

'Clementina? You're joking!'

'I'm asking.'

'You don't know her!'

'No. Then if she'd been alive this morning she'd have made her bed?'

'I should say so! Oh . . . I see now what you're getting at. You think that all this time . . . I mean since last night . . .'

'Go on.'

'Where was I? Oh, I came in here then and I saw her. She was half lying, half kneeling there,' he pointed to the cooker, 'with her head inside and the gas turned on.'

The Marshal looked at the small window.

'Was that open?'

'No, I opened it. That was the first thing I did because of the smell—no, I went and touched her first. She looked dead but I'm no expert and you never know. So then I opened the window—'

'Didn't you turn off the gas?'

He hesitated. 'You're right, the gas, I suppose I must have done . . .' He looked at the cooker as if to make sure. 'I must have done . . . and then I opened the window and came back to get her head out of there. That was when I realized . . . she was going stiff. I've never had much to do with . . . you know what I mean. My mother died in the house but then you send for the woman that lays them out and until it's all been done you don't . . . I came across a dog once—must have been run over—that was going stiff like that. I managed to drag her away from the oven. I suppose I was thinking of putting her on the bed but in the end I couldn't manage it with her being—anyway I covered her face up and then went to the front window and shouted to Franco to come up. I opened the door for him.'

'Did he touch anything?'

'Nothing at all. He said not to. As a matter of fact, he said I shouldn't have moved her but I—'

'Don't worry.' The Marshal's opinion of Franco improved.

'What if there'd been a chance, you see—'

'You did your best. How long do you think you were in here before you went to call Franco?'

'How long . . .? I couldn't tell you.'

'Five minutes? An hour?'

'Oh, nearer five minutes than an hour but it may have been ten.'

'And you didn't feel sick? Wasn't the room full of gas?'

'I suppose so.'

'You suppose so?'

'It did smell awful.'

'But not enough to make you sick?'

'Well, I opened the window.'

'But it wasn't the first thing you thought of doing. You went to look at Clementina's body first so I imagine you could breathe all right.'

'I suppose . . . I remember holding my breath a bit because of the smell.'

'And you're not absolutely sure at what point you turned the gas off.'

'I did turn it off, though . . .' But he still hesitated, frowning.

The Marshal got off the edge of the table and went to look at the cooker.

'You see? It's off.'

'I see.'

He looked behind it and then pulled back the flowered curtain next to it. Behind it there were three shelves with a few plates and cups, a mug with some cutlery in it and, as he had expected, a blue gas canister underneath. Few of the houses in the old Quarter were connected to the town gas supply. The Marshal took the canister by the handles and rattled it.

'Empty.'

'But there must have been enough in it to kill her, poor soul,' pointed out Pippo. 'Why should she do a thing like that? Of course she hadn't a bean . . .'

'I need to make a phone call.'

'There's no phone here.'

'I didn't think there would be. What about the flat below?'

'They've probably got one.'

The Marshal made for the door.

'What about me?'

'Stay where you are. Don't touch anything.' Though what use it was saying that at this stage, thought the Marshal as he plodded down the steep stairs.

The door of the flat below was shut tight which surprised him a little. Not the nosey sort. He pushed the bell. The flat must have been as small as the one above it since he could hear voices and cutlery going quite clearly, noises which stopped when he rang. Even so, it was some time before the door was opened by the plump-cheeked young woman he'd seen before.

'Yes?'

'I'm sorry to disturb you but I need to telephone urgently. If you wouldn't mind . . .'

By the look on her face she did mind but she opened the door and let him in.

'Good evening.' The Marshal turned his hat in his hands and excused himself again to the young man sitting at the table in the kitchen to his left. There had been no hurried clearing of plates, which made the Marshal wonder why they had been so long answering the door.

'He needs to telephone.'

'That's all right.' The young man got up, smiling.

'Don't interrupt your meal.'

'I'll just show you where the phone is. Don't want you to get lost in these great halls.' He passed in front of the Marshal and switched on the light in another room. It was a cheerful living-room, filled with books and with brightly coloured rugs scattered on the floor. 'Help yourself. I'll leave you in peace.'

The Marshal made just one call, to Headquarters in Borgo Ognissanti. His commanding officer, he knew, was away on holiday in the mountains and he was put through to a young lieutenant he didn't know. Giving the facts as briefly as he could, he finished: 'I'll stay on here until somebody from the Public Prosecutor's office arrives.'

'Good. Well, if you feel you can cope with everything . . . You can't imagine how difficult things are here with just a skeleton staff.'

'Of course. Don't worry, I can cope.'

When he had hung up he glanced around the room and then switched off the lamp and opened the door. As he did so he heard the man say quietly, 'Don't worry.'

They were sitting at the table but not eating. The Marshal told them not to get up.

'I'll see myself out—but I'm afraid I might have to disturb you again later, or perhaps tomorrow morning. Routine inquiries, you understand.'

'Of course—if you could make it tomorrow I'd be grateful. We'd planned to go out tonight.' His wife watched him as he spoke and then looked at the Marshal for his answer.

'Tomorrow, then.' It was amazing. They hadn't asked him a single question or even so much as mentioned their dead neighbour's name. It was true that he hadn't mentioned it himself. For reasons of his own he didn't want the truth getting about just yet. He closed the door softly as he went out. They looked a nice couple, intelligent too, but odd not to be at all curious.

He dismissed them from his mind when he heard voices coming from above and, since he had left Pippo alone, that meant new arrivals. This could hardly be an instant result of his phone call. He was annoyed and quickened his step, arriving on the landing above breathless, his hat clutched to his chest. The door was open and the tiny flat seemed to be full of chatter and cigarette smoke.

'For God's sake . . .' He hadn't been gone five minutes!

Pippo was talking animatedly to a stocky young man in dark blue. An elderly woman was sitting on an upright chair in the bedroom, apparently waiting for something.

'What's going on here?'

Pippo interrupted himself and the younger man turned, cigarette in mouth, grinning lopsidedly.

'Galli!' The Marshal recognized the journalist from the *Nazione*. 'How the devil . . .'

'I have my methods.' Galli held out his hand and the Marshal was obliged to shake it. Not that he didn't like the man, he'd always found him honest in his job and you couldn't say that for so many journalists. But he had an infuriating way of turning up too soon. Too soon for the Marshal, at any rate. And there was that story of the time he not only turned up at the scene of a crime before the police got there but found a witness, which the police had failed to do, and instead of informing them he published the man's statement in the paper, pointing out that the police hadn't . . . Oh well. There he was.

'I'll go if I'm in the way,' Galli offered.

'You mean you've already got what you want.' He hadn't, though, not from talking to Pippo, the Marshal consoled himself. Unless he'd taken a good look at the body. He was no fool.

'You won't get more than four lines out of a story like this,' he hazarded, without actually lying.

'Are you kidding? In the middle of August? If my gran's cat committed suicide I'd give it half a page and a photo!'

The Marshal was relieved. Even so, he said: 'I'd rather you went before the Substitute Prosecutor arrives.'

'Right you are. If it turns out she had a bag of diamonds on top of the wardrobe or anything, or was the rejected daughter of some foreign prince, let me know.'

'Hm.'

'Or even if the old girl had been crossed in love we'd do a special edition. God, it's hot. It's foul working in August.'

'Go on holiday, then.'

'And leave you in peace, you mean? Not me. I can see myself, squashed into a square inch of beach with the riff-raff. I went to London last month. It was so damn cold I wore an overcoat the whole time.'

He was certainly suffering from the heat. His face had a greyish pallor and there were dark circles under his eyes. He mopped his forehead with a handkerchief.

'I'll be off, then. If I can be of any help to you, just shout.'

It was impossible to stay angry with the man even when he was as cheeky as this. And it was no more than the truth since he often had been of help.

'I'll bear it in mind.'

'So long, then!'

The Marshal glowered at Pippo who flushed.

'Have I said something I shouldn't?'

'How should I know? I don't know what you told him.'

'Nothing I hadn't told you. I never thought . . . You didn't tell me not to let anybody in.'

Which was true. The Marshal gave it up and looked towards the bedroom where the elderly woman was still sitting perfectly still, staring straight ahead of her as if in a dentist's waiting-room.

'And who's this?'

'Franco sent her up.'

'Oh yes? And did Franco send Galli up, too?'

'Who?'

'That journalist.'

'I don't think so, no. He just turned up. Said he was on his way to supper with friends and saw the crowd outside.'

'I see.'

'If you don't want her, you can send her away.'

At this point the Marshal, too, fished out a handkerchief and mopped his brow. Perhaps he'd do better to go home and leave Franco to deal with the whole business. The woman continued to stare straight ahead. What on earth did she want? He went in to her.

'Well? Did you want to speak to me?'

The old woman looked at him as if he weren't quite right in the head.

'Just tell me whether you want me to stay or go,' she said.

Since he couldn't find a reply to that, it was just as well that she added after a moment, 'I haven't touched her. Franco said to wait for your permission.'

'I see. You've come to lay her out, is that it?'

'Of course. As she has nobody I'll stay the night.'

'No, no. She'll be taken away.'

'I understand. Franco said there might be formalities.'

'Formalities, that's right. I'd rather you left, if you don't mind.'

'I said, didn't I? Just tell me whether you want me to stay or go. As you want me to go . . .' She stood up, very tiny and neat.

'Wait . . . Did you know her well?'

'Clementina? Of course. Everybody knew her.'

'But some must have known her better than others.'

She thought for a moment and then said, 'No.'

'How do you mean?'

'They didn't. Everybody knew her the same way.'

'Well, would you mind leaving me your name and address, anyway.'

'There's no need. I live next door, and if you want me just tell Franco and he'll give me a shout.' And she was gone.

It was Pippo who let her out. He had lit a cigarette, perhaps absent-mindedly, and now he hovered on the landing, shuffling from one foot to the other and wishing that he, too, could leave.

The Marshal, who had remained in the bedroom, called to him, 'Somebody down there wants you.'

The noise below the window had increased and a number of people were calling Pippo's name. He went to the window, the cigarette dangling from his mouth, and leaned out. The Marshal stood back and watched him without comment. Pippo's white shirt, no doubt his best one put on for the holiday, was stuck to his back with sweat. The sunset had faded but it was no cooler.

'What's up?'

'Your wife said to say she's gone back up. The kids have to eat.'

'All right.'

'What's going on up there?'

Pippo shrugged his shoulders and then leaned out further as a car horn hooted and the crowd began to open up. Somebody shouted, 'Second floor!'

Pippo withdrew his head.

'Somebody's arriving. I can't see who on account of the scaffolding.'

The Marshal went to the door. It sounded like a whole army was pounding up the stairs. The Substitute Prosecutor appeared first, looking up at the Marshal and taking the steps two at a time.

'Good evening, sir—' the Marshal began.

'Where is she?'

'Here, in the kitchen. I don't think there'll be room for you all at once.' For the Prosecutor had his registrar with him and behind them came the lab people and the photographer laden with equipment.

'What's in there?' demanded the Prosecutor.

'The bedroom.'

'Doctor!'

The doctor from the Medico-Legal Institute emerged from the group on the stairs and pushed his way forward.

'In here.'

The Marshal barely had time to remove the ridiculous tea-towel from the corpse before the Prosecutor snapped, 'Who moved her?'

'The man who found her,' the Marshal said, straightening up slowly. Surely the Prosecutor couldn't imagine he'd done it? 'He found her with her head in the gas oven and thought he might be in time to—'

'*Gas oven?* Doctor . . .'

The doctor had made his way into the kitchen, stepping across the body. Now he bent over it.

'Who's moved her?'

The Marshal mopped his brow and began again, 'The man who found her. It seems—'

'Found her with her head in the gas oven,' interrupted the Prosecutor.

The doctor frowned.

'Well, we'd better talk about it after the autopsy . . .'

The Marshal was more than a little annoyed. He knew

as well as they did that those wine-coloured marks on the body showed how it had lain after death and that if she'd really died of carbon monoxide poisoning they'd have been a much lighter red. But they weren't going to discuss it in his presence. They would discuss it privately and then the Prosecutor would give him his orders. It was their way of telling him, in case he didn't know, that he was only an NCO. The Marshal knew from his captain, however, that the worst of them treated officers in the same way. The best of them didn't do it to anybody. This looked like being one of the worst of them, to judge by the way he'd swept in without so much as a good-evening, let alone introducing himself, since the Marshal didn't know him from Adam. Probably annoyed to have his meal interrupted. And then when the case goes badly, thought the Marshal, summing the man up, yours truly will be to blame.

As these thoughts passed through his mind, his face remained impassive and his large bulging eyes stayed fixed on the peeling wall in front of him like those of a bulldog waiting for a command.

At nine-thirty, all the rooms in the tiny flat were lit with weak, unshaded light-bulbs and the Marshal was alone. The Prosecutor, the doctor and all the technicians had gone through the rituals attending sudden death and taken their departure. Pippo, having told his story, rather better the second time round to the Prosecutor, had gone home to his wife and supper and the TV. The body still had to be taken away and seals put on the doors and windows, but in the meantime the Marshal was alone, expressionless, looking.

He looked in the fridge first. It was tidy and clean enough but so old and scratched as to look a bit sleazy, and all the more depressing for having so little in it. A small box of milk in the door, one egg and a paper-thin slice of sausage on a tin plate.

'Sometimes she'll ask him for an egg, just like a child asking for a sweet.'

'And does he give it to her?'

'Wrapped in a bit of newspaper . . .'

One of the last things the Prosecutor had said, wondering why anyone should have wanted to kill her, was 'Had she money?'

And the silent Marshal had opened his big eyes wider than ever to suggest the man look around him and see.

'It doesn't necessarily follow.'

It was true, of course, as far as it went. Even Galli, the reporter, had quipped, 'If it turns out she had a bag of diamonds on top of the wardrobe . . .'

The thought sent him wandering into the bedroom. He wasn't searching the place systematically. Perhaps he should have done but he didn't want to. He was content to sniff about the place with no aim in mind. He pulled the one straight chair towards the scratched wardrobe and climbed on it carefully, not at all convinced that it would bear his weight. It creaked a little but it held. There was no bag of diamonds up there and nothing else either, except a thick layer of dust and fluff. The crazy woman's cleaning mania had been as unsystematic as the Marshal's searching. He got down and opened the wardrobe door.

'Who the devil . . .' He couldn't have been more surprised if he'd found someone hiding in there. As it was, his first thought was that someone had removed Clementina's clothing, and who on earth could have done it? Yet there was nothing in there except a few wire coathangers and a plastic-wrapped bundle lying at the bottom. This, when he opened it, contained two old woollen dresses that reeked of mothballs. He replaced the bundle and straightened up to look about him. There was a small chest of drawers against the opposite wall and he went over to it, opening the three drawers one after the other and making a mental inventory. It didn't take long. A few pieces of much worn underwear, a heavy cardigan, darned on both elbows and a lighter one in rather better condition, two pairs of thick stockings and another old woollen dress, this one, too, wrapped in polythene and filled with mothballs. That was all. Hadn't she even a coat? And what about shoes? The shoes, at least, he found under the bed. She'd been wearing nothing on her feet when she died and he found her slippers under the bed, too. She'd probably been asleep when it happened then, and that housedress with no buttons was her nightdress which would account for her appearing at the window in it at siesta-time that day last week. Still, she must have had a summer dress. Hadn't his wife said so, and that she wore it every day? So where was it? There was only one place it could be, and yet the scaffolding . . . He went to the window and looked out. It was there all right, tied on to the scaffolding itself, washed and dried, hanging there in the lamplight. The scaffolding had prevented her from using the washing-line on a pulley below her window, and from seeing out properly too. Had she been the one to pull away the netting that should have covered all of it? Perhaps not, since the planks hadn't been laid at that level, only lower down. A funny way of doing a job to half finish it and leave it there all August.

He leaned out and retrieved the dress. The lights were on in the flats of the house opposite and he could hear a television from an open window. He heard a voice calling up from the street below in the hot, lamplit night.

'Martha!'

'What is it?'

'I'm going to Franco's if you want some cigarettes.'

'Get me two packets, then, will you?'

'How is she?'

'No different. I can't leave her. If only it weren't for this heat . . .'

The Marshal withdrew and closed the window. He looked at the flowered frock. All she had. And one egg and a slice of sausage in the fridge. If the evidence weren't against it, it would be easy enough to believe she'd committed suicide, though there were people in even worse condition, ill and in terrible pain, ill-nourished, lonely, and still they hung on to life at all costs. Besides which, there was no forgetting the day of his black eye, and Clementina as he had seen her outside the bar afterwards, noisy and bumptious, threatening all comers with her sweeping brush. Crazy she may have been, but she was full of life even if she did only have one frock that she washed and hung out every night. What the devil did she live on, anyway . . . a pension most likely. He returned to the kitchen, stood in the middle of it, looking about him and then looked behind the bit of curtain again. At the back of one of the shelves, in such a gloomy corner that he hadn't seen it before, was a biscuit tin. He sat down at the table and opened it. He found a thousand-lire note and a few coins. There was no pension book and no rent book either, but at least there was her identity card.

Anna Clementina Franci, born 14 May 1934 in Florence. Citizenship: Italian. Residence: Florence. Civil Status: widow Chiari. Profession: none.

The Marshal was surprised that she was only in her fifties.

There was nothing else in the tin. The absence of a pension book was disturbing since it might mean she had another hiding-place that he hadn't managed to find. The lack of a rent book was less odd, though he very much doubted that the house was hers. There was such a desperate housing shortage in the city that thousands of people had rented houses with no contract or rent book, often at exorbitant rates. Whoever had a house to rent could call the tune, and even those who offered contracts often expected a bribe each time they were renewed. Not that crazy Clementina was a likely customer for that sort of landlord . . . unless it was true that she had cash hidden away, in which case someone who knew about it . . .

'Well, I'm not convinced,' said the Marshal aloud in the silence of the gloomy kitchen.

No, the rent book wasn't worrying him but something else was. Something else was missing. There might be another tin somewhere, or a drawer. He got up to check. Every house had a drawer where things accumulated. In poor houses it was always in the kitchen, in richer households it might be in the entrance hall. It was where you went to look when you needed a bit of string for a parcel—though you never found the scissors that should have been there—or a candle when the lights fused, last year's Christmas cards for the children to cut up or a pair of gloves that some visitor had left and never reclaimed. There were always keys in it that no longer fitted any lock, lost receipts for gas bills, spare plugs and tiny coils of wire. It was a drawer that was never difficult to find and the Marshal found it now at the first try by lifting the plastic cloth on the table, since there was no other piece of furniture with drawers in the room. He soon discovered a bit of candle and two or three postcards sent to her from the seaside, one of them from Franco, dated the previous summer. He rummaged further and found a few remnants of knitting wool, an empty chocolate box, a few screws and nails, the handle of something and a sheet of yellowed newspaper which had probably once lined the drawer but had got pushed to the back. But he didn't find what he was looking for. It was true that women sometimes had another drawer of this type in their bedrooms, where broken bits of cheap jewellery, unused presents of scent and old headscarfs accumulated along with precious letters and childhood prayerbooks. But he had already been through Clementina's bedroom drawers and found nothing.

'Odd,' he muttered.

The doorbell rang and he went to open it.

'We understood you'd finished here . . .' said the first of the porters to appear.

'We have. You can take her.'

They went about their business. When they were struggling down again, the Marshal heard one of them shout crossly, 'Upright! Keep her upright or you'll not get round this corner, blast these old stairs!'

He went on waiting patiently until someone turned up to affix the seals, then he put the housekeys in his pocket and made his way down the gloomy staircase to go and pay a visit to Franco.

CHAPTER 3

The diffused yellow light of the street lamps and the sweaty warmth of the August night gave an indoor atmosphere to the tiny square which, as the Marshal's wife had said, was little more than a widening of the road. At the tables outside Franco's bar the men were gossiping or playing cards. Above their heads their wives leaned out of lighted windows, fanning themselves with handkerchiefs, smoking, exchanging bits of news or complaining about the humidity. Every television in every house was blaring out the same film soundtrack. Franco himself was standing in his doorway, unshaven, hands resting comfortably on his paunch. The Marshal squeezed between the tables.

'I thought you'd be coming,' the big barman said. 'Come inside and sit down.'

His television was on the loudest of all since it was turned to face the street so that the men could watch it from outside.

The Marshal sat himself down at the table where he had once nursed his black eye and Franco went behind the bar to get two glasses and a cold bottle from the fridge under the counter. He held the bottle up and said something the

Marshal couldn't possibly hear over the film music which was now giving way to gunfire. However, seeing the label on the bottle, Pinot Grigio, he nodded. It was fortunate that once the bottle was open and on the table Franco smiled and said, 'I'll turn the sound down a bit so we can talk.'

A howl of protest went up outside as the sound diminished but Franco went out and raised a hand.

'Just be patient a minute, I have to talk to the Marshal.' The protests died down. He ran the square as though it were a school. The Marshal couldn't help admiring him for it, but at the same time he realized that he was only going to find out what Franco decided he should find out, and that if the big barman should take it into his head to protect someone there'd be little or nothing he could do about it. It remained to be seen whether Franco was disposed to be helpful.

'I'd turn it off altogether,' the barman remarked, sitting down and filling their glasses, 'but it's better to let them go on watching the film. We want to hear each other but we don't need everybody else listening in.'

'True.'

'Your health.'

'And yours.'

'So, how's it going?'

The Marshal's eyes opened wide as he drank from the misted glass. Naturally, Franco would ask the questions! And he was by no means put out when he didn't get an answer. His mild voice just rolled calmly on.

'I didn't touch anything up there myself. I didn't even look at her. I thought it would be a mistake to create unnecessary confusion, leave more fingerprints everywhere, and so on.'

'Fingerprints?'

'This is between ourselves, you understand. Don't think I'm telling you your business, but I know the people round here and if you take my advice you'll let them go on thinking it was suicide for the time being. I haven't said anything.' He winked confidentially. 'I think you'll agree it's best . . .'

The Marshal was too astonished to sort out the questions that were tumbling through his head and he was wise enough to keep quiet. If Franco hadn't even looked at her—and it was absurd to imagine that he knew enough about forensic science, anyway . . . What did he know? The Marshal would not have been too surprised if Franco had disposed of the whole case there and then, plucking a murderer out from among his customers and serving him up as simply as he had served the bottle of cool white wine.

'I don't need to tell you that I'll do anything I can to help. Not to put too fine a point on it, I feel a bit guilty, you know. Of course, the wife's quite right in saying that nobody would have done otherwise—after all, she was crazy, not so crazy as some people might think, but when it comes to things like that—Do you know, she once tried to telephone the Pope? She was in here one Sunday morning and she got all het up about something he'd said in his speech on the telly and if she'd been able to find the number there'd have been no stopping her. She's done that sort of thing before, so you can understand why I didn't want her bothering you at that time of night, besides which she encouraged kids to climb up the scaffolding by behaving the way she did—I mean, chucking buckets of water out at them only made it more fun. You can understand that, I'm sure.'

Up to now, the Marshal hadn't understood a word but his face didn't show it and he took another draught of wine before deciding that perhaps the best place to start might be a bit further back in the story.

'Did you know Clementina well? Has she always lived here?'

'No, no. She's not from round here. Other side of the river, Santa Croce. She's not been here all that long.'

'I see. A pity.'

'Ten years at the most.'

'As little as that?'

'Might only be nine and a half but ten at the most. My family now, we've been here, in this same building, for a hundred and thirty-eight years. People move about more these days. War's often to blame. We haven't budged since the 1848 revolution, but then in the last war we were lucky and in the flood, too—lost all our stock, of course, but we live on the floor above and it didn't reach us. I remember—'

'Yesterday,' interrupted the Marshal firmly—at the back of his mind was the memory of a call to a disturbance referred to Headquarters but he wanted to take things one at a time. 'Yesterday, did you see Clementina? Was she much as usual?'

'Yes and no—I'll explain in a minute. Yesterday, you see, we had our big "do" on.'

'I've heard about that.'

'Did Pippo tell you? Well, we were busy all day getting ready for it, especially as my wife did most of the cooking. Clementina was hanging around here all day, as excited as a kiddie. She liked eating and she stuffed so much down so fast it's a wonder she wasn't ill. I've never seen her so cheerful as she was last night when her cheeks were full to bursting with ravioli.'

The Marshal remembered the fridge with one egg and a slice of sausage. 'I suppose she didn't often get a really good meal.'

'Not a meal like last night's, no. But she always had enough to eat. She hadn't a penny—well, you've been up there so you've seen how she lived, but everybody did their bit and I don't think a day passed without her getting a dish of something from her neighbours. In fact, the wife was making up a nice plate of stuff left over from last night for her when Pippo came for me to say she wasn't answering.'

Even so, to be dependent on whatever somebody thought to give you . . . The Marshal was feeling the effects of missing supper, despite his having eaten too much rabbit at lunch.

'And if it comes to that,' Franco went on, 'Pippo's wife had prepared a bit of something for her, as well, and that's how they came to notice—'

'I know,' the Marshal said, 'he told me.'

'Well, there it is. We did our best. She had a good blow-out on the last night of her life. I'm pleased about that, though, as I said, I'm not happy about that business of her phoning you.'

'Tell me about this phone call.'

'You must know all about it already, they'll have told you at your Station, of course.'

'Of course. But tell me your end of it.'

'Well, it must have been towards three in the morning . . . or maybe only two-thirty, say two-thirty.'

'You went on as late as that?'

'Well, yes and no . . . It had finished really, the party, but there were a few of the lads hanging about afterwards and Clementina's one who . . . the women had all gone home to bed long since but she was still here.'

'With all the men?'

'You must remember she wasn't right in the head. When they made a grab for her she'd think it was serious, and of course they encouraged her to. They went a bit far at times but she was almost always the one to start it. She liked attention.'

'And were they the people who were tormenting her by climbing up the scaffolding as Pippo said—did that happen last night?'

'That happened almost every night but it was the youngsters, not the men. Ever since that scaffolding's been there . . .'

'How come it's there in August?'

'You tell me. They're supposed to be doing the façade of the building by order of the town hall since there were dangerous great lumps falling off it, but if you ask me there's a shortage of money there. The scaffolding was put up but the work was never started, and in the meantime Clementina's torn the netting away to feed her pigeons.'

'Is it true she threw buckets of water at the boys who climbed up?'

'Many a time. I used to go out and tell her, "Shut your windows and go to bed and they'll soon go away." But after two minutes she'd open up and start shouting and throwing water again. And what was the use of shouting at the kids? They knew as well as I did that she enjoyed it.'

'Not very pleasant for the people underneath her.'

'You're right there. And of course with their having . . .'

'What?'

'Nothing. Poor things. He studies, you know, and the noise must often have annoyed him. They're a nice respectable young couple.'

'Yes. Well, if this racket went on every night, how is it that last night Clementina wanted to send for me?'

'I'm coming to that. We were closing up here, as I said. The lights were still on in here and the outside shutter was half down, if I remember rightly. When I went outside to roll it right down there was a racket going on under her house fit to wake the dead, and one of the kids—I couldn't see who it was—was swinging on the scaffolding. I shouted across to them to pack it in, that we all wanted to get some sleep. I waited until the lad had climbed down and everything was quiet and then I came in. That's why I interrupted when she tried to phone you. Things had been perfectly quiet for a good half-hour when she came banging at my shutter saying she wanted to call the Carabinieri. You see what I mean?'

The Marshal was beginning to see but he wasn't sure whether things might not get more difficult if he said so. He stared into his glass for so long, wondering what line to take that Franco picked up the bottle and filled it for him. When that didn't rouse him, he repeated, 'You do understand? She'd drunk a fair bit, a lot, in fact, for her. I remember how red her face was when she was dancing. She was a bit drunk—well, why not, once in a while? She enjoyed herself. But things had been quiet for over half an hour. I let her in under the shutter and I took a look outside at the same time. There wasn't a soul in sight. Even so, she grabbed the phone, shouting that someone was trying to get into her house. I tried to reason with her but the others who were still here were egging her on as they always did when she started anything like that. One fellow even went so far as to find your number for her. Well, you know how it went after that. Whoever answered told her to ring Borgo Ognissanti. I said I'd do it for her and took the receiver from her. She didn't notice that I didn't make the call because she was by the door shouting at whoever she thought was out there to fuck off and leave her alone. She swore a lot but there was no harm in it, it was just her way.'

'Hm.'

'I'd a job to get her to go home again because she was convinced that you'd be turning up. In the end I told her I'd wait for you and went up to the flat with her. I had a good look round every room to convince her there was no one there and by the time I left she'd calmed down. I'm sorry about what happened, but even now I can't think what more I could have done. When somebody's as crazy as Clementina was you've no way of knowing when, for once, there's something really wrong. How could I have known that something must have happened to really frighten her? She must have been upset and I just thought she was drunk. More than likely she was a bit of both. You understand?'

'I understand.'

'Franco!'

One of the card-players was looking in at the door, his eyebrows raised in a question.

The big barman didn't move from his chair, only lifted a plump finger and gave the slightest negative sign with it. The man in the doorway vanished. The Marshal read both question and answer but he had made his mind up by this time to notice nothing. If he got on the wrong side of Franco he would never get to the bottom of this case. He was aware of Franco's glance, checking to see if he'd noticed anything, but all he did was to take sip of wine, gazing out at the night through the open door, his face blank. Among the group of card-players, voices were raised in some brief, friendly argument. A woman's voice called out from a high window, 'I'm off to bed . . .'

The film on TV was drawing to a close to judge from the music. Everything in the piazza had returned to the normal rhythm of a summer night and it was difficult to believe that anything dramatic could have happened there, that any outsider could have penetrated this closed little world and done violence to it. This was a world where tragedies were small and familiar; the wail of the ambulance when somebody's mother had a stroke, then the daily slog to the hospital until it was all over. At worst, a heartbroken mother whose son had been caught for some petty crime. Even Clementina's madness had been an accepted daily fact of life. They made soup for her, teased her, bawled her out when she went too far. In all the years he'd been in Florence nobody had ever called him to intervene here. They settled their own differences or Franco settled their differences for them. That was how it had always gone on and how it would continue to go on. The killing of Clementina was an anomaly. It had to have been done by an outsider, and whoever had done it had been clever enough or intuitive enough to choose the gas oven as something appropriate to this district, though not efficient enough to have made a convincing job of it. Perhaps he hadn't cared that much, or had assumed that nobody else would care that much. A crazy old woman, poor and harmless, whom nobody would miss.

'I'll miss her, in a way,' said Franco, staring out at the night like the Marshal, 'though she was a pest at times. She was part of things, you know? I keep expecting her to appear out there with her brush . . .'

Nobody appeared out there.

'Seven of clubs.'—'Mine.'—'Your deal' . . .

'She once cracked the council refuse collector over the head with it.'

'What?'

'She used to go for people with her brush, especially if they got in the way of her cleaning. She was fanatical about it.'

'My wife mentioned that, said she swept the whole square.'

'Swept it? She washed and polished it. She was forever down on her hands and knees. And I've seen her go out of a shop and take her receipt straight to the skips, struggling away to lift up those high lids—she was only small—despite her little bag of shopping and the inevitable sweeping brush that was always under her arm. What a case she was. She got much worse when it started going dark, sweeping and mopping as though her life depended on it.'

'Franco?' A woman appeared from somewhere at the back of the room. She was as large as Franco and just as placid and smiling. A big brooch decorated her dress on her ample breast and she was smoking a cigarette.

'My wife, Pina,' Franco said. Evidently there was no need for him to tell her who the Marshal was.

'Eeh, poor creature . . .'

The Marshal took this to be a comment on Clementina rather than a greeting to himself.

'I'll sit down a minute,' she went on with a sigh, 'my feet are swollen. The doctor says I should walk more but I don't know where he thinks I'm supposed to walk to or how I'm to find the time.' Her beringed fingers slapped a packet of cigarettes and a plastic lighter down on the formica table and she sank on to a chair that looked far too fragile for her. Franco started to get up.

'I'll get you a glass.'

'No. I don't want anything. What were you talking about? Clementina, I suppose.'

'About the way she cleaned the square,' Franco said, 'even at night.'

'She was a strange one all right.'

'Did she always have this mania?' the Marshal asked.

'As long as she's been here and that must be ten years—isn't it, Franco? You never know, maybe she got that way when she lost her husband. It takes some women funny.'

'When did she lose her husband?'

'I couldn't tell you. I'm only guessing she was a widow because she wore a wedding ring. It's funny, now you mention it, but although she always had plenty to say for herself in her own way, she never said a word about her past.' Pina took a long drag on her cigarette which was stained with bright red lipstick. 'You can see somebody every day and in the end you don't know that much about them. I do know she had a bit of a job up to not so long ago, though goodness knows who was good enough to give it to her.'

'What sort of job?'

'Cleaning, of course!' Pina laughed. 'I know it sounds like the ideal job for her, poor creature, but she had her own ideas about cleaning and they weren't everybody's. I wouldn't have wanted her cleaning my house, I can tell you.'

It was true that when the Marshal had been in Clementina's flat he had found it tidy enough but certainly not fresh and sparkling. He'd put it down to everything in it being so old but perhaps it hadn't been too clean, at all. There was all that fluff on top of the wardrobe . . .

'Somebody doing her a good turn,' Pina suggested,

'though I don't know who. She hadn't a soul in the world to care for her.'

'Where was this job?'

'Some sort of office, wasn't it, Franco?'

'That's right. Not far from here, near the river. I don't know the name of the place.'

'I ought to know,' Pina said, 'she mentioned it many a time when she was going there . . . What the devil was the name of it?'

The Marshal didn't urge her or insist on its importance because he knew that would make it harder to remember. He couldn't even be sure that it was important but he still felt that the murder had been an 'outside job', nothing to do with the people here in the square, and anything which connected Clementina with someone outside the area might be useful.

After racking her brains a while longer, Pina stubbed out her cigarette and heaved herself up from the small chair.

'I know who'll remember. Maria Pia! Pippo's wife,' she explained to the Marshal. 'You've met Pippo.'

'Yes, I've met Pippo.'

'Well, if anybody remembers it'll be her. She never forgets a name or a face. I'll give her a shout.'

'Now?'

'She won't be in bed. She never goes to bed before midnight.'

And Pina waddled slowly to the open doorway. The Marshal saw her pause there on the pavement. One of the men at the tables must have said something to her in an undertone. Whoever it was couldn't be seen from inside. Pina shrugged and murmured something of which the Marshal only caught the word 'Franco'. He looked across at the barman, who smiled and said, 'She won't be long. Do you mind if I leave you a minute and wash a few glasses? We can still talk.'

'Of course.'

They heard Pina outside calling up in the darkness.

'Maria Pia! Maria Pia!'

Shutters creaked and banged open.

'What's up?'

'Can you remember what the place was called where Clementina worked? That office?'

'Why?'

'The Marshal's here and he wants to know.'

'But she stopped going there a while ago.'

'It doesn't matter, he still wants to know.'

'Wait . . . it's on the tip of my tongue . . .'

Why did Franco, behind the bar, remind the Marshal of some sort of mechanical toy? He was so big and his bald head was so shiny . . . and now he wrapped a huge apron round his paunch—but it wasn't his shape that did it . . . That was it. It was because whether he was talking or silent, working or doing nothing at all, his large head bobbed slightly as if it were on a spring. It was that, along with his constant gentle smile, which made him look like a giant toy.

'There! I knew she'd be the one to ask.' Pina waddled back in, triumphant, and smiled at the Marshal. 'It's called "Italmoda". Something to do with the clothes trade but I don't know exactly what.'

'Did she work there long?'

'As long as I can remember. She always worked there, didn't she, Franco?'

'Ever since she moved here. Only three mornings a week, though.' Franco lifted a steaming wire basket of glasses out of the sink.

'Make me a camomile tea, love, while you're there. And then we might as well close, what d'you think?'

Franco only nodded and smiled. He dropped a camomile teabag into a white cup and held it under the boiling water spout.

'Don't close early on account of my being here,' said the Marshal placidly. How could he make them understand that he didn't want to disturb their normal habits without admitting that he had guessed what they amounted to? On the contrary, it was essential that things went on as usual, but there was no way he could openly say so. All he risked saying was, 'I'm not here to keep an eye on you, you know . . .'

If they started closing early, he would lose his best watch-dogs. The best thing he could do might be to gain their confidence by taking them into his. He was pretty sure he could trust them not to gossip, and in any case, Franco had already said he knew it wasn't suicide. Their amiable solidity and their position of trust in the neighbourhood convinced him. Even afterwards, when the story got out with tragic consequences, it never crossed his mind to blame them. He remained convinced that he had done right in saying as he did: 'There's something I'd like to say to you in confidence, to both of you.'

He waited as Franco dried his hands and came back to the table with the teacup for his wife.

'Sit down a minute.' He glanced around him, but the television was flickering in front of empty chairs and no one was playing the computer game that was beeping somewhere out of sight. Everyone was outside, hoping for a whisper of cooler air that never came.

'Whose deal is it?'—'Mine. One more hand and I'm off to bed . . .'

The Marshal leaned forward a little towards the couple facing him across the round table but his gaze was averted, fixing the doorway to be sure no one appeared there to listen in.

'Clementina didn't commit suicide. I'm sure of that.'

'There! It's what you said, Franco.'

'The Marshal knows I know. I told him.'

'I must say, though,' pointed out the Marshal, 'that I

can't begin to imagine how you found out. You didn't even look at her.'

'There was no need to. As soon as Pippo said he'd found her with her head in the oven I knew. There wasn't enough gas in that canister to kill a sparrow. I checked it myself yesterday. She was forever running out of gas. They're not that keen on delivering just one and she sometimes hadn't the cash for two. She was pestering me yesterday when we were up to our eyes in work getting ready for the party. She thought I might have a spare canister but I didn't, and with the two-day holiday coming up she thought she was going to be without. I managed to find time to go up and check and I told her she'd enough to make her coffee and that she'd be eating here that evening and I'd see she got some leftovers or something tonight. They'll be open tomorrow so I was sure she'd manage. No great mystery, you see. Even she wasn't crazy enough to try and gas herself without gas.'

'No. Well, there it is. The fact that she was left with her head in the oven like that can only mean that somebody wanted us to think it was suicide.'

'Oh, Franco, just imagine.'

'How did they do for her, then.'

'I don't know. There'll be an autopsy. Now . . .' He turned his gaze on to them, one by one, 'You were right in thinking it had better not get about. I've told you two, not just because you already suspected something but because I think you can help, and I don't want anybody else round here to find out.'

'You surely don't think that anybody round here—'

'No,' the Marshal reassured Franco, 'I don't think anything of the sort. But if people get to know, the papers will get to know and so on. I prefer to let whoever did it think he's pulled the wool over our eyes. It's the only advantage we have over him at this point.'

Franco mulled this over for a few minutes, his shiny head

bobbing gently as he thought. Pina watched him, sipping her tea daintily.

'If it's nobody round here,' Franco pointed out, 'I don't see what help we can be to you—not that we're not willing, you follow me, it's just—'

'Don't worry, I'm not expecting you to do anything. Just keep your eyes open. If I start asking questions around here the story will soon be out, but you can chat to your customers, it will be natural enough for everyone to talk about Clementina after what's happened. You might pick something up, anything odd that involved her in the last few weeks, for example.'

'Everything about Clementina was odd,' put in Pina.

'But perhaps some stranger visited her recently.'

'Nobody as far as I know.' Franco's brow was corrugated.

'When did she stop working, do you know that?'

'I can tell you that,' Pina said, 'because it was my birthday. July 15th it was. I offered her a glass of something on the strength of it—she liked a glass when she could get it, and she said "Here's to that bastard and good riddance" and I said "What's this? Have you packed in your job?" To tell the truth, I thought it more likely that she'd got the sack, probably cracked the boss with her sweeping brush, but I didn't say so. Anyhow, all she said was, "I know my rights and what he says isn't true! I won't go!" So what the truth of it was I don't know.'

'I'll find out.'

'I suppose you will, but I don't imagine anyone would—you know—do that . . . because they were having trouble sacking her from a cleaning job. Well, you know more about these things than I do.'

'But you'll be better at keeping a watch on things round here. I'm sure you realize as well as I do that it wouldn't be worth my while putting even a plainclothes man on the job here where everybody knows everybody.'

'He'd stick out like a sore thumb,' Franco agreed. 'I see

what you mean and you're right, of course. They did once send a plainclothes man round here for something or other, and eveyone knew right away.' He glanced at his wife and then back at the Marshal. 'You don't think the chap would come back?'

'We're not safe in our beds, then!' cried Pina.

'I'm sure you are,' the Marshal assured her. 'Don't worry.'

'It gives me the creeps, I don't mind telling you,' Pina said. 'After all, Clementina wasn't safe in her bed—d'you think she was asleep when it happened?'

'Quite probably.'

'I'll bet she was,' Franco said, 'because if she'd had the chance to get one scream out she'd have woken the whole of Florence with that voice of hers.'

'You know,' said Pina thoughtfully, 'it's a shock. I mean, nobody expects somebody they know to get murdered, but I think I'd have been more surprised to hear she'd done away with herself. Whatever her faults, she wasn't one to feel sorry for herself. She might crack you one with her brush, she might swear like a trooper and even criticize the food you gave her as if she were in a restaurant, but she never asked for pity or felt sorry for herself. From the minute she got out of bed in a morning to the minute we could persuade her to go home and get back into it, she was out there and doing; cleaning, quarrelling, playing cards, swearing, giving as good as she got . . . She'd never have committed suicide in a million years, no matter what troubles she had. Am I right, Franco?'

'I think you are. And to my way of thinking it's just as well she was crazy. Given how poor she was and that miserable flat and not a soul in the world, she'd have had a miserable life if she'd been normal and kept herself to herself. It's just as well she was the way she was.'

'You may well be right,' the Marshal said. 'Anyway, let your customers have their say, and if it turns out anybody noticed anything unusual or saw any stranger about lately, let me know.'

'You'll be back, then?' Franco asked.

'At some point. I'll phone you in a day or two if I don't get a chance to come round. And now I'll be on my way and leave you in peace.' He got to his feet.

'You can rely on us,' Franco promised.

Only about half the tables outside were still occupied. At one of them, Pippo's white shirt glowed yellow in the lamplight.

He interrupted his deal to say, with a touch of self-importance, 'Good night, Marshal. Will we be seeing you again? I imagine there'll be an inquest.'

The Marshal only gave a noncommittal grunt and then added, 'Good night to you all.'

CHAPTER 4

The drawer was stiff and he had to give it quite a yank before it opened.

'Salva! Is that you?'

'Mm.'

'I thought I heard you come in. What on earth are you up to out there?' She was already in bed and he hadn't meant to wake her but he couldn't resist taking a look in the drawer in the hall.

'I'll be with you in a minute,' he called.

There . . . a box of buttons, another box with just his uniform buttons . . . the first aid kit that wouldn't fit in the bathroom cabinet, a sewing kit, the pliers . . . the pliers? He'd spent an hour looking for them the other day . . . Before long he unearthed what he was looking for, a shoebox full of old snapshots. They were the snaps that hadn't been considered worthy of the photograph album. Some were out of focus, some had been taken into the sun and some were even superimposed, showing two-headed monsters or background ghosts. He found one of the boys on the beach down at home and was amazed to see how small and plump and babyish they looked. He couldn't remember them being like that. Of course he'd seen very little of them at that age because of being posted here. He looked at the date scribbled on the back and dropped it back in the box. The photos right at the bottom were old and faded and had belonged to his mother. He had no idea how they came to be there, but there they were. Some things seemed to follow you about wherever you went without anyone thinking to take care of them, while other, more important things got lost when you moved. He was sure it was the same in every family. And yet in Clementina's flat he hadn't seen a single photograph. She'd been married but there wasn't a wedding picture. And even if she'd had no children, she'd been a child herself. She had a past, a family like everybody else. How was it possible that there wasn't so much as a single snapshot in her home? He closed the shoe box carefully and the drawer with difficulty.

'Salva! What on earth . . .?'

'I'm coming.'

She was sitting up in bed with the bedside light on. The air was heavily perfumed with mosquito-killer and a fan was whirring in one corner, though it seemed to be doing little except redistribute the hot air.

'Did I wake you?' He began unbuttoning his shirt.

'I wasn't asleep or you would have done, banging about. Whatever were you doing?'

'Looking at old photographs.'

'Ours? What for? Which photographs?'

'The snaps in that box in the drawer.'

'At this time of night? They're none of them any good, anyway. They want throwing out.'

'But they never do get thrown out, that's the point.'

'I don't know what you mean. I'll go through them one of these days, but they do keep on accumulating, year after year.'

'Exactly.'

'I wish I knew what you were talking about.'

'About Clementina, I suppose.'

'That madwoman?'

'That's right. She's dead.'

'No!'

'Yes. And there wasn't a single photograph in her flat, not one snapshot.'

'But—is that why you were called out?'

'Yes. I think I'll get a glass of water, do you want anything?'

'No, but have you eaten?'

He'd forgotten about that. 'No . . . I might have a sandwich.'

'I'll make it for you.'

'No, no. Stay where you are.'

Sitting alone in pyjamas at the kitchen table with a sandwich in front of him gave him an odd feeling which he didn't identify at once because he was distracted. He was trying to think whether he'd ever in his life been in a house without a photograph or two in it, but he couldn't. He'd known peasant families down at home when he was small who hadn't enough to eat and certainly never owned a camera, but even they had pictures of First Communions and weddings. Clementina might have been crazy, but in his book that didn't account for it. The trouble was that once a person was labelled as crazy, everything they did or said was put down to that. How many times had it been said up to now? 'Of course, she was crazy.' 'Everything about her was odd.' 'You have to remember she wasn't in her right mind.' Well, he wasn't convinced. He wasn't convinced because somebody had killed her. You don't kill a woman because she's a bit funny in the head and goes cleaning the streets after dark. You kill her for a good reason which probably had nothing to do with her being mad.

The clock on the shelf ticked softly against the sawing rhythm of the cicadas in the Boboli Gardens behind the Palace, and it struck him, at last, that sitting here alone with his sandwich reminded him of his grass widower days. It wasn't an unpleasant memory since it made him feel all the more satisfied with the present. It would be even better when the boys came back. How babyish and fat they'd looked in that photograph . . . He got up and rinsed his plate. He was wakeful, despite the late hour, and he wanted to chat to Teresa for a minute if she wasn't already asleep. He switched off the kitchen light and was pleased to find the lamp still on in the bedroom, though his wife's eyes were closed. He switched the fan off.

'Are you asleep?'

'Almost . . . What time is it?'

'Late, but you can always sleep in tomorrow.'

'I never sleep in. You know very well that once I'm awake . . .'

He got into bed and picked up the alarm clock.

'I've already set it. What happened to that poor old woman?' Her eyes were wide open now. 'Or don't you want to tell me?

'I'll tell you . . . but you mustn't say a word outside these four walls because I don't want it to get about yet. It was set up to look like suicide but somebody killed her.'

'Killed her? That harmless old thing? But surely she hadn't a penny!'

'What's that got to do with it?'

'Well . . . I don't know. I just thought—I don't know.'

'As far as I know she hadn't a penny, but somebody killed her, even so. Not a word to anybody, think on!'

'I won't say anything. You needn't have told me if you didn't want to. There's no need to get annoyed.'

'I'm not annoyed.' But the truth was that he was annoyed

and it showed in his voice. Annoyed with himself because he'd got so distracted by the photograph business and the old woman's madness that the obvious idea of her being killed for money had quite gone out of his head. And when all was said and done, what did he or anyone really know about Clementina? She might have been a miser. There could be money tucked away that they hadn't managed to find, however unlikely it seemed. Her past was a mystery. which brought him back to the photograph problem. Who was she? Where was she until ten years ago? That's what he needed to know.

'Well, if you'd rather not talk about it I'll switch the light off.'

'What? No . . . I was just thinking, that's all. But switch it off, anyway.' All of a sudden he was tired. It had been a long day, and tomorrow looked like being a longer one still.

Morning, in August, was the best time of day, the only time when the body felt cool enough and light enough to be active and the head clear enough to make the decisions of the day. The Marshal was in his office a good hour before the boys on day duty came down. Before that he had heard them getting up and showering upstairs, their voices thick with sleep when they muttered the occasional remark to each other. Outside his window the air was still and birds were chinking among the laurel bushes. He heard the park keepers arriving on the ground floor, where their office was directly below his. On a morning like this it would have been nice to live out and to walk to work through the Boboli Gardens. He got up and opened the window. The morning air was just warmed by the sun and smelled of the trees instead of the heavy traffic that burdened it for the rest of the year. He leaned out a little for a glimpse of the red dome and white marble tower of the cathedral against a pale, misty blue sky. It always pleased him. His freshly-ironed uniform felt good against his skin. He would have given a lot to get out of his office at this hour, but he had things to do and by the time he was ready to leave both the air outside and his uniform would be hot and sweaty. So he stayed where he was for a moment at the open window, making the most of it until he heard the boys come clattering down the stairs.

''Morning, Marshal.'

''Morning, lads. Sit down a minute, both of you. Everything all right?' This remark was addressed to the boy on the left, a big, cheerful lad doing his National Service.

'Yessir!' He would insist on saying Sir and saluting with a snap of his heels at the most unexpected moments. The Marshal found him disconcertingly military. The other boys laughed at him. Di Nuccio was smirking now. The Marshal maintained a pop-eyed solemnity.

The door burst open while somebody was still knocking on it.

'We're going to get the post, Marshal.'

'Wait.' The Marshal pushed the preliminary report of last night's events into a large envelope. 'Deliver this to the Public Prosecutor's office first—and put a spurt on this morning because I want to send Di Nuccio here out as soon as you get back.'

He had good reason to tell them to hurry. Going for the post at Headquarters was everybody's favourite job, since they were bound to bump into old friends over there and always got in a quick coffee and a few minutes' gossip. The Marshal knew this and pretended not to.

When they'd gone he had a few words with the National Service boy whose name was Bruno, taking care to avoid Di Nuccio's smirk as he did so. You couldn't help liking this lad although he was so eccentric. When he'd first arrived he'd been a physical fitness fanatic and spent every spare minute exercising with dumb-bells and chest expanders. Three weeks later he took up painting in watercolours and the dumb-bells vanished. And it wasn't as though you could criticize him for doing things superficially. As long as his enthusiasm lasted he gave himself to it heart and soul and got results. The boys got endless fun out of him but there was no denying that his muscles were impressive and only the week before he'd won some sort of prize for one of his paintings. The Marshal, for his part, couldn't complain. If he'd wanted to, the lad could have gone straight to university and put off his military service for years but he had accepted his call at eighteen and bounded into uniform, bursting with enthusiasm even for that. He was the only boy the Marshal had ever come across who seemed to be enjoying the experience, even when it consisted just of standing around in a draught on guard duty. Nothing deflated him and nothing dismayed him.

'Can I ask you something, sir?' asked the bright-eyed Bruno as soon as he lit on a pause in the Marshal's fatherly lecture.

'Don't call me "sir".'

'Nossir—Marshal, are you allowed to eat with us?'

'What . . .?'

'Can we invite you up to eat a meal with us, sir?'

'Don't—!'

'Sorry.'

'He's taken up cookery!' put in Di Nuccio, stifling a burst of laughter.'

'Chinese cookery,' corrected Bruno seriously. 'I've always been a good cook. I'm planning a special dinner—not yet, because I can't get the ingredients I need until the shops all re-open. But I want to invite you, too.'

'We'll see . . .' muttered the Marshal, nonplussed. 'You'd better get on duty. I want a word with Di Nuccio.'

Bruno jumped to his feet, fired off a salute and marched out as though he were under guard, slamming the door behind him.

'That boy . . .' began the Marshal, but he tailed off, at a loss for words.

'He's taken over all the cooking, all of it!' said Di Nuccio, letting his laughter out. 'We're in clover!'

'You haven't been exchanging duties without—'

'Oh no. He does all his regular duties and cooks as well. We might as well enjoy it while it lasts.'

'I suppose so . . . Does this mean he's given up painting?'

'Looks like it.'

'Hm. We'd better get to work. First of all, do you know anything about a call, the night before last, concerning a disturbance in the San Frediano district?'

'I remember seeing it on the report yesterday morning—but there was nothing to it. It was referred to Borgo Ognissanti and the lad on duty called Headquarters himself so they'd inform the nearest patrol car. Apparently they passed by but there was no disturbance—and whoever the caller was never did try Borgo Ognissanti so that was that.'

'I'm afraid it wasn't,' the Marshal said, and explained.

When he'd finished, Di Nuccio said, 'Do you think there'll be a claim of negligence?'

'No, no. The caller was correctly referred to the emergency service and the lad had the good sense to send a patrol there himself. I don't see what more he could have done even if he'd known what was going to happen.'

'That's true.'

'Now, what I want from you is some information and I want it unofficially. What's the name of that friend of yours over at Borgo Ognissanti? The one who broke his leg skiing last winter?'

'Mario?'

'That's the one. He was a neighbour of yours down home, wasn't he?'

'Same street.

'Well, as you're old friends and neighbours, both from Naples, I imagine you can get what I need from him. If I make inquiries myself action will have to be taken as a matter of course and that's the last thing I want. There's a bar in the square just across from the dead woman's house. It's my guess that there's a bit of gambling going on there —small friendly stuff, nothing to worry about—after the place shuts at night and sometimes going on until the small hours.'

'I see. Well, Mario's bound to know since it's on their night beat.'

'Just check for me. But think on, I don't want anybody poking their nose in there.'

'You don't want it stopped, then?'

'No, no. On the contrary. I want it to go on, if that's the way things are, because as long as it does go on the shutters will be down to give the impression that the place is closed and somebody, somewhere, will be keeping a lookout.'

'I see what you mean. It could be useful—provided that they're willing to report anything they might see.'

'They're willing. Nobody likes the thought of a murderer lurking about the area. But their habits mustn't be disturbed. I need their help. So, all I want to know is what time they go on till, more or less, and whether anybody who didn't know could guess from the outside that there were people in there.'

'I doubt that. I'll have a word with Mario, then, making it sound casual.'

'Don't get too complicated. Tell him the truth, if you like. As long as it doesn't come officially from me nobody's obliged to do anything about it. Understood?'

'Right.' But Di Nuccio looked disappointed. He liked a bit of intrigue to make life interesting but the Marshal preferred him to reserve this taste for his dealings with women, which, from the snatches of conversation the Marshal picked up, should have provided enough intrigue for anybody's needs.

When Di Nuccio had gone he sighed. With a business like this he'd have been glad to have his young brigadier,

Lorenzini, with him, a straightforward lad and bright, too. But Lorenzini had left for the seaside with his wife and small baby yesterday morning. He would have to make do with Di Nuccio, half a dozen or so young regulars with very little experience, and, God help us, Bruno the artist—or rather, the cook.

And, to his dismay, he realized that the temperature had already risen and sweat was beginning to trickle down his back. Why the devil did a thing like this have to happen in August?

'You know what it's like in August,' said the voice at the other end of the line apologetically.

'Of course,' the Marshal said, keeping his temper with difficulty. 'I'm in the same situation, with so many men on holiday, but—'

'Then you'll understand. I can't say at this point how much of a delay there'll be, but there are three other post-mortems which have precedence, so . . .'

'I realize that, you told me last time I called, but the point is I need as much information as possible before the story breaks that it wasn't a suicide. Otherwise it wouldn't matter so much.'

'Well, frankly, I've already spoken to the Prosecutor on the case and I must say he didn't seem so concerned as you are.'

So that was how things were. A prosecutor who was neither use nor ornament, the sort who then came down on you like a ton of bricks when things went badly.

'Have you spoken to him about it yourself?' went on the other.

'No . . .'

'Well, that might be your best bet if you really feel it's that important. It may be that if you can convince him he could put pressure on at this end. You know there's not much I can do.'

'I suppose not.'

'If you want so speak to the doctor about his on-the-spot findings . . .'

'No, there's no need. I was there. That's not what I want to know.'

But what *did* he want to know? he thought as he hung up. He knew the most important thing: that Clementina hadn't gassed herself.

'I want to know who she is,' he answered himself aloud. He would also have liked to know if she'd ever had children. That photograph business was still sticking in his mind, though, needless to say, he hadn't mentioned that in his preliminary report to the Prosecutor this morning. Was there any point in trying to get him to put pressure on about the post-mortem? There was no harm in trying. He might have read the report by now. The Marshal mopped his brow with a handkerchief and dialled. The Prosecutor hadn't read his report. It was apparently still lying on his desk unopened, according to the registrar who answered. He was in court at the moment but would certainly receive the Marshal's message as soon as he was free. 'He's got a very heavy workload, and this being August . . .'

The most important thing in the heat is to keep your temper. Once you let it boil over you feel ill for the rest of the day. To distract himself from the Prosecutor and the post-mortem, the Marshal doggedly ran his finger down the list of things he had set himself to do, looked up the number of Italmoda and dialled it. But no sooner had it started ringing than he felt a rising tide of anger against the Public Prosecutor's office and all who dwelt therein, with special reference to the sort of substitute prosecutor who didn't so much direct an inquiry as sit on it, only shifting every now and then to derail it when it was going along nicely without his help. And all the talk there was these days about their defending their precious autonomy. A good deal less of it was what they needed, and some sort of outside watchdog to keep them under control. A bunch of prima donnas, that's what they were, and not above such childish tricks as calling the police in on a case to spite the Carabinieri and vice versa. 'Keeps them on their toes.' He'd actually heard one of them say it. Well, if this one wanted a scene, he could have it—no, he couldn't! He'd keep perfectly calm, that's what he'd do. Blast the man—and blast the people in this office who couldn't be bothered to answer their phone! A fine way to run a business. No wonder the country was going to the dogs.

The ringing at the other end went on and on and the Marshal's head felt fit to burst. Suddenly he slammed the receiver down and slumped back in his chair, passing a finger under his damp collar. Of course nobody was answering the phone. Whoever heard of an office being open in August? He shut his eyes and tried to breathe slowly, but his heart was beating too fast, and somehow his breathing insisted on keeping up with it. He'd done it. He'd boiled over. If he had any sense he'd just go quietly on with his routine work and let Clementina's case hang fire until September when it was possible to work properly because the world was functioning again. Of course, if he did try that on, the Prosecutor would appear from nowhere and start harassing him. He went and closed the window and switched on the fan. Then he switched the fan off again and got his jacket from behind the door. There was one possibility left on his list, and if the day was going to be that sort of day then he might as well go on blundering through it. Why spread the agony out over two or three days? He poked his head into the duty room as he left. Bruno was holding forth.

'A wok, since you're so ignorant, is a special sort of pan with sloping sides—'

'All right, all right, but we haven't got one,' said Di Nuccio, stabbing at the switchboard with a plug.

'No, but I'm going to get one as soon as the shops open.'

'I'm going out,' interrupted the Marshal, and shut the door.

Down in the entrance, he blinked in pain as the light hit his sensitive eyes and he fished out his sunglasses. Only a very few cars were dotted about the sloping courtyard in front of the Pitti Palace and the tourists rambled about freely in their bright new holiday clothes. Someone had dropped an ice-cream which had melted into a slimy pink and brown puddle around a sodden cone. He walked slowly down and crossed the road to take a short cut down a dark alleyway. The streets smelled sweaty and the large ochre stones of the high buildings shimmered with heat. He crossed Piazza Santo Spirito, where the absence of market stalls had a depressing effect. There was just one peasant farmer in from the country with a few limp-looking greens for sale on a small table. An old woman was poking about in them, grumbling.

It was cheering to find Franco's bar open. The butcher and the greengrocer wouldn't open until tomorrow. The Marshal stepped under the scaffolding in front of Clementina's building and rang the first-floor bell. A trickle of sweat rolled slowly down between his shoulder-blades until it reached his belt. Another was forming at the bridge of his nose under the sunglasses. He dabbed at this one with his handkerchief, replaced his glasses, rang the bell again and stood back a little in the road.

'They're out,' said a voice behind his head. He turned. Pippo's wife, Maria Pia, was leaning out of the window, dangling a dripping white shirt. 'I think they've gone to her mother's.'

'Oh yes? And where would that be?'

'Arezzo.'

'Arezzo . . .' If they'd gone that far they'd be gone all day. And surely, when he'd told them he'd be back the young man had said, 'Tomorrow would be better.' Much better. They'd be gone! Well, he might have expected it, the way things were going today.

'You don't know when they'll be back?' he called up.

Pippo's wife had pegged the shirt to the line hanging below her window and was squeaking it along on the pulley to make room for another.

'Moh . . .' she said with a shrug, and a second shirt sent a flurry of cool drops down on the Marshal's upturned face. 'Oh dear . . . watch out!'

'Good day to you,' said the Marshal and turned away.

''Bye,' she said, and then as an afterthought called out, 'Franco might know!'

So he might. But if they were out they were out, and what the Marshal needed, as those few cool drops had reminded him, was a shower. And maybe a cup of coffee, too. The heat had gone to his head to the extent that he couldn't care less that the wretched young couple had gone off. All he cared about was getting in off the hot streets and under a cool shower. That was all he wanted now.

What he got was a waiting-room full of tourists, one of them an elderly lady who was crying quietly into a paper handkerchief.

'Thank goodness you're back.' A harassed-looking Di Nuccio put his head round the duty room door and the Marshal glimpsed two more tourists in there behind him. 'There's been a pickpocket at work in the galleries and as these people are all foreigners and can't understand a word I say this is going to go on for ever.'

The elderly woman went on crying quietly and the rest of the group all turned reproachful eyes on the Marshal, as though it were his fault that their holidays had taken this unexpected turn for the worse. His first thought was that, given the sweaty condition of his shirt, he wouldn't be able to take off his jacket before tackling this lot. His second thought was that at least there was somebody else working in this heat and, judging by the row of woeful faces before him, the pickpocket had had a more successful morning's work than himself.

'You haven't even glanced at the paper.'

'It's late . . .' He buttoned up his collar and picked up his jacket.

'Well, you came in late for lunch so I don't see why you can't have ten minutes' rest. There's an article about Clementina . . .'

'Hmph.'

'They've given her almost half a page.'

'What . . .? It doesn't say anything—'

'Oh no. The headline says suicide. I suppose there isn't much news, so . . .'

'Well, I haven't time to look at it.'

'I just thought you'd be interested.' She was disappointed. He knew that she was feeling more and more at a loose end as time passed without the children, and it was beginning to weigh on him as much as the weather.

It was with this in mind that he said, 'We'll go out for an hour after supper,' remembering that it was because of Clementina that they had missed their walk out the night before. A logical sequence of thought, as he pointed out later, that needed a woman's convoluted mind to interpret as a snub. This came out towards nine in the evening when supper was cleared away and they were on the point of going out. The idea had been to take the paper with him since they intended to find a not too expensive café where they could afford to sit outside, a privilege that doubled the price of a drink.

'What d'you mean, you threw it away? You never throw it away the same day.'

'Well, I did today,' she said calmly.

Which didn't stop him stumping around the house, grumbling under his breath, apparently still looking for it.

'What are you doing, for goodness' sake? I've thrown it

away, since you said you didn't want to read it.'

'I said I hadn't time to read that one article at that one moment!'

'Are we going out?'

'Going out? What's the point of going out?'

Being accustomed to what she privately referred to as his 'brown bear act', his wife went into the bedroom to touch up her hair and put a bit of lipstick on. As she took a white cotton jacket from the wardrobe she could still hear him growling to himself in the middle distance.

'These things wouldn't happen if everybody did what he was supposed to do . . .'

A remark familiar to the boys upstairs. He occasionally forgot that his wife wasn't one of them. When she was ready she picked up her handbag and they left in sedate silence.

At twenty past nine they were crossing the bridge and the lamps came on, stage-lighting the embankments and making the water glimmer. As was their habit, they paused to look down at the river.

'That boy . . .' he began suddenly.

'I suppose you mean Bruno. I don't know why you let him worry you so much. I think he's a lovely boy and so cheerful.'

'He's taken up cooking. Whatever next?'

'And why not? He's such a nice boy.'

'Nobody's saying he's not nice, but for goodness' sake . . .' As usual, he tailed off, baffled.

At which point his wife felt safe in saying, as they strolled on, 'I'm sorry about the paper.'

'Hmph.'

'It was a good picture of her, too, poor old thing.'

'What?' He stopped in his tracks and stared at her.

'I said it was a good picture of her. The one in the paper. Very like.'

'Come on!'

'What are you hurrying for?'

The broad street between the bridge and the cathedral was warmly lit and the tourists strolling out from their hotels after the evening meal filled the air with a heavy mixture of perfumes and after-sun cream. The Marshal and his wife all but crashed into a heavily built and finely dressed couple who turned to stare after them.

'Excuse me . . .' mumbled the Marshal, when they were already well out of earshot.

'Where are we going in such a rush? Salva?'

'The nearest open bar. I want to see that paper.'

But the bars and cafés in this area served the tourist trade and didn't find it necessary to provide the local paper. The Marshal glowered at a tray of drinks being taken to an outside table at one place, garishly coloured drinks in outsize glasses with paper flags stuck into the fruit floating on top. 'Good God . . .'

'We should try a side street,' suggested his wife.

They found the sort of bar they wanted in a cul-de-sac not too far away.

'Have you got today's *Nazione*?'

'Of course. It's in the back, I think. I'll get it for you.'

'Good. You can pour us a drink first, in that case.'

There was a jug of Sangria on the counter which looked tempting. They were each sipping a glass of it when the barman came back to say apologetically, 'I'm afraid my wife must have taken it home with her . . .'

'Don't worry,' Teresa said twenty minutes later, 'after all you've only got to ring the paper tomorrow morning and they'll give you a copy.'

Which was true. Even so, his curiosity had got the better of him. Where had they found the photograph when he had found none? It was usual for the journalists to ask the Carabinieri for a loan of one of the photos they found in the house in these cases. If that fellow Galli had found one while he was up there in the Marshal's absence and made off with it, there'd be trouble!

'What was it like, anyway,' he asked his wife. 'Did it look recent?'

'It must have been. I recognized her straight away.'

Their walk was ruined. He quite forgot that they had intended to stop and sit down for a while and his wife was almost trotting to keep up with his determined strides.

Nevertheless, out of habit, they were following their usual route, and it was when they were back on their own side of the river and passing the little garden where they often sat down to look at the view that the Marshal spotted a man in shirtsleeves seated on what they regarded as 'their' bench, reading the paper by lamplight. The Marshal turned in by the path.

'Salva,' whispered his wife, 'you're surely not going to . . .'

The man was a bit surprised but not too put out.

'Help yourself. Is it in the main paper or the local pages?'

'The local pages, I imagine.'

His wife kept her distance, too embarrassed to look.

When he rejoined her they walked on in silence until she became exasperated enough to say: 'Isn't that just like you!'

'What?'

'You drag me all over town looking for a newspaper photograph as though it were the only thing that mattered on this earth and when you find it you don't say a word!'

And he still didn't. He had nothing to say. The photograph had certainly been recent and it was a very good one, too, with a professional look about it as opposed to the usual blurred and formless look of the enlarged snapshots often used in such circumstances. But what was keeping him silent more than anything was that he was convinced he'd seen it before.

They were back at the Pitti Palace and turning in under the arch on the left to the barracks before she tried again.

'What about the article? Did you look at it?'

'No. How could I? I'll ring Galli tomorrow.'

She gave one of her ostentatious sighs and began: 'It's just like your mother always used to say . . .'

He fished for his keys as they climbed the stairs.

'You were the same as a child. She told me once . . .'

To the comforting background of this familiar speech, he went on searching his memory. Where had he seen that picture before?

CHAPTER 5

'No mystery about that, it was in our archives—if you want to phone back this afternoon Galli should be in. He's out on a story but he'll be here about three.'

'It doesn't matter, if you can tell me about it.'

'I doubt if I can be that much help. Galli told me all about it the other night—I live just further down the road from Clementina and he was on his way to supper at my house that night. The supper was ruined but Galli got himself a scoop—not that he let me in on it until the next day, the bugger, but that's journalism for you.'

'Not much of a scoop, a suicide.'

'In August? Are you kidding? I gave two columns to the plight of abandoned animals in the city yesterday! You know the sort of thing . . . people who get a pet and as soon as the holidays come round they don't know what to do with it. They just throw them out to roam the streets. Anyway, as to Galli's scoop, he squeezed as much mileage out of it as he could and he even went through the archives just in case we had anything on her, found that photograph and slapped it in as padding. If you've seen it before it's because two summers ago, when we had the same problem of too much space and no news, we ran a series of articles—July, it was, if I remember rightly, not August. "Florentine characters" it was called. Well-known eccentrics, colourful characters of the Quarter, that sort of stuff. Each of us contributed a couple of short pieces based on our own neighbourhood. I did three of them, as a matter of fact, because San Frediano's full of characters like that. I did the old flower-seller who used to stand on the corner of Piazza Santo Spirito—he's dead now, run over by a bus, and then Torquato who sells a few vegetables and a lot of backchat on the market there. He's still going, you know who I mean?'

'Oh yes. He was there yesterday when I passed.'

'Well, and then I did Clementina, just for a laugh, really, and because I knew how much she'd enjoy having her photo taken. She liked attention.'

'So I've heard. And did she enjoy it?'

'I'll say. The whole square was in an uproar. They were falling about laughing at the way she posed for us and she was so insistent that we ended up taking twice as many shots as we needed. It's not bad, though, is it, the one we used? You have to admit she's photogenic—was, I should say.'

'You didn't give her a copy?'

'I don't know whether she ordered one or not—they have to be ordered and paid for. Our photographers are an independent firm though they're here in the same building, so anyone who wants a copy of a photo has to fill in one of their forms and pay for the print, and so on. I expect our Clementina just kept the one out of the paper.'

'I expect so. You don't know anything else about her, do you, given that you live so near?'

'Not really, except that it's a lot quieter at nights now she's no longer with us. She used to be shouting and creating until all hours. You'd do better to ask people who've lived there longer. I'd only been in the area a couple of months when I did that piece.'

'But to write that you must have talked to her, asked her some questions about herself.'

The young reporter burst out laughing. 'I tried to! But for all the good it did me I might as well not have bothered.

She made up all sorts of rubbish. I remember one of the things she said was that she was going on a cruise for her summer holidays. One of the local chaps shouted "That's right, down the Arno!" This was out in the square, so of course everybody was standing round, joining in and taking the mickey out of her. Whoever made that crack about the river Arno got cracked himself, over the head with Clementina's sweeping brush—she never put it down, even for the photographer.'

'"Who's paying for your cruise?" one of the others shouted. "The Pope? Is that what you were ringing him up about?"

'"Not the Pope, though I might go and see him sometime. It's a man I know who's paying for me."

'"Eeh! Clementina, if you go away with another man it's all over between us." This chap tried to clasp her in his arms and she was struggling like mad to get her brush free and lay into him. But her face was pink and you could see she was delighted to be at the centre of attention. Then she stopped fighting and started giggling.

'"All right, then, maybe I won't go."

'"You go, Clementina, and we'll all come with you." Then they started singing to her. You can imagine how much useful material I got for my article. Afterwards, we had a drink in the bar there and I talked to a chap called Franco—I don't know if you've met him.'

'I've met him.'

'Well, anything useful I got, I got from him, and he'd been the one to come out and shut them all up because they were getting out of hand. So there you are . . . I said I couldn't be much help to you.'

'Thanks, anyway.'

'If Galli had been here . . .'

'Never mind. It was really just the photograph that interested me for a particular reason. I won't keep you from your work any longer.'

The young man laughed again. 'If you really want to know, I'm trying to fill in time by tidying out my desk drawers. It's amazing the things you find when you're not looking for them.'

When he'd hung up, the Marshal sat staring at the photograph in yesterday's paper which he'd just begged from the park-keeper's office downstairs. His mind was a blank. Only a couple of weeks later, when the first faint breeze began to refresh the September air, was he to wonder at himself. Was it his innate stupidity or was it the heat that made the tiniest mental or physical effort seem huge? What, after all, would it have cost him to say Yes instead of No to the young reporter's suggestion that he talk to Galli? Looking back on it, nothing at all. And it would have saved a man's life. But at the moment, his brain, never a great force, felt like an overboiled cauliflower. The facts went in but then lay stagnating until it was too late. So he sat there, staring at Clementina's bright, excited eyes peering out at him over the handle of her sweeping brush, his mind, if you could call it that, rambling round and round on the same course. Why were there no photographs in her house? Why did she seem to have no past? It wasn't that they were the wrong questions. On the contrary, they were exactly the right questions, but he just went on asking them without finding any answers. He felt hot and weary and fed up with himself. That, as far as it went, was understandable, but that he could have sat gaping at that picture of Clementina without reading the article underneath was almost beyond belief, even for a man with his record of what his mother used to refer to as 'being asleep on his feet'.

The only piece of luck, if you could call it that, was his leaving the wretched thing there on the desk while he got on with some minor paperwork. Because of this he was able to save face when, half an hour later, the phone rang.

'Substitute Prosecutor for you, Marshal.'

'Put him on.'

'Guarnaccia? I've just read your report.'

The Marshal coughed and shuffled in his chair. 'I'm afraid there isn't much to go on at present.'

'I can see that,' snapped the Prosecutor. 'We'd cut a better figure all round if these journalists got their information from us instead of the other way round. I gather that's the situation since there's no mention of San Salvi in your report. If you did know anything about it I'd have appreciated your letting me know before the Press, whether you thought it relevant or not! Are you there?'

'Yes . . .' The Marshal was sliding the newspaper towards him, trying to open it without making any tell-tale rustling noise. Never had he been so grateful for being in receipt of such a long-winded roasting which went in one ear and out the other as his big eyes scanned the article until the words *San Salvi* jumped off the page at him, the name of the city's mental hospital. He went on reading until the Prosecutor ran out of steam and then said, 'It was the journalist who found out. There was something in their archives, which is where they found the photograph. I've already called the newspaper.'

'In that case, you might also have been good enough to call me, too, before this article was published.'

'I telephoned you yesterday but you weren't in,' the Marshal said, hoping the Prosecutor wouldn't inquire too closely into the sequence of these events.

'I see. Well, at least, first thing this morning then.'

'I thought I'd better look into it first. A newspaper is hardly a reliable source of information.' Not bad, that, for somebody asleep on his feet, and he was still reading the article.

'Ten years in San Salvi . . . released as a result of the new law . . . inadequate supervision . . . poverty . . . suicide . . . is this the Ministry of Health of a civilized country . . .'

'I take it you're going up there, then?'

'Almost immediately.' Well, he hoped he could count on their not shutting for August, at any rate.

'In that case, get in touch with me as soon as you get back.'

'Of course.'

'I shall push for the post-mortem to be done tomorrow. I don't see why August should be an excuse for the lackadaisical attitude one finds everywhere.' A remark obviously aimed at the Marshal's own deficiencies. Still, at least he was showing a bit of interest, which was unexpected.

'I may well decide to break the news of its being a murder tomorrow. It might bring in more information.'

'I wonder . . .' The Marshal tailed off uncertainly.

'What's that?'

'I was thinking that perhaps if we waited . . .'

'Waited for what? The paper's making altogether too much of this business and the chief public prosecutor wants it cleared up with no loose ends. I'm leaving for my holiday on September 4th so I'd appreciate a bit of effort on your part.'

A succinct enough explanation of his sudden interest.

'I'll do my best,' the Marshal said, 'and I'll be in touch the minute I have something from the asylum.'

This time, when he hung up, he read Galli's article with great care.

By eleven o'clock he was ready to pay a visit to San Salvi, but he only got as far as the stairs when Di Nuccio called him.

'Phone for you, Marshal. They say it's urgent.'

He went back to his office and picked up the receiver.

'Is that you, Marshal? I've got a bit of news for you.'

There was no need to ask who it was. There was no mistaking the calm, slow voice of Franco. As if well aware of this, the barman didn't bother to identify himself.

'Has something happened?' the Marshal asked him.

'No, but I've been chatting to my customers, like you said, and I've found out that somebody called on Clementina a bit ago, a stranger.'

'How long ago?'

'I can't tell you exactly but about a month. It's a long time ago, I suppose, for it to have anything to do with what happened. All the same, I thought I should tell you because nobody ever came to see her before.'

'You did right. Who was it told you?'

'The young woman who lives underneath her, when she came in this morning for a bottle of wine.'

'I see. They're back from Arezzo, then?'

'Late last night. You knew, did you, that they'd been to her mother's?'

'Yes, I did.' And it gave the Marshal a mild feeling of satisfaction to have known something without Franco's telling him. But then Franco took the edge off it by saying:

'That's right. Of course, you were ringing their bell yesterday, I remember Maria Pia saying.'

'Hmph . . . Did you get a description of this stranger?'

'How do you mean exactly?'

'Did this young woman—what's her name?'

'Signora Rossi.'

'This Signora Rossi. Did she tell you what the man looked like?'

'Oh yes. Every detail. She saw him on the stairs, you see, going up, and then she watched for him coming down and got a good look at him.'

'Why was she so interested that she watched for him coming down?' It was a habit of old people with nothing better to do than watch the goings-on of their neighbours but it seemed odd in a young woman. It was true, of course, that she'd been looking out the first time that the Marshal had gone up to Clementina's flat. 'Is she the nosey type?'

'No, I wouldn't say that.'

'Then why was she watching for him coming down?'

'I couldn't tell you . . .'

You won't tell me, thought the Marshal, but I'll find out.

'So what did he look like?'

'Well, she said he wasn't all that tall but he was big, stocky like, with a thick bull's neck. He was balding but not that old. She said he looked a real brute—oh, and that he walked with a limp.'

'Anything else? How was he dressed?'

'It was a wet day and he had some sort of dark raincoat on. Wait—she said he wore a very big ring with a jewel in it, size of a knuckle-duster. She said he gave her a fright.'

'Why? He was calling on Clementina, wasn't he?'

'Even so, he was in the building and he looked like a nasty specimen. Well, there it is. That's all. Nobody else seems to have seen him.'

'What time of day did he call?'

'Lunch-time. That's probably why nobody else saw him because everybody eats about the same time round here.'

'I see. I'm very grateful to you.'

'D'you think it might be him?'

'What do you mean?'

'Him. You know . . .' He lowered his already quiet voice to a whisper: 'Could it be him . . . who did it? Don't worry, I'm ringing from the flat, not down in the bar. I didn't want anybody listening in.'

'That was sensible of you. I'll be in touch.' And the Marshal hung up without answering Franco's question.

Whether it was 'him' or not, there was no saying. The Marshal was just as interested to know what the problem was with that couple downstairs. Well, it was something that would have to wait. He had a fractious prosecutor and the San Salvi story to deal with first. He went off down the stairs again, fishing for his dark glasses as he went, and this time nobody called him back. By the time his phone started ringing again, he was driving along the river bank and it was too late. Had he been there to answer, he'd only have had to make the same journey he was making now, and without knowing, even then, that it would only lead to a dead end.

The gates of the asylum stood open and the tree-lined avenue was deserted and silent except for the chirping of birds. The Marshal began to wonder, as he drove past a tightly shuttered villa on his left, if he would end up finding nobody even here because it was August. He'd never had occasion to visit the place before but he knew, as everyone knew, that it was supposed to have closed down about ten years ago, according to a new law which abolished asylums. But he also knew, as not everyone did, that it was still operating for the benefit of such chronic patients as had nowhere to go.

He passed yet another deserted building. Had the patients been farmed out somewhere for a month? He was relieved to see a few cars parked outside the next villa and someone disappearing through the main door. He parked his car near the others, pushed his dark glasses under the dashboard and then got out and locked up.

'Hello.'

The Marshal looked about him, blinking, but he saw no one at first, unaccustomed to the sudden light.

'Hello.'

A tall, fat man was standing on the lawn in the shade of a big magnolia tree to the Marshal's right. He was dressed in a soiled white T-shirt and cotton trousers which left his enormous belly bare, and he was standing so still that it had been difficult to spot him right away.

'Hello,' he repeated.

'Good morning,' answered the Marshal.

'Hello. Hello.' Apparently satisfied, the fat man turned away and lowered his trousers, crouching to relieve himself in the grass.

The Marshal put his keys in his pocket and entered the building. The entrance hall was bare and the whitewashed walls badly scuffed. There was a porter's lodge on the right and he looked in at the window; the porter was buried in his newspaper. Rather than tapping on the glass, the Marshal knocked on the door and went in.

'Good morning. Marshal Guarnaccia's the name. I'd like a word with—'

But the porter had already jumped to his feet and picked up the telephone, saying as he dialled, 'I'll get you the archivist right away.'

'Archivist . . . ?' The Marshal frowned. 'It was the director I wanted.'

'Director? There's no director here—hello? Mannucci? They've sent somebody from the Carabinieri. I'll send him straight to you, shall I? Yes . . . Right.' He hung up. 'Mannucci's coming to fetch you himself. I can't leave the lodge unattended. You were quick about it, I must say.'

'What do you mean?'

'Mannucci sent for you, didn't he?'

'Nobody sent for me, as far as I know.'

'Well, that's a turn-up for the books. Here he is.'

A bustling, grey-haired man appeared at the lodge door. He had a pleasant face and very bright eyes but he was looking anxious.

'Ah, Marshal, good morning.' He shook the Marshal's hand briskly. 'You were very prompt. Come this way, will you.'

The Marshal made no protest but followed the archivist down a series of corridors to his office, where he was offered a chair in front of the desk. The area around this desk was a little island of colour and cheerfulness in a sea of grey. There were reproductions of paintings on the walls and a clutter of photographs and personal belongings on the desk, which gave a human touch in contrast to the otherwise unrelieved drabness of steel filing cabinets occupying the rest of the room. There was a stack of dusty old files on the floor labelled with spidery brown handwriting, looking even more depressing than the grey cabinets.

'A sort of hobby of mine,' Mannucci said, following the Marshal's glance. 'Those files there contain reports on deaths occurring in the asylum since it opened. I've reached the year 1919. I'm compiling a survey on the history of this place before it disappears altogether. But I'd better not get on my hobby-horse or I'll waste your entire day. I called you in, rightly or wrongly—'

'Just a minute,' interrupted the Marshal, 'before you go any further, I don't know who you called and why but I'm not here because of that. I'm here on my own account to make some inquiries concerning a case I'm looking into at the moment. Whoever you've called in will no doubt turn up in due course, but if you don't mind—'

The telephone rang.

'Excuse me . . . Speaking. Put him on . . . Yes, yes, he is. I'll pass him to you. It's for you.'

The Marshal took the receiver, puzzled. It was the lieutenant he'd called the night they found Clementina.

'I telephoned you at Pitti and they said you were on your way up there, though I don't know how you got on to this business by yourself.'

The Marshal was more puzzled than ever. 'I came here because of the . . . suicide case. It seems the woman was a patient here for some years and I thought they might be able to give me some information about her.'

'I see. Well, they called here about the same thing so I wanted to put you on to it. It seems somebody's been up there already making inquiries and they got suspicious.'

'When was this?'

'Yesterday afternoon. Apparently, the archivist you're with now had some doubts and told the man to come back this morning so as to give himself time to consult his colleagues. When the man didn't come back, he got worried and called us. I'll leave you to deal with things there, though I suppose I'd better give the Substitute Prosecutor a ring and let him know.'

'He won't be too pleased.'

'You think not? Why's that?'

'He's already annoyed that the paper was better informed than we were and now it looks as though if I'd at least read that article as soon as it came out I'd have got here before this mysterious visitor. No, he won't be pleased at all.'

'Hm. Well, if it makes you feel any better I hadn't read that article myself until I got the call from the asylum. Don't worry about it. Get on with things there and I'll see to the Prosecutor. I've worked with him before and it's not easy, I know.'

'Thanks.'

The Marshal hung up and sat back, looking at Mannucci.

'So, tell me all about it.'

'It was yesterday afternoon, 'Mannucci began, 'about three o'clock, I think, though I can't be exact to the minute.'

'It doesn't matter. Go on.'

'There was a knock at my door—well, I'll not waste your time with all the ins and outs and ifs and buts—what this chap wanted was the medical file of Anna Clementina Franci.'

'You didn't give it to him, I hope?'

'Certainly not. We don't give people's files out just like that. In certain cases the patient's family doctor can ask to consult it and in even rarer cases we let medical students doing research consult our files. On the other hand, we can release a photocopy of the file if the patient, after being released from here, supplies a written request for it. This man claimed to be a relation with authority to act for Anna Clementina Franci and he had the written request signed by her—don't worry, I still didn't give him what he wanted.

It so happens that I heard about this woman's death even before it came out in the paper because I've got friends in that Quarter and I met them strolling round the centre that very evening. The wife and I usually go for a stroll after supper. She likes to look at the shop windows and since it's too hot to sleep anyway . . . So, as I was saying, we met up with these friends of ours and they were telling us how they'd seen a big crowd outside a house on their way out, and when they'd asked what was going on they were told that crazy Clementina had committed suicide.'

'Did they know her?'

'No. They're from the same Quarter but two squares away. They've got their own version of a crazy Clementina who writes slogans and insults on the walls inside their building, like a juvenile delinquent though she's pushing eighty. Anyway, I was pretty sure that this "crazy Clementina" was Anna Clementina Franci, so I rang the newspaper the minute I got back home. It was very late but they put me on to the journalist who was writing the thing up in a rush so it could go to press that night.'

'Excuse me, but why did you ring the paper?'

'To get publicity. That must sound odd to you but I'm always on the lookout for a chance to get this place named in the papers or on TV because, I can tell you, we can't go on much longer—I'm sorry . . . another hobby-horse of mine. I'll try to stick to the point. Suffice it to say that the journalist was very obliging. Despite the fact that he had already got his story together and was half way through writing it he let me convince him to do a different version, giving as much emphasis as possible to the plight of the mentally ill and the situation here. "No problem," he said to me. "To tell you the truth I don't give a monkey's what goes into the thing as long as it helps fill the paper. Just leave it to me." Of course I know only too well from experience that I've got more of a chance in the summer when there's not much news, which is why I jumped to it as soon as I heard. So when this character turned up with his written request for the file, I'd known since the night before that the woman was dead.'

'You think the thing was a forgery?'

'Not necessarily. It was dated before her death. Not that that proves anything, but I knew Anna Clementina Franci and I knew her signature—she was already a patient here when I took this job—so the first thing I did was to look into her file there and then and compare the signatures. I'm not a handwriting expert, of course, but it didn't look genuine to me, though it was like enough to have convinced me if she hadn't been dead.'

'You had her signature?'

'On her transfer documents—I'll explain in a minute.'

Was he always so energetic and enthusiastic or was it the novelty? To judge by his 'hobby-horses', the former, thought the Marshal. He seemed quite undaunted by an environment that would have reduced a less buoyant personality to tears.

'Now, the next thing I did, because for some reason, despite the plausible date and signature, I wasn't convinced—'

'Why weren't you, exactly?'

'Well, legally, I could have let him have a photocopy but, after all, the woman was dead so he wasn't intending to give it over to her. And if she had written the request, why had she? I mean, if she was intending to kill herself . . . there's no knowing, of course, but I got the impression that he was the one who wanted it. It went through my mind that if I should commit suicide after being a patient in here for years, maybe my family wouldn't want it publicized. But the harm was done in this case. It made no sense. Wouldn't you have thought it odd? So, I thought to myself, I'll get to the bottom of this because there's something fishy about it. I said to him, crafty as I am, that there was no difficulty, that I'd put the request through and a copy would be made and that he should come and pick it up this morning.'

'And he didn't come, is that right?'

'Not a sign of him. So I called you people, just to be on the safe side.'

'I'm very glad you did.' Was the Prosecutor right, after all, in thinking it would be better to let the true story out? It was lucky that the archivist was both quick-witted and cautious, but if he'd known it was a question of murder he might have managed to keep the man waiting and called the Carabinieri straight away . . . But what was he thinking of? Whoever the fellow was, he wouldn't have had the nerve to show his face here if it weren't that he thought he'd pulled off the suicide trick. I'm beginning to lose my grip, he thought, annoyed with himself. An impatient prosecutor and this wretched heat will be enough to make me mess things up good and proper if I don't keep calm.

'I even gave him an appointment for 9.30,' Mannucci said, 'to make it sound more convincing.'

'Is the file still here?'

'Of course. It's—you surely don't think he could have . . .'

'If he didn't come back,' the Marshal said, 'it might be because he caught on to your being suspicious, but more likely it was because he'd got what he wanted.'

'No!' Mannucci got up and went to one of the filing cabinets. 'No, I'm quite sure that when he left I closed the drawer and it was in its place—yes. Here it is.'

'Can I be permitted to see it?'

'Well . . .'

'I'd better tell you at this point—but please keep it to yourself—this woman didn't commit suicide, she was murdered. And the man you talked to yesterday might well have been the murderer.'

'In that case . . .' Mannucci came and sat down at his desk and opened the file. He was neither upset nor surprised at this piece of news. No doubt, after working many years in a place like this, nothing shocked him.

'If you feel you want to consult your superior first . . .' the Marshal began.

'There's nobody to consult in this place, Marshal. It runs itself as best it can. Surely you know that it's officially closed?'

'But somebody must run things. Isn't there at least some sort of administrator?'

'Certainly there's an administrator. He keeps a record of how many slices of meat we consume and how much we spend on laundry.'

'I see. Then perhaps the senior doctor.'

'We have no doctors, either. Not in residence. There are a number of doctors who each do a short spell of duty here each week. We have a few of our own nurses and some nuns, the few that remain—they once had a house here but since the place closed there are only a handful still with us. There used to be almost three thousand patients in here, Marshal, many of them chronically insane and many more without a soul to care for them, and then along comes some bright spark, full of fancy new ideas, and makes a law closing the asylums. All nice and tidy on paper. Once these places cease to exist it's that much easier to pretend the people who were in them no longer exist either!'

'Three thousand . . . but where did they all go?'

'According to popular rumour, home to their loving families who were waiting for them with open arms. In reality, we found homes for a few, a very few. A large part were transferred by their families to a private asylum run by the Church, and those of them who knew how to wangle it got the National Health to foot the bill. Short-term patients who used to be brought in here just the once, or who were in and out of here when they needed it, now go into the psychiatric wards of regular hospitals—and even those wards officially shouldn't exist, according to the new law. The psychiatric patients are supposed to be mixed in with the physically sick ones, but you tell me how that can be managed. The patients you see here now are the chronically insane who have nobody to retrieve them and dump them elsewhere. They'll be here until they die, with no director, no resident physician or psychiatrist, and precious little money even to keep the place decent because you don't get votes by pouring money into an asylum that everybody likes to think doesn't exist any more. That's how we get along here, Marshal, and if you want to know what it means in real terms I'll give you an example: last week a visiting doctor was kind enough to stay overnight because there wasn't a nurse available for night duty on one of the wards. That should give you an idea.'

'I see,' the Marshal said. 'Of course I hadn't imagined . . .'

'No. Nobody can imagine and you can be sure that pretty well nobody wants to. I'm sorry. I shouldn't be sounding off like this, but if you knew what it was like to struggle on here day after day—if this were a dog's home we'd get a lot more sympathy and help. That's why I called the paper, and I'll go on calling them and anybody else who'll listen to me because somebody's got to defend these people. Now, I'll stop sounding off and we'll take a look at this file. She was quite a character, was Clementina. Did you know her at all?'

'I saw her once.'

'Let's see what her file has to say . . . These are her transfer documents, which mean that, according to a law passed in '68, she became a voluntary patient where before she'd been committed—that was in '67. There's her signature. That was long before my time. I only knew her in her last years here when she was pretty settled. Here's a medical report from just before she left us. She didn't ail a thing, healthy as a baby. And she'd been taken off the tranquillizers she'd been taking in the evenings. She used to get a bit agitated towards dusk . . .'

'Did she clean up a lot when she was here?'

'She certainly did—if you could call it that. She always had a brush in her hand as long as I knew her and she'd sweep and sweep, even the grass out there. She was no trouble to anybody as long as she was busy with that. We did have problems with her, though, I remember—there's a note on it here . . .' He looked up from the file. 'It's something that needs to be seen in context or you'll get a false idea. One of the everlasting problems in a place like this is the women getting pregnant. You can imagine that not many people, however desperate for a child, are willing to take one born in here. Despite all our efforts, quite a few children have been born here.'

'The wards are mixed?'

'The departments are separate but the patients aren't locked up. They need to go out in the grounds, they have to have fresh air and exercise. Every effort is made to keep an eye on them, but needless to say . . . We introduced the contraceptive pill at one point but the thing was hopeless. The nursing and supervision was mostly done by nuns in those days—and don't get me wrong here because we don't get on nearly so well without them now they've almost all gone—but as for putting the women patients on the pill, it was useless for the doctor to prescribe them even after getting the family's consent because the nuns simply didn't administer them so what could we do? Anyway, that's just to give you the background. It's a constant problem and an understandable one. Clementina was one of those who went after the men. She liked attention and when she didn't get it she'd invent it, making out that this or that man was after her.'

The Marshal was on the point of saying 'She still does' until he remembered that Clementina was dead. Nevertheless, this opened up a new line of thought.

'She didn't have a child in here?'

'No, she didn't.'

'But she was here long before you, you said.'

'True, but it would be in this file.'

'I see.'

'Is there anything else I can tell you?'

'I don't know.' The Marshal was silent for a moment, then he said, 'Nothing particular seems to have happened to her while she was in here . . . A lot of patients were released under this new law, you said; was that when she left?'

'Yes.'

'Well, I'm trying to imagine what reason anybody could have had for killing her. As far as we can make out, she had no money or anything at all worth stealing. She was harmless and seemed to have no contacts much other than her neighbours . . .'

'What you're trying to say is, could it have been another patient, or ex-patient, some sort of homicidal maniac.'

'I suppose so.'

'This isn't a criminal asylum, Marshal, and however disastrous the new law was, we didn't release a gang of homicidal maniacs on to the streets.'

'No, of course not.'

'I'm not saying it can be excluded absolutely. After all, sane people up and murder somebody and a mentally sick person could, by the same token, up and murder somebody too. But there'd still have to be a reason.'

'Somebody came to see her last week. A stocky man, balding slightly and with a limp. That doesn't ring a bell?'

'I'm afraid not.'

'It doesn't fit the man who came here?'

'Not at all. He was nondescript . . . About my age, though, and very well dressed. He didn't limp.'

'Did Clementina have any visitors while she was in here?'

'Not that I remember, but she could have done without my knowing anything about it. Remember we had three thousand patients then, and it's not my job to deal with them personally; my time's spent in here. What I can tell you about Clementina comes mostly from her file, though I used to see her about the grounds with her sweeping brush, and occasionally picked up news about her goings-on from other members of staff.'

'I see. But she had a husband. Her identity card states that she's a widow.'

'I can't remember anything about a husband—wait a minute! If I'm not mistaken, what triggered off her illness was a bereavement, so perhaps she lost her husband before she came here. It was long before my time, of course, but the circumstances of her admission should be mentioned in this file. What if we look through it right from the beginning?'

'It was so long ago,' murmured the Marshal, 'but perhaps you're right.' It would have looked more hopeful if Clementina had only just been released and somebody didn't want her in circulation, but she'd been living in that same house all those years without anything happening to her. There had to have been something new and it seemed useless to go so far back. 'Well,' he said, 'anything that helps me to get to know her and, if possible, her family—she couldn't have been committed wrongfully?'

'That wouldn't be easy,' said the archivist, 'because there are too many checkpoints. No patient ever comes straight in here—or came straight in here, I should say, since we no longer admit anyone. I'll explain the procedure as it was in the days when Clementina was admitted. The first thing they needed was a certificate stating that the person was considered dangerous to himself or others—herself, in this case. That had to be made out by the police, but in some cases it was made out by the mayor. In either instance, we don't have a copy. It remains with the police or in the mayor's office. With that the patient could be admitted to the observation ward in a hospital, a normal hospital such as Santa Maria Nuova. After that, the patient would either be released or an admission order made out and the patient sent here—but she wouldn't be committed even then. She'd be put in our clinic, which was a University clinic—you may have noticed the large building on your left as you came in the gates. At that point, a time-limit came into operation, because a patient could only be kept there for up to thirty days. Once the thirty days were up she would either have to be released or committed to the asylum proper here. I think you'll agree that it would have been impossible for her to have been wrongfully committed. That's a lot of people to get past.'

'Yes, it is. Do any of these certificates state the exact reason . . . I mean the cause of her illness?'

'Not the certificates, no. I'll show you. The dangerous persons one, as I said, we don't have here. What we do have is the admission order that sent her to the clinic and then the committal order . . . somewhere . . . that's funny, it should be right at the beginning . . . perhaps I've mixed things up.'

The Marshal watched Mannucci go through the file from beginning to end, sure that he wouldn't find what he was looking for. Then he said: 'I presume that few people present themselves to the police claiming to be dangerous?'

'It does happen,' Mannucci said, still turning over the pages one by one, working backwards this time. 'In fact, it happens fairly frequently these days, since we stopped admitting people. A great many ex-patients who found they couldn't cope outside tried to get back in.' He paused and looked up. 'There was one last week who set his house on fire and then went to the Carabinieri saying they had to re-admit him to a hospital because he was still mad. When they sent him home he went to the next village, smashed up a car that was parked in the central square and tried the Carabinieri there. When that didn't work he got himself a shotgun and killed the first person who happened to walk by his house. When they came for him he said: "Now will you believe I'm mad?" And he's not the only one by any means. There was another case—'

'But,' interrupted the Marshal firmly, 'if Clementina didn't give herself up to the police, somebody else must have done it.'

'Yes,' said Mannucci, 'the name and address would be on—you're not still imagining that she was wrongfully committed?'

'No. I'm just trying to think why anyone would come in here and remove his name and address from that file.'

Mannucci gave up his search. 'You're right. It's gone—and not only that, there should be the notes from the observation clinic . . .'

'How long did you leave him alone?'

'I didn't! No . . . You're right, I did. He'd just arrived and presented his request. As I told you, it struck me as odd right away with Clementina being dead.'

'Try and remember your movements exactly.'

'Well, I looked at the date first, obviously.'

'And then?'

'And then at the signature. I thought of looking at Clementina's signature in her file. I didn't have anything definite in mind because it might well have been all above board. Just instinct, I suppose.'

'So you got Clementina's file out and then, for some reason—'

'No. Nothing of the kind. I thought of checking the signature but before I could get the file out my assistant called me from the door. She's in the room just across the corridor, there, and she needed me . . . It couldn't have been more than five minutes.'

'If you'd intended to get the file out you probably walked towards it.'

'I may have done.'

'Well, it wouldn't take him more than a matter of seconds to find it, then. They're in alphabetical order, I imagine?'

'Yes. The cabinets are all labelled.'

'Is anything else missing?'

'I don't think so.'

'What's missing, then, is not anything that refers to her years in here but to her past life and to whoever got her admitted and why. Well, it's a pity, but it's also a help.'

'A help? I'm mortified. I obviously wasn't suspicious enough . . . Wait! Perhaps he didn't know about the first certificate, the one we don't have, and if he does know he'll have a job to get his hands on that. You'll be able to find it in the archives of one of the police stations. It won't have much on it but it will have Clementina's home address at the time she was first taken into hospital.'

'In that case,' the Marshal said, 'I'll get on to it right away.'

CHAPTER 6

Mannucci accompanied the Marshal to his car. The fat man had disappeared but in the doorway of the next building a middle-aged woman appeared naked, trailing a dress of some sort on the floor. A tiny nun wearing a big rubber apron over her habit came out to persuade her to come away. The woman allowed herself to be led inside. She was laughing in a raucous, uncontrolled voice that sounded all the louder for the desolate silence of the grounds.

'I suppose,' the Marshal said, 'that there's no chance of any patient who knew Clementina . . .'

Mannucci shook his head. 'At one time, when there were short-term patients . . . With the poor creatures who are left in here now . . . Wait, though—there's Angelo. Clementina, I think, used to sit with him in the grounds.'

'Sit with him? Is he crippled?'

'No, he's not crippled. You'll see for yourself. He's a

reasonable enough soul when he's not in a crisis—but don't expect too much, he's very childish. I doubt if he can tell you a lot.'

'To be honest with you,' the Marshal said, 'I don't even know what I want him to tell me.'

They walked together along the tarmac between rows of pollarded trees, and the Marshal fished in his top pocket for his dark glasses without finding them.

'It's just that I know so little about her. She seems to have had no contacts other than her neighbours and yet someone . . . There must have been other people in her life before she came in here. Family, friends—do you think her being in here so long would explain there not being a single photograph in her house from her past life? It's something that bothers me.'

'It could explain it,' Mannucci said. 'It does happen but usually only in really bad cases, people who have no contact with reality at all, such as those who are severely retarded from birth. But I'd have thought someone like Clementina would have had her little box of treasures. Even Angelo has, and he's a great deal worse than Clementina was or he wouldn't still be here. There he is on his bench. Neat as a pin and as good as gold . . . Angelo!'

He was indeed as neat as a pin, and he sat with his feet together and his arms tightly folded, watching their approach with dark, shining eyes. His face would have been handsome but his forehead was far too big and the back of his head very flat. He could only have been in his early forties, the Marshal judged, as they came up close.

'I haven't done something bad, have I?' Angelo asked Mannucci at once. 'Because I don't think I have, I don't think so.'

'No,' said Manucci very gently, 'the Marshal here's been paying me a visit and he wanted to know about Clementina. You remember Clementina?'

'Yes, oh yes. She used to sit with me, she used to . . .'

'Well, the Marshal would like to talk to you about her.'

'Will he sit with me, will he?'

'Yes, of course. Sit down, Marshal. I'll nip in and tell the nurse on duty what's going on.'

The Marshal was a little disconcerted at being left alone with Angelo. Since he had no idea how to proceed when dealing with the mentally ill, he proceeded in his usual way.

'Excuse me for disturbing you,' he began.

'It's all right. It's all right. I'm very sick, you know, very sick, and that's why I have to stay in here but I'm all right at the moment. I've been very well all morning. I've been . . .'

'Can you remember Clementina?'

'Oh yes. Yes. She used to sit with me. I liked Clementina. She kept herself clean, you see. She kept . . .' He looked hard into the Marshal's eyes, his own full of distress. 'It's terrible in here, terrible. There are dirty people, filthy . . . who think nothing of . . . out here on the grass, anywhere. And some of them are dangerous. I know. I know! I'm dangerous when it comes over me, I know that. But the rest of the time I'm frightened, the rest of the time . . . you see . . .'

'I see,' the Marshal said, 'but you weren't frightened of Clementina?'

'Clementina no. Clementina . . . Is she coming back?'

'No, she's not coming back.'

'She went home.'

'Yes.'

'I—I could have gone home only I'm very sick. Very, very sick . . . when it comes over me . . . My mother's at home waiting. They let me go home once, but it came over me. I get frightened . . . I get frightened and it all goes up in my head and then it comes over me, that's why it happened. I didn't want to hurt her, I didn't want . . .'

'You hurt your mother?'

'Yes. And she hit me. She hit me . . . It all goes up in my head and I can't—I have to stay here, I know that. I have to . . . I'm very sick. Nobody's forcing me, I understand I'm very sick. Nobody's . . .'

'Was Clementina very sick?'

'Clementina wasn't frightened like me. She used to sit with me but she was very busy. She was . . . Clementina had her cleaning to do. She had a lot of cleaning to do and then she wouldn't sit with me.'

'Did she talk to you?'

'Yes. Yes.' Angelo's arms were folded so tightly it must have hurt him. A blackbird hopped by and he jerked himself forward to watch its movements, his eyes bright. Then he sat back just as suddenly and smiled at the Marshal, his face radiant.

'A bird . . .' he whispered.

'How long have you been here?' the Marshal asked him.

'A long time. A long . . . maybe since I was twenty. Before that I was in another place but I can't remember it. I *have* to stay.'

'I understand. You were here before Clementina, were you? You were here when she came?'

'Yes. I *have* to. . . .'

'I understand. What did Clementina talk to you about?'

'She didn't talk. Not for a long time. She didn't talk for years and years . . . Then she . . . maybe she was frightened then. But when she started to shout she shouted wicked words. Filthy . . . she shouted.'

'But not when she sat with you? You liked her to sit with you, didn't you?'

'Oh yes, but she wanted to marry me, she wanted. She had her pension, she said. She had . . . I've got one too and my mother . . . No—it's not true. Don't be angry with me.'

'I'm not angry.'

'Don't be angry with . . . I know I shouldn't tell lies. Perhaps I have got a pension but I can't remember. Sometimes when I'm frightened I can't remember things. But Clementina had a pension and they used to send it for her and she kept some money in her apron.'

'Who sent it for her?'

'If you can't go they get it for you. She told me.'

'Who got it for her? Did somebody come to see her?'

'Her sister. Sometimes her sister came.'

'Clementina had a sister? What was her name?'

'I don't know.'

'Try and remember.'

'I don't know. Don't get angry with me. Don't get . . . Sometimes I can't remember things because I'm sick.'

'That's all right. It doesn't matter.'

'Is it all right?'

'Of course. Don't worry.'

'I can't help it.'

'No, no . . . It doesn't matter at all. I'm very grateful to you for telling me that Clementina had a sister. I didn't know that.'

'She had a house, as well. That's why she could go home, but I can't because I'm not well enough.'

'She was married once, did she tell you that?'

'No. But she had a ring and I saw it. Everybody said her husband was dead and her baby, but she didn't say. Perhaps she couldn't remember things, like me, because she was sick.'

'I expect that's the reason.'

'I wish she'd come back . . .' He turned his pleading eyes on the Marshal. 'I'm so lonely.' His breath was shallow and halting. 'I'm so lonely I could . . . I'm *frightened* of being by myself, they know that. I'm all right if somebody's near me. I'm all right now you're here, or if there's a bird . . . I've been all right this morning, I've . . .' He loosened one arm, keeping the other tight to himself. 'I've sat here by myself and felt lonely in my chest but I've sat still, sat still, and kept it in my chest because when it goes up in my head . . .'

He clutched at his huge forehead with his free hand, then looked up, quicker than the Marshal to catch the sound of footsteps.

'Signor Mannucci's coming back.' He regarded the archivist with earnest eyes. 'I've been all right this morning.'

'So the nurse said. She's been looking at you from the window and she noticed how quiet you've been.'

'Is she going to come out and sit with me?'

'She can't do that, Angelo. You know she has a lot of people to look after. Don't you feel up to going in for a while?'

'I can't. The smell . . . the noise is so terrible, terrible. I need to be quiet.'

'All right, old chap. You sit here and be quiet. We'll leave you now—if you've finished, Marshal?'

The Marshal got to his feet. He'd already learned more than he'd hoped for and he was afraid of exciting the unfortunate Angelo.

'We have to go now.'

'But we were having a talk about Clementina. I'll remember her sister's name, I'll remember. Wait . . . just let me think, I have to think. Wait . . .' He flung his head down on his knees and put his fists to his temples, suddenly silent, rocking slightly.

Mannucci touched the Marshal's shoulder. 'We might as well go now,' he said quietly, 'he stays like that for two or three hours at a time.'

The Marshal allowed himself to be led away. When they were far along the drive he turned to look back. Angelo was hunched over on the bench, exactly as they had left him.

'I'm afraid you're upset, Marshal,' Mannucci said with a note of curiosity in his voice. 'I suppose anyone who's not accustomed . . .'

'No, no,' said the Marshal, realizing with some embarrassment that Mannucci was staring at his watering eyes. He pulled out his handkerchief. 'I'm allergic to strong sunlight. Left my sunglasses in the car, I think.'

But he was convinced that Mannucci didn't altogether believe him.

'Poor Angelo. He was much better when there were milder cases and short-term patients here. He had more company. There was one old man who used to sit with him for hours. That's all he needs. When the fear gets too much for him he becomes violent. All day and every day he battles with his fear and if he reaches bedtime and his sleeping pill without having had a crisis, he's happy. When the nuns were here they saw to it that he was never left alone, but now we haven't the staff and such patients who are left frighten him. Ah, Marshal . . . I badger the newspapers and the Council as much as I can but there's no news and no votes in an Angelo. Was he any help to you?'

'I think so, yes. He thinks Clementina lost not only her husband but a child, and that she never breathed a word about it herself. He also said she had a sister. Could it be that her sister collected her pension for her and brought it or sent it here?'

'It's more than likely. That's the case with most long-term patients. I only wish there was somebody here from Clementina's day who could be more helpful. I'm afraid Angelo and I are the only survivors.'

When they reached the Marshal's car, the first thing the Marshal did was to unlock it and reach inside for his sunglasses which he put on rather ostentatiously. Only then did he say: 'Thanks very much for all your help.'

'I'm only sorry it was so little. I just wish I'd called you straight away when that character turned up here. It's a long time, I must say, since we've had to get the law in.'

'Did it happen often in the past?'

'Now and then, when a patient went completely wild. These days they're kept under control with drugs but I remember one chap—weighed over 25 stone—and when he let loose even five or six men couldn't hold him. It often ended with them locking him in wherever he happened to be and sending for the police who'd throw tear gas in through the window. It was the only way, though there was one doctor here at the time who could get him under control just by throwing a wet sheet over him. An old trick, but it worked. Well, I'll let you get about your business. If that chap turns up again . . .'

'I'm afraid he won't,' the Marshal said, getting into his car, 'but if by any chance he should, keep him waiting and telephone me directly. Here's my number.'

'At the Pitti Palace? I didn't know there was a Station there. Right you are. I'll do what I can, but I'm inclined to agree with you. He got what he was after and won't be back.'

The Marshal drove towards the exit. The car seat was burning through his trousers and the steering-wheel was red hot, too. The spacious grounds had been full of trees and he had stupidly parked out in the open. He wound down his window, hoping for a bit of a breeze as he drove along the river bank. In his quarters the shutters would be closed and the rooms fairly cool. His meal would be ready and there would be a misted bottle of white wine in the fridge. With a sigh he drove past the Pitti Palace, leaving it all behind him, and turned right towards Clementina's house. For a moment he wasn't sure whether he had the keys with him but then he found them buttoned into his top pocket. Even so, he changed his mind and rang at the street door. The last thing he wanted was to give the young couple a fright by appearing unannounced on their stairs. It seemed to him that for some reason he hadn't yet fathomed they were frightened already. Of course it would disturb anybody, having a suicide in the building, but he wasn't satisfied with that as the only reason. He rang again and waited, hoping they hadn't slipped away a second time. The window above his head opened and a face peered down through the scaffolding. The street door clicked open.

The Marshal stepped inside and began climbing the stone stairs, hat and sunglasses in hand. It had been the young woman who had looked down at him but it was her husband who let him into the flat. The Marshal was puffing a little from the steep steps and he didn't speak at first, only looked around him. The flat was very tidy and the young people who had struck him as a nice couple the first time he'd seen them looked even nicer. The wife was wearing a freshly ironed apron and had probably been about to serve their meal. The Marshal noticed two small wet stains on the bodice of her cotton dress, one on each side of the apron bib. The husband must have been laying the table and was still holding the cutlery in his hand. When the Marshal didn't speak at once he perhaps took it as ill-humour, for he said quickly:

'I'm afraid that yesterday . . . We hadn't forgotten you said you'd call but we had to go to my mother-in-law's rather urgently.'

'I'm disturbing your meal,' the Marshal said as he got his breath, ignoring this apology, 'but I won't keep you long.'

'That's all right,' the young woman said, 'it can wait.'

They looked uncertainly at each other and then Rossi said, 'Perhaps you'd like to sit down.'

'Thank you. Your stairs are a bit steep.'

'Yes. Of course, we're used to it.'

'How long have you lived here?'

'Just over three years.' It was always Rossi who answered. They were both as tense as springs.

'I suppose you can tell me something about Clementina, then, having had her for a neighbour for three years.'

As soon as he asked the question he felt them relax a little. Rossi even sat down opposite the Marshal, though his wife remained standing. 'She must have been a bit of a nuisance by all accounts, with the noise she made.'

'Clementina? Well, not so much during the day but she

was often pretty rowdy at night. We never said anything to her because that would only provoke more noise. She was always ready for a fight when she was in a rowdy mood.' Rossi glanced up at his wife and, getting his message, she sat herself on the arm of his chair and tried to smile.

'What I was wondering,' began the Marshal carefully, 'was whether she had any visitors recently. You see, by all accounts, she was a cheerful sort of character even if she was a bit off her head. It makes me wonder if somebody or something could have upset her or frightened her enough to make her kill herself. You see what I'm getting at?'

'Yes . . .' said Rossi, 'I suppose you're right. She was cheerful enough as a rule.'

'There's nobody been round here bothering her recently, that you know of?'

'No.' He said it too quickly and his face was red. So was his wife's. They were poor liars, which made him sympathetic to them since they obviously weren't accustomed to telling lies. And the thought gave him no pleasure, really, because they were believing every word he said and he was lying through his teeth, talking about suicide and pretending not to know about Clementina's visitor. He was a better liar than they were. Occupational hazard, perhaps.

'Think back more carefully,' he insisted, 'you just might recall something that's slipped your mind up to now and I'd be so grateful to you. You see, in the course of my inquiries—not hereabouts, as it happens—' he wasn't going to blow his best spy—'I've come across a man who knows Clementina and says he came round here a few weeks ago. I'd rather not mention his name and we've no proof, of course, that he did or said anything to upset Clementina, but we have to check everything in our business, as I'm sure you understand.'

They both nodded, their eyes fixed on him as though he had them under hypnosis.

'This man,' he went on, 'is a biggish chap, not tall but

bulky, and he has a limp . . . and the thing is, he said he saw the signora here . . .' He stared at Signora Rossi with his big, bulging eyes. 'And that made me think that with a bit of luck you might remember having seen him.'

There was a silence. They knew they were trapped, all right, and he was sure it would be she who spoke first because she was much more agitated than her husband.

What happened next was so unexpected that the Marshal got to his feet in alarm and dismay.

Instead of speaking, the young woman burst into tears, putting her head down on her knees and covering it with both hands as great sobs shook her. Both men were standing over her. Rossi placed a hand on her hair and she threw her head up, shouting, 'Tell him! For goodness' sake, tell him! I don't care any more, I'm sick of the whole business. We'll go and live at my mother's, anything! Tell him . . .' She collapsed, sobbing again.

Rossi took her by the shoulders and brought her to her feet. She kept her head down but her hands were now covering her breast.

'Go and see to yourself,' her husband said quietly, 'and try to calm down. Leave it to me.' She shook him off and left the room, still crying.

The two men sat down again.

'Where's the baby?' asked the Marshal.

'At her mother's—we didn't tell her why because her heart's bad and she hasn't to be upset, so . . .'

'Where on earth was the baby last time I came in here? It wasn't here or in the room where I telephoned.'

'I took the carrycot into the bathroom before we let you in.'

'So that's what you were doing to keep me waiting so long.'

'There were other bits of stuff to hide, as well—how did you guess?'

'I didn't, then. But just now, your wife's dress . . . I've

got two children myself . . . It's not good for her, you know; she could get a fever if she's been feeding the baby herself up to now. Not good for the baby, either.'

'We didn't know what else to do. It's in the contract that we're not supposed to—'

'I understand. But all this has nothing to do with me. Surely you didn't think I was spying on you?'

'Of course not, but what difference does that make? If we have to give evidence at an inquest—or even if some journalist puts our name in the paper—It's not just the baby. My wife was the one who signed the contract for this flat before we were married and there's meant to be just one person living here. We've been trying to find another place for over eighteen months but every time we go and look at one it turns out they only want foreigners who'll move on quickly so they can keep raising the rent without problems, or else they expect an enormous bribe. The worst flats are those that claim to be rent-controlled. Then they not only expect a bribe but they want double the official rent and give you a receipt for half of it. It's a jungle. If we can't manage to hang on to this flat we'll be on the streets.'

'What about your mother-in-law?'

'She lives in Arezzo. I'm still trying to get my degree at the University of Florence, plus I've got a job. I can't get here from Arezzo every day and there's no work there.'

'What is your job?'

'I work as a draughtsman and I'm studying to be an architect.'

The Marshal sighed. There was nothing he could do.

'Have you been to get advice from the Tenants' Association?'

'We went to them immediately when we got notice to quit.'

'And what did they suggest?'

'They think we'll have a better chance by telling the truth about the baby even though we have broken the contract, because it always takes longer to evict a family than a single person. But it's risky and a lot depends on the personal sympathies of the judge. There's a hearing coming up soon and we still haven't made up our minds what line to take. Then there was that thug who came round here.'

'The man with the limp?'

'Yes.'

'Then it wasn't Clementina he came to see?'

'Oh, he went up there, too. My wife saw him. She's always on the alert because the agency we rent through could always send someone round unexpectedly. They do that sort of thing.'

'She could have refused to let him in, you know.'

'He got in under false pretences. The trouble was that Linda, my wife, was so panic-stricken, thinking it was somebody come about the flat, that when this man claimed he was checking on TV licences she was so relieved she let him in without thinking and went to get the licence from the drawer in the kitchen. When she came back he was looking round the place in a way that disturbed her. She showed him the licence and he just grinned at her. Then he said:

'"Have you got somewhere to go when you're thrown out of here?"

'"Who are you? You haven't come about the licence."

'"Just my little joke. It's a nice place, this, for one person, not for a couple with a baby."

'What could Linda do? If only I'd been here, but I was at work. I suppose he knew that, the bastard!'

'He must have given some explanation of who he was.'

'Oh, he gave a name—Bianchi—false, I imagine. He said he reckoned things would go badly with us if anyone found out about the baby but that he could help us. He said he'd come from the agency to check up on us but that he could always keep his mouth shut. He said he even knew about one or two other flats.'

'How much did he ask for?'

'Three million.'

'Did you pay up?'

'On a draughtsman's salary? We haven't a penny to spare. We thought of my mother-in-law but because of her weak heart we were afraid to tell her the real reason and that would have meant inventing some other excuse, even supposing she could afford to help us. In the end the only thing we could think of was to go back and tell the woman at the Tenants' Association.'

'And what did she say?'

'At first she said it was a pity we had no proof of what had happened, since it would have put the owners in the wrong and could have helped us. Of course there was no proof, there was only our word for it. Then she thought of telephoning the agents on our behalf without saying who she was. Then they might have let something out and she'd be a witness.'

'But they were too clever for her?'

'Not at all. She simply asked for Signor Bianchi, saying she had some money for him and wanted to make an appointment to come to the office with it. She didn't give her name but she managed to mention the address, ours that is, so that they could easily have thought she was Linda. The girl who answered simply said, "There's no Signor Bianchi here. You must have the wrong number."

'She insisted, saying perhaps she'd got the name wrong, but the girl on the other end said there was only the owner of the agency who was a woman and another girl besides herself working there.

'"He said he came from here?" she asked. "Do you mind holding the line a moment? I think I should tell my employer."

'In the end the owner of the agency came to the phone herself and when she heard the full story she was furious and wanted to call the police, though she didn't in the end.'

'Hm,' the Marshal said, 'then it sounds as though our friend Bianchi was here on his own account. There might well be a good living to be got out of people in your situation. It would only be a question of getting the right information.'

'But how could he? How did he come to know we were threatened with eviction?'

'I don't know. He could work somewhere where he could get information about cases coming up for a hearing. It wouldn't be that difficult. You don't happen to know what he said to Clementina?'

'No. Linda tried . . . wait, I'll ask her.'

He was gone for some moments and then brought his wife back from the bedroom to which she'd retreated. She had changed her dress. 'It's all right,' he was saying, 'I've told him everything. Don't worry. He wants to know about Clementina.'

They sat down close together and he kept her hand in his.

'I can't really tell you much,' she said, 'but I knew he'd been up there because I saw him go up the stairs when he left here. I waited behind the door until I heard him going down—I think that was when I first noticed his limp. He dragged one foot. When he'd gone I went up and knocked on her door. When she opened it she was almost stark naked. It was just after lunch and she often used to take a siesta wearing an old cotton overall with no buttons down the front. On a warm dry day she'd even wash her dress through so it would be clean for the evening. Then she'd wash it through again at night. People thought she was out of her mind completely but it's not true—oh, it's true that she had that mania for cleaning the square and that she tended to get worse as it went dark, and it's also true that she liked flirting with the men. But most people only saw her at her worst, that is, when she was out there shouting and creating. But, you know, the rest of the time she often behaved quite normally and got on with her life, such as it was, in quite an organized way. She was very poor.'

'I know,' the Marshal said, 'I've been in her flat.'

'Then you probably noticed that there's no heating at all in the place, not even a little stove.'

He hadn't noticed. It had been so hot . . .

'In winter she'd sit in Franco's bar all day watching TV because it was warm there. I always thought—I'm no expert, of course, it's just my idea—but I always thought that she was much more normal than she let on to be, apart from her mania, which she really couldn't control.'

'What made you think so?'

'I don't know but—yes, sometimes when I saw her during the day when she was quiet, there was something about the way she looked at me—she had very piercing blue eyes—and she seemed to be saying, "You know I'm not as crazy as they think but I have to keep up the game." At those times she seemed very lucid and it made me think that playing up to her image as a madwoman had become her method of survival. I don't know if I'm making any sense?'

'I think so. I'm beginning to understand. Especially as she wouldn't have been let out of San Salvi to live alone if she'd been all that bad.'

'I didn't know about San Salvi until I saw it in the paper. She never talked about her past. But after all, just think how many old women are dragging out their existence without enough money to eat properly or keep warm. If they've no family they're often left to fend for themselves because they give nobody any trouble, they're too proud, so no one notices them much. Everybody always used to say that Clementina liked attention, especially when she hung around the men—but if she hadn't behaved the way she did she wouldn't have got half the help she got, if any. Because of her pottiness she was an institution.'

'And you think she worked all that out for herself?' Even as he questioned it he believed her, thinking of Angelo sitting there alone hour after terrified hour, trying to be good while the noisy, disruptive patients got all the attention. Clementina had been in a good school, watching it silently before forming a new survival personality. Ten years of that . . .

'I said it was only an opinion,' Linda Rossi said, taking his silence for dissent. 'And it wasn't as cold-blooded as that since she really did go batty at times. I just think she kept the image up the rest of the time, that's all, because it served. Apart from that, who's to say she wasn't clever? Clever people do go crazy, perhaps more easily than stupid ones. Anyway, I'm supposed to be telling you about that day when I went up there. I was upset, of course, by that dreadful man, but I was curious as well because I'd always understood that Clementina didn't rent her flat.'

'Did she say so?'

'Not in so many words. She did say something to that effect but not then, a long time ago, about a year and a half ago. Our rent had been raised and I remember thinking: Poor Clementina, she must have had the same bad news this morning in the post. I'll take her something up. She wasn't there, and I was amazed when I eventually found her down at the front door mopping at the step with a dirty old rag as usual, chirpy as ever.

'"I've made you a bit of soup", I told her.

'"Is there a bit of bread with it as well? Because I have none."

'She was never humble or grateful and she would even go so far as to complain if she didn't think much of your cooking. I mentioned that the rent had gone up and that if she hadn't had a letter about it already one would arrive.

'"Not me," she said, "I don't pay rent."

'She may have been inventing it, but I'd swear she was telling the truth.'

'Well,' the Marshal said, 'I found no rent book or receipts of any kind in the flat. Did she explain why?'

'No. But I didn't want to appear nosey, though I was curious. That's another thing—I often got the impression that she was very secretive and that acting crazier than she was kept people at a distance. Everybody knew about her craziness but nobody really knew *her*. I don't think a soul knew about her being in San Salvi until yesterday.' She turned to her husband who had been stroking her hand throughout the conversation. 'You said you felt the same, that she was secretive.'

'About her flat?'

'About everything! We talked about it!'

'I know, but we're not psychiatrists. If she was all those years in San Salvi . . .' He gave the Marshal one of those man to man glances as if asking him to make allowances for his wife's emotional state. The Marshal privately wished Rossi would go out and have a coffee somewhere. Up to now, the only person who had told him anything useful about Clementina had been poor Angelo. And now this young woman was embarrassed and was sure to clam up.

Avoiding the husband's eye, he said, 'I'm no psychiatrist, either, but I'm inclined to think there's a lot in what you say. One of the things that bother me about Clementina is that she appears to have no past. There isn't so much as an old snapshot in her house, for instance, which struck me as odd.'

'Isn't there? That *is* odd . . .' Linda frowned. 'She had that picture she cut out from the newspaper, though. It wasn't from her past, of course, it was an article they did last year or the year before, I forget. But it shows she does keep photographs of herself, even if it was only cut out from the paper. She once showed it to me.'

'Where did she keep it?'

'In a drawer in the kitchen table with a lot of bits and pieces. Didn't you see it when you were looking about up there?'

'No, I didn't . . . unless . . .' There had been a crumpled

sheet of newspaper in he drawer but it was very old and yellowed and looked as though it had been lining the drawer. 'Was it a full sheet, or even a double sheet?'

'No, it was just a small picture with a short piece written underneath it. She'd cut it out very carefully.'

'In that case it wasn't there. She must have thrown it away.'

'It was there that day I went up after the limping man had been here.'

'What makes you so sure?'

'The drawer was open. I told you Clementina was undressed. She was looking through the drawer for a button to sew on her frock which she'd just washed—she had hardly any clothes—and the cutting was right there on top in the open drawer. It struck me because in the picture she was wearing that same frock. Goodness knows how long she'd had it. I remember wishing I could give her something to wear but she was much shorter than I am and plumper.'

'Well, if you say she was busy with her dress and so on when you went up, I gather she was no more upset by that man's visit than she'd been when you told her about the rent going up.'

'Oh no. She was upset this time—she always got more active when she was disturbed. There she was, half naked, looking for a button in the drawer and her dress was half in and half out of a little bowl of soapy water in the sink so that it was dripping on to the floor, and her face was all red. She was talking and swearing to herself loudly and she hadn't answered my knock so, since the door was ajar, I went in.

'"Clementina, it's me."

'She didn't answer but went on talking to herself.'

'What was she saying? Try and remember, it could be helpful.'

'She seemed to be just rambling. I couldn't make any sense of it, I'm afraid. Oh—she did repeat a number of times “I won’t go . . . Whatever happens I won’t go and they can’t make me!” That’s all I can remember having heard clearly. I gathered that Bianchi, as he called himself, had threatened her in some way as he had us. I knew she had no money and couldn’t have paid him off. What I didn’t understand, though, was what he could have threatened her with. She lived alone and didn’t have our problem. Of course, there was this business of her not paying rent and I did wonder if she’d simply not paid up—you know, playing her crazy old dear act and thinking she could get away with not paying.’

‘She didn’t explain anything to you?’

‘No. She was working herself up into hysterics. It happened now and again. She started swearing senselessly, just a string of foul language without rhyme or reason. At the end she was crying too. I tried to tell her that the man had been to me with his threats, too, but she took no notice. She wasn’t just being her crazy self then, Marshal, she was really frightened and I’m sure that’s why she killed herself. Even I—it’s true that we don’t have money to spare and we’ve been pretty desperate about being evicted—but I’m not alone in the world and not so poor as she was. I wasn’t surprised when I heard what had happened.’

‘Are you sure,’ the Marshal asked, ‘that she’d received an eviction order, too? It’s not the sort of thing you throw away and I didn’t find it . . .’

‘I’m not sure, since she never told me so. All she ever said was that she didn’t pay rent—and since Bianchi went up there too . . .’

‘Yes, but if he was on the make on his own account he may just have been guessing.’

‘Then why was she frightened? And why did she kill herself?’

The Marshal considered telling her the truth but then he said nothing. What good could it do at this stage? It would only serve to frighten her since she was alone in the house all day. At last he said, 'Bring your baby home—is it a boy or a girl?'

'A little girl. She's two and a half months old. Do you have any children?'

'Two. Both boys.' He looked at Rossi. 'If that fellow should come back, don't give him money.'

'We won't.'

'Did he give you a deadline?'

Rossi looked at his wife.

'No, he didn't . . . I assumed he'd just come back again, but he never did and it must be about four weeks . . . Now that you mention it, there was something odd about that. I was too upset to take it in at the time but I've got a clearer idea about his behaviour now. There was something . . . improvised about the whole thing. I think, looking back on it, that he wanted what he could get out of me then and there.'

'Come on, now, Linda,' said her husband, squeezing her hand. 'He could hardly have expected you to produce three million from your purse.'

'Listen to me!' She removed her hand from his, 'Marshal, I'm convinced he was improvising and that he wanted or needed money right away. After all, I could have given him a cheque if I'd had the money to cover it—and I told you I found him looking about in a way that bothered me. I'll bet he was sizing us up and deciding how much to ask for.'

'He decided wrong, then,' said Rossi, 'since we haven't a penny.'

'But I'm right, even so. Marshal, look around you. This is a very tiny flat but everything in it is good. That's because when his mother died we inherited a bit of good furniture. My husband has a brother and sister so that when everything was divided there wasn't all that much, but you see that coffee service? It's silver, and the two rugs are Persian. The few things we've bought ourselves come from the cheapest department store, but the general impression is of more money than we have.'

'That's true . . .' The Marshal was no expert. The first time he'd come in here he'd only noticed how cheerful and pretty it was, especially after Clementina's flat, but this Bianchi had been looking with a different pair of eyes.

'I'd swear,' said Linda Rossi, 'that he'd have gone away contented if I'd given him that coffee service, and that it was only because I was too terrified about the rental contract and the baby, etcetera, to realize, that stopped him getting what he wanted.'

'Did he seem desperate?'

'No, not that . . . no, because he was too cheerful in a leering, sarcastic sort of way. Not desperate, just improvising and definitely in a hurry. It's true, I thought at the time he'd be back, otherwise we couldn't have gone to the Tenants' Association, but I wasn't thinking very straight because I was frightened—not just of him but because of the hearing coming up, everything.'

'You don't know if he asked Clementina for money?'

'She didn't say so, but I've told you she wasn't very coherent. The next day, I told her we were going to the Tenants' Association and asked if she wanted us to take her with us. She calmed down by then and was downstairs as usual mopping the doorstep.

'"If I want to go there, I'll go! I can find my own way!"

'She was down on her knees and she looked up at me with that sharp, blue-eyed glance that meant she was lucid and only shouting to keep up appearances. I wonder if she went . . .'

'I'll check,' the Marshal said. He got to his feet and took a card from his top pocket. 'This is my number. If you remember anything else or if Bianchi comes back . . .'

'But surely,' Linda Rossi said, 'if you've already talked to him and he admits he's seen me . . . Can't you arrest him?'

The Marshal, much embarrassed by his deceit which, to tell the truth, he'd quite forgotten until now, could only say, 'I'd rather just keep watch on him until I have more to go on. I can't arrest him yet or I would.'

Well, that was true enough, he thought as he stumped off down the stairs. They had promised to call him if anything happened, but where the use was in leaving his cards all over the place in case two men about whom he knew nothing should be so kind as to make a second visit for his convenience he didn't know. What he did know for sure, as he lowered himself gingerly on to the burning car seat yet again, was that he wanted a cold shower and a meal and, if humanly possible, a rest.

All he got was the shower. He barely got time to put on a fresh uniform before he was summoned to the Public Prosecutor's office.

CHAPTER 7

By four o'clock that afternoon the weather was so sultry that it was becoming difficult to breathe. Almost everyone in the streets was wearing sunglasses like the Marshal because the blinding white glare of the vapour-screened sun was so painful. He had a headache which was getting steadily worse. It might have been hunger or the bad temper provoked by the Substitute Prosecutor, but it was more likely the weather since, as he looked about him, everyone else seemed to have the same beaten look. He walked across the Santa Trinita bridge slowly. On days like this there was no point in hurrying because everything you tried to do went wrong, so the fewer things you tried to do the better. You can fight against some things but not against August. The only thing to do in August is wait for it to be over. The Marshal had reached this conclusion at half past two when he had got back into his car ready to leave for his interview with the Prosecutor on an empty stomach and found that the engine refused to start. It was his own car, of course, not a squad car, but he would normally get one of the mechanics over at Headquarters to look at it. What was the point of telephoning when they would be sure to say that since it was August . . .

All the anger and frustration that had welled up in him when the car wouldn't start sagged, leaving a sort of blank lethargy behind it. He could have taken the van that was parked next to his 500 but he just got out and walked away, perhaps to spite himself or perhaps to spite the Prosecutor who would, in turn, be annoyed when he arrived late.

The Prosecutor had been annoyed. Not because the Marshal was late, since he had even kept the latter waiting for a quarter of an hour. He was angry in the first place about the San Salvi business, and the Marshal's account of it in which there was no avoiding the fact that, had he got there yesterday, he might have encountered the mysterious visitor, was bound in the nature of things to make him angrier. He had been annoyed, too, by what he saw as the Marshal's sullen attitude, the way he didn't rise to the bait when criticized. Couldn't he see that it was just too hot to bother? For his part, the Marshal could understand well enough that the Prosecutor was as exhausted by the weather as everyone else. His face was pallid and damp and there were dark rings under his eyes. Not only was he at the end of his tether because of the heat but he was also threatened with having his long-awaited holiday postponed. The Marshal couldn't in all conscience blame him but nor could he work up any energy to react to him. It wasn't a pleasant interview. The Prosecutor concluded it by saying:

'If you have the keys to the flat on you, leave them here.'

'Of course.' The Marshal had taken them from his top pocket and placed them on the desk.

'The agents dealing with the letting have been in touch

with me and I see no good reason, at this point, for asking them to wait. I'm having the seals removed today and I'll give them back the keys tomorrow.'

'You don't think—'

'Think what?'

'This man I told you about . . .'

'What about him? I've no reason to believe he has anything to do with this case.'

'They didn't say, the agents, whether they'd had any problems with Clementina not paying her rent? Or that she'd received notice of eviction?'

'Nothing of the kind. It seems to me that these people in the flat below—what did you say their name was?'

'Rossi.'

'Rossi. These people are just trying to attract your attention to their own little problem by making out that the Franci woman upstairs was somehow involved. If you keep your mind on this case and the things that really are relevant to it we might get somewhere.'

The Marshal thought of the young couple whose 'little problem' might end in their being out on the streets with their two-month-old baby in its mother's arms and their furniture piled up around them on the pavement. He stared down at his big hands which were planted on his knees and then across the desk at the Prosecutor whose thin fingers were fidgeting with a pen that left red spots on their tips. What was he agitating about now?

'I'll inform them this evening. I can see nothing to be gained . . .'

He kept on saying that, the Marshal noticed. 'I can see nothing to be gained . . . I can see no good reason . . . I can see no point . . .'

Well, no doubt he was right. There was probably nothing to be gained by finding Clementina's murderer. No point . . . No good reason . . . You just went through the motions and life continued as before. Somebody had once thought there was a good reason for closing the asylums and now the same patients were in private asylums at public expense and everything went on as before. What was the point, the good reason, for looking after human wreckage like Angelo? Or for neglecting him?

'Are you following me?'

The Marshal gave a little start and his big troubled eyes met those of the Prosecutor. Just like school when he would suddenly hear the teacher rap out: *Guarnaccia! Are you paying attention?*

Yes, sir.

What was the last thing I said?

That . . . that . . . .

You've no idea, have you, Guarnaccia?

No, sir.

The Prosecutor could hardly go so far as to ask him, What was the last thing I said? There were some advantages to being an adult. He just went on talking and the Marshal arranged his features into an attentive expression and did his best to pick up the threads. Evidently, he was going to inform the newspapers that it was a case of murder and not suicide. Well, so be it. They'd be pleased. Better than stray dogs. He stood up when the Prosecutor stood up. The interview appeared to be at an end.

When he was half way down the corridor, he heard the Prosecutor behind him talking to his registrar in the open doorway.

'The blank incomprehension of the man . . .!'

Perhaps he had meant the Marshal to overhear.

Now, as he reached the other side of the bridge, he saw a middle-aged couple arguing with weary fractiousness over a tourist map. The Marshal couldn't understand their language but he didn't need to. He saw them walk off, the woman marching in front, tight-lipped, the husband trailing ten paces behind dejectedly trying to refold the bright-coloured map which wouldn't cooperate. The Marshal understood the one word he let out when the map ripped. When it came down to it, even working was better than trudging round Florence as a tourist in a strange city. There was an open bar on the corner of the embankment and he was about to go into it and get himself a sandwich when a brass plaque on the wall next door caught his eye. *Italmoda, Export Agency. 1st Floor.* Was it worth going up and ringing the bell? Hadn't he decided that the less he tried to achieve today the better? In the end he compromised: he'd have that sandwich while the going was good, after which there was no harm in just ringing the bell since he had no hope of finding anyone there and so couldn't be disappointed.

He chose a big slice of bread with fresh tomato, basil leaves and a sprinkling of olive oil, then ordered a coffee.

'It can't get any worse than this,' the barman grumbled. There was no need to say what.

'No,' agreed the Marshal, munching. He was so hungry he decided to have another.

'Tomato, the same?'

'Yes.'

'It's been like this every afternoon for a week, and every day I'm convinced there'll be a storm but it never comes. I like the hot weather, myself, but when it's humid like this . . . I've taken three aspirins already; my head's bursting.'

'I'm the same,' the Marshal said, 'and I don't suppose there's a chemist open for miles.'

'Here,' the barman said, handing the box of tablets over the counter, 'though you shouldn't if you're going to drink that coffee. What about an iced tea?'

'I expect you're right.'

'I'll pour you one—don't worry about the coffee. The way I look at it, August has to be treated like wartime conditions. We have to help each other out. Remember the flood?'

'I wasn't here then—'

'It was the same then. People helped each other. I remember going round in a boat distributing all the mineral water I had in stock. Water everywhere and not a drop to drink. Three thousand lire. I'm not charging you for the coffee.'

'Thanks very much.'

'You're welcome.'

Italmoda, Export Agency. 1st Floor.

A fancy big building with a carpet running up the centre of the marble staircase and polished brass plaques on each door. He rang the bell on the first floor left and waited only a few seconds before turning, ready to start down again. When he heard the door click he stopped in his tracks.

'Well, that's a turn-up for the books,' he muttered, and pushed open the door. Someone had let him in and yet the place was silent and seemed deserted. He walked along a short, broad corridor where boxes were piled half way to the ceiling all along one side.

'Is anyone there?'

'Who's that?' called a surprised female voice. A door opened behind the Marshal to his left. He turned.

'Oh!'

'I startled you, did I?' the Marshal said. 'But you let me in.'

'I thought you were someone else. Somebody's supposed to call for this stuff.' She indicated the stacked-up boxes. She was small and pretty and had a slight foreign accent. She was also crying and took no trouble to hide the fact, although she did blow her nose before asking, 'What do you want?'

'Are you the only person here?'

'As you can see.'

'Then I'd like a word with you, if you can spare me a minute.'

'You'd better come in here.'

There were more cardboard boxes just inside the office door, one of them open on the floor with a cotton skirt half out of it. The girl sat down behind a desk and took another tissue from a box by the typewriter.

'Sit down, if you like.'

The Marshal took his time about it, looking around him. The room was large and carpeted and two tall windows looked out over the river. There were two other desks with covers over the typewriters.

'Your colleagues are all on holiday?'

'Everybody's away except me because I deal with Germany and they don't think much of the way you can't do any business here in August. I had ten days off in July and I should get some more holidays in September if I don't get sacked first.'

It was really very odd. She spoke in quite normal tones without a break in her voice and yet tears continued to roll down her cheeks. She went on talking, ignoring them.

'What was it you wanted?'

'I'm just—excuse me asking but have you got something wrong with your eyes? I only ask because I—'

'No. I'm upset.'

'I see. I beg your pardon. I'm here to make some routine inquiries. Nothing to worry about.'

'If that's true it's the first time anything's happened in this office that's nothing to worry about. What do you want to know?' At last she seemed to notice the rolling tears—and no wonder, since they were trickling under the collar of her cotton-blouse—and she dried them with the tissue.

'Have you been here long?'

'No. Nobody stays here long.'

'How long exactly?'

'Less than two months.'

'Then do you remember a cleaner who worked here up to about a month ago?'

'We haven't got a cleaner and if that bitch of a woman thinks I'm going to start vacuuming the carpet she's got another think coming. She already expects me to make coffee for her every time she shows her face here—not that I object to making anybody a cup of coffee, but in the first place it's not my job, and in the second place I can't stand vulgar women who imagine they've got class when what they've got is money and bad manners. Well, how would you feel?'

'I—Can you remember the cleaner who worked here up to a month or so ago?'

'I suppose you mean that madwoman?'

'That's right.'

'What about her?'

'Did you know her?'

'Office cleaners go off before the staff arrive, but I've seen her once and that was enough—to see she was crazy, I mean. You have to be, mind you, to work here, but in any case the day I saw her she was getting the sack. It was the first time I'd seen anyone get the sack because I'd only just started here, but two more people have got the sack in the last month. I'll be next.'

'Who does all this sacking? The owner, or is there a manager?'

'Both of them. And since the manager's the owner's husband it's all one. She's the real rotten apple but thank God we don't see much of her. But he's been getting worse and worse, forever having hysterics about every little thing.

'And the cleaner? Who sacked her?'

'He did, but she was behind it, I'll bet.'

'Why was she sacked?'

'Maybe she didn't do her work properly—not that it makes much difference in this place whether you do your work properly anyway, since nobody can do anything right.' She had rolled up the tissue into a ragged ball and was tearing it to shreds with the fingers of one hand.

'If you're so unhappy here,' the Marshal said, 'why do you stay?'

She changed her tune at once. 'I suppose it's no worse

than anywhere else, all things considered. Why do you want to know about that cleaner?'

'She's dead.'

'Oh . . .'

'It's thought she committed suicide . . .' What was the point? It would be in the paper tomorrow, in any case. 'But really she was murdered.'

She stared at him and reached for another tissue. It was all one to her, good news or bad, since she went on weeping just the same.

'Are you in some sort of trouble?' he asked her gently. He'd never seen such an abundant flow of tears.

'No! Yes . . . I mean with *him*. First he screams at me for not taking any initiative and then when I do he says I've no right to take decisions without consulting him!'

'I see. Well, perhaps when you've had more experience you'll manage better. You're still very young.'

'I'm twenty-six. And how can I get experience if I can't keep my job? You can't imagine how difficult it is to find work here.'

'Where are you from?'

'Germany. Do I have an awful accent?'

'No, no . . . very slight. But wouldn't you find it easier to get work in Germany?'

'I can't go back—my parents . . . Oh well, I won't bore you with all that. I can't tell you much about your cleaner, except that she was crazy.'

'I know that, but what made you think so?'

'The way she screamed and swore—good for her is what I thought—give him as good as you get. You'd think she'd been an overpaid executive the way he was sounding on about how nobody else would give her a job like he'd done and how she'd be sorry. I'm not sure she didn't go for him, to judge from the banging and scuffling we heard, and then she went screaming off down the corridor shouting "I won't go! I'm not going!" But she went, of course, and that was the last we saw of her. I wouldn't be surprised if he didn't sack her because he was too mean to pay her. We didn't get our July salaries until last week.'

The Marshal looked around him again before remarking, 'This is a fancy sort of outfit to employ a crazy old woman for a cleaner.'

'I don't suppose it's that easy to find cleaners. Maybe I can get a job cleaning if the worst comes to the worst.'

'If your boss thinks so little of you, how come you're left in charge here alone?'

'Because *she* has to be taken on holiday, no matter what, and he's not the sort to trust his wife alone at the seaside like other businessmen do. She's a lot younger than he is and flashy with it. He has to be at her beck and call twenty-four hours a day and woe betide him if he doesn't give her everything she asks for.'

'Where are they on holiday?'

'They have a house by the sea in the Maremma. He'll be ringing up any minute and if all this stuff's still here that'll be my fault, like everything else. It's already late and when orders are delivered late the client can refuse to accept them. If that happens I'll be sacked, I know I will. But is it my fault that nothing gets done round here in August? Is it?'

'No, no, it's the same for everybody.'

'But it's not! You try making anybody in Northern Europe understand what August in Italy means! They don't want to know and who can blame them? That's why I did what I did—just look at this skirt! Would you say there was anything wrong with it?' She got up and snatched at the skirt trailing out of its box on the floor.

The Marshal stared down at it as she thrust it under his nose. 'Well . . . I don't know much about these things . . .'

'But just look at it!'

The Marshal sighed. Everywhere he went he seemed to get lugged into other people's 'little troubles', as the Prosecutor called them. The run-down asylum, the Rossis' eviction order and now this. The girl had an endless supply of tears. He didn't know what to say. He watched her fling the skirt back towards its box any old how.

'Do you know what I was supposed to do? Have the button on the waistband changed to a slightly darker blue. Right? I couldn't get it done before September and the order had to be filled by August 20th—and there were still our labels to be sewn on. He's told me so often to buck up and show initiative that I got the labels sewn on and sent the stuff off as it was. There was no specification on the order about the buttons being a particular shade of blue and they look perfectly all right as they are. Well, don't they?'

'I suppose . . .'

'The truth was that they were supposed to be delivered to us without buttons but, since they weren't what was the use of making the order late? He went completely berserk, screaming at me over the telephone. "You had no right to take things upon yourself! You don't know what you're doing! Get that order back before it goes through Customs and if it happens again you're fired, do you hear me? Fired!"'

She sat down in her chair again and began crumpling a fresh tissue without drying her tears.

'Now they've got to be taken to have the buttons changed and the driver hasn't turned up. They'll be late arriving in Germany now, anyway, and when they refuse to take them he'll blame me.'

'I'm sorry,' the Marshal offered, wondering how he could politely take his leave from this unfortunate girl. 'I'm still inclined to think you should look for another job.' He had understood something of what was going on, though the girl clearly hadn't. She might as well get out before he reported the matter as he would have to do, though he was in no hurry about it. There were worse things happening in the world than what her boss was up to.

'Would you mind giving me one of your firm's cards?'

'I've got some in my drawer. Here, take a few.'

'One's enough if your boss's name is on it.'

'It's there. Antonella Masolini. He really runs everything, if you could call it that, but the business is hers.'

'Thank you. And you can't tell me anything further about Clementina?'

'Clementina?'

'The cleaner.'

'Oh, that crazy woman. I didn't know her name. No. I never spoke to her even the one time I saw her. All I can remember about her, now, is how much she swore.'

She might well have forgotten already that Clementina had been murdered, she was so wrapped up in her own problems.

'I'll leave you my card in case you think of anything further. When will your boss be back?'

'September 1st. Do you want me to tell him you were here?'

'If you like. I'll be back, anyway.'

When he was down in the street he looked up and saw her at the window, blowing her nose and watching, no doubt, for the driver who was to come and take away the pile of boxes.

The air was so humid that the stones of the buildings had begun to look damp and the few cars passing through Piazza Pitti seemed to make the soft, swishing noise they made when the road was wet. Perhaps the dampness had made the dust settle on the tarmac, or perhaps it was just the Marshal's imagination, but everything, the sounds, the smells, the light, were those of a rainy day. Only the rain was missing. He crossed the road and started up the sloping forecourt towards the palace. As he reached the top and went left, he took off his dark glasses and turned back to look at the sky.

The first crack of thunder split the air and went rippling and shuddering away. The hills that should have been visible beyond the roofs to the south had disappeared. The Marshal felt as relieved as if that first explosion had gone off inside his own head. A big fat raindrop splashed on to his hand but he didn't hurry. His headache, long dulled by the aspirin, lifted suddenly and as he passed beneath the great iron lantern under the stone archway it was with pleasure that he saw more big raindrops falling on the gravel ahead and bending the leaves on the laurel bushes. He climbed the stairs with a quicker tread than he had done for months.

'Just in time, Marshal,' said Di Nuccio, looking out from the duty room.

'In time for what? Has something happened?'

'It's starting to rain!'

'Ah.' The Marshal removed his khaki jacket and went into his office to hang it up. A second explosion of thunder made the windows rattle and the rain began to pour down in earnest. He sat down at his desk, looking out at it with satisfaction. As a rule he disliked wet weather as much as a cat but today he was pleased to watch it rain. The more ferociously it rained, the more pleased he felt. Nothing would have induced him to be so foolish as to go out and get wet, but he liked to think of the whole hot, grubby city being washed clean by the deluge as it soaked into the red clay roofs, gurgled along the gutters and streamed down the marble statues. He could hear it drumming on the roof of the van parked below his window and on his own little car that wouldn't start. Every so often a greenish flash lit the room.

'Good . . .' he murmured to himself. 'Right . . .' without meaning anything in particular. The telephone rang and he picked up the receiver.

'Guarnaccia.'

'Salva.'

'Oh, it's you.'

'You didn't come in to lunch so I wondered . . .'

'Sorry, I didn't get a chance to phone you. I was with the Substitute Prosecutor.'

'As long as everything's all right. You didn't get caught in this rain?'

'No.'

'Well, thank goodness for that. What a storm! I shan't stir this afternoon. I'm going to get out the children's winter clothes and go through them.'

'Already?'

'Well, this weather makes you feel like doing something. And by the time they get back and start school I won't have a minute.'

He could tell she was feeling the way he felt himself and was just as relieved at the break in the weather, in spite of her saying how terrible it was.

'I'll see you later.'

'You're not going out again?'

'No, no.'

He didn't hang up but searched on his pad for the number of the Questura, Headquarters of the State Police. He'd just found it when Di Nuccio knocked and looked in.

'I talked to Mario . . . am I disturbing you?'

'No. Tell me all about it.'

'There's not much to tell. It's more or less as you imagined. The bar shuts by eleven, or even before, after which the regulars play cards for money. Friday and Saturday nights they play Bingo as well and the wives stay, too. A stop was put to it once years ago, but of course it soon started up again so nobody bothers them any more since it's small money and local and the bar owner doesn't profit by it.'

'How late does it go on?'

'That depends. During the week not much after one, but Fridays and Saturdays the men sometimes stay until three-thirty or four.'

'Is there any sign of it from outside?'

'None at all, except at the time when they leave.'

'And somebody must keep a lookout. Good. Thanks. Oh—before I forget, Clementina Franci had a sister, or I believe she did. Get on to the registry office tomorrow morning and see if you can find her residence papers.'

The rain was certainly clearing his head! When Di Nuccio had shut the door he dialled the number of the Questura. This was a tricky business since the police were unlikely to put themselves out for the rival force.

'Questura. Good afternoon.'

Well, here goes, thought the Marshal, and began to explain what he wanted. He was put through to two different offices before being told that his best bet was to ring the Commissariat of San Giovanni, right in the city centre.

'If you're not sure which Commissariat was involved, that's your best bet because it's the nearest to the hospital of Santa Maria Nuova where people like that are usually taken.'

'Thanks.'

The man who answered the phone at San Giovanni was a Sicilian and from the Marshal's own province, to judge by his accent, so things couldn't have been better.

'Guarnaccia, did you say?'

'That's right.'

'Over at the Pitti Palace? Well, that's a turn-up! My cousin's little boy used to be at school with your two—wait, don't tell me . . . Giovanni and . . . Totò! Am I right?'

'Quite right.'

'They left last year—are they up here now with you?'

'Yes—at least, just now they're down at home for the holidays, at my sister's.'

'So's my little girl, and the wife, too. It's no joke working through August. Just listen to that thunder! I can hardly hear myself speak. This rain's a relief, though.'

'It is.'

'Well then, what can I do for you?'

'I want to trace a Dangerous Persons certificate—though I'm only guessing that it might have been made out there as you're the nearest to Santa Maria Nuova.' He explained the situation as briefly as he could.

'How many years ago, did you say?'

'1967—at least, that's when she was taken to San Salvi.'

'Right you are, I'll have to go to Records where they'll tell me they're short-staffed but don't you worry. Just leave it to me. If it's here I'll find it.'

'Thanks very much.'

'I'll phone you the minute I get it—and if it turns out it's not here, leave it to me just the same. A couple of phone calls will do the trick and it's better if they come from me. You know what I mean . . .'

'Of course. I can't thank you enough.'

'Don't mention it.'

Good, said the Marshal to himself again as he hung up, and this time with reason. Whether it was because the two of them came from the same place or because the other man, too, was feeling bucked up by the change in the weather, or even a bit of both, things could not have gone more smoothly.

Di Nuccio tapped at the door again and came in with a large envelope.

'This just arrived from the Public Prosecutor's office.'

'Thanks.'

The envelope contained a copy of the pathologist's report. It was a wonder the Prosecutor had been good enough to send it rather than have him go and collect it. No doubt he'd seen enough of the Marshal to last him a while—or had he cheered up because of the cooling rain, too?

The Marshal opened the envelope and started reading.

At the end of half an hour he had learned only one thing. Clementina had been given a blow to the back of her head, an extremely efficient and bloodless blow which had probably been meant to stun her before her head was thrust in the gas oven but which had killed her. Her lungs had taken in no carbon monoxide. But then, there was little enough of it available in that almost empty canister. The assailant, thought the Marshal, had too much muscle and too little brain for the job. That Clementina had had a child he'd already heard, albeit only from Angelo. There was nothing else that interested him. She had been in fairly good general health and she had died in the early hours of the morning, between three and five was the pathologist's estimate. That was all. And if the pathologist had given him an analysis of every cell in Clementina's body, it wouldn't have told the Marshal what he wanted to know. He got up and went to the window. A rivulet had formed on the path coming down from the gardens to the gravelled area below and the heavy rain bounced up from it as it swirled along. Once, Clementina had been somebody's young wife with a child to look after. What had happened to her husband and child that had sent her into an asylum for ten years, to be then turned out into the world to play the part of a village idiot? What if it were something violent? Had she witnessed their violent deaths? A witness not in her right mind shut up in an asylum was no danger to anybody—especially as she didn't speak for years—but when she got out . . .

'No, no.' The Marshal frowned. She'd been out for years, so why now? Why now? And what the devil did happen to the husband and child? Well, if it was something criminal he could find out. He went back to his desk and, without sitting down, rang Borgo Ognissanti and asked for Records. At first he asked them to check 1967 but then, on second thoughts, he added:

'Try '66 as well.' For all he knew, her illness could have begun at the end of '66 or the very beginning of '67—damn the man who'd got away with those documents. And shouldn't he have thought of that when he asked for the Dangerous Persons certificate?

He rang the San Giovanni Commissariat again and was embarrassed to realize that he hadn't thought to get that helpful policeman's name. It was lucky for him that the boy on the switchboard didn't wait for him to ask. When he heard who was calling he said at once: 'Do you want Extension 12 again?'

'Yes. Thanks.' And the familiar accent was soon coming over the line, though sounding surprised.

'I'm afraid I haven't got anything for you yet.'

'No, no, it was just that it occurred to me that you should check 1966 as well as '67 because I don't know what month she arrived at San Salvi, and if it was January, for instance . . .'

'I get you. I'll check the second half of '66, then.'

'And there was something else. I shouldn't be asking all this of you . . .' Not that there was any reason why he shouldn't but it did no harm to say so.

'Ask anything you want,' said the policeman, impelled by this remark to show himself even more generous than before, 'What's the problem?'

'I'm trying to trace, in that same period, any case of violence involving the deaths of a man and a child. All I have is the surname, Chiari, and they were the family of Clementina Franci.'

'You can't specify the type of crime? It might be a help to Records.'

'I don't even know that there was a crime, let alone what type. I only know that the husband and child died. I'm even guessing as to their dying together, and that the circumstances were unusual or violent enough to have driven this woman out of her mind. All you can do is check that period and that surname.'

'Mm. Could have been a road accident, though, couldn't it, or a gas explosion. Anything.'

'People don't usually lose their wits after a thing like that. Oh, you're right, of course, it could have been anything, but I still think it's worth checking, if you don't mind.'

'I don't mind. Anything to oblige. You've got me curious

by this time . . . I mean, I saw it in the paper about this Franci woman. She committed suicide, didn't she?'

'And you think I'm going to an awful lot of trouble for a suicide? I'm sorry, I might have told you before since by now the Prosecutor leading the inquiry will have let it out to the papers. She was murdered.'

'I see. Keeping it quiet, were you?'

'It was set up to look like suicide and it seemed as well to let the culprit think he'd got away with it for the time being.'

'Might get cocky and show his hand, you mean? Seems a good idea to me. What are you letting it out for?'

'I'm not. The Prosecutor is.'

'Enough said. Who've you got?'

The Marshal named him.

'Christ.'

'Yes.'

'Not his sort of case, at all. Won't hit the national papers and he's ambitious. I suppose he got saddled with it because it's August and there's nobody else.'

'Didn't we all.'

'Including me, now, eh? Well, I'll do all I can.'

'Thanks a lot.'

And the Marshal hung up, still without having thought to ask the man's name. At least he had the extension number, which he wrote on his pad, and with a bit of luck his wife might know who the man was.

'That'll be young Spicuzza.'

'You know him?'

'I've never met him—do you want another slice of ham?'

'I wouldn't mind.'

'You may as well finish it. He's a cousin of Annamaria Rizza, Annamaria La Rosa she was, before she was married. You must remember the La Rosa family. Their eldest boy gave them a lot of trouble at one time. Finish the melon as well, it won't keep.'

'What sort of trouble?'

'The father was a baker—on the corner of Via Gramsci next to that shop that sells fishing tackle, you know the one—and the son . . . now, what was he called . . . Corrado, that's it, didn't want to go into the business. He wanted to be a mechanic. He had a passion for cars and could fix anything, even as a boy. His mother was quite ill over it. After all, to let the business go out of the family, it would have been the end of the world—it had been her father's. Anyway, it turned out he met a nice girl and that settled him down. He runs the baker's now his father's retired, but I think he still does car repairs at weekends. The sister has a boy who was in Giovanni's class. We used to chat once in a while outside school when they were smaller. I remember her mentioning once that her cousin was in the police up here. I suppose it came out because of you being here. What did you want to know about him?'

'Just his name.' But he couldn't help thinking that in his small home town there could be no Clementina with a complete blank in her past. Florentines had long memories but each Quarter was like a separate village and that complicated things. Clementina wasn't from San Frediano.

'I've made a cake,' said the Marshal's wife, interrupting his wandering thoughts. 'It's the first time I've ventured to use the oven unnecessarily in weeks. I've made one for the boys upstairs as well.'

'You've no call to be doing that,' growled the Marshal, pleased. 'They're old enough to look after themselves.'

'A treat now and then does them no harm. They're good lads.'

'They're not here to be mollycoddled. They get enough of that at home and it takes me all my time to toughen them up.'

'Well, I don't think a slice of cake will ruin their characters,' said his wife mildly, knowing he was pleased but allowing him to pretend he wasn't. 'And young Bruno's given up cooking so they're back on spaghetti and tomato sauce every night.'

'Given up cookery?'

'I saw him this morning when I was going shopping. He said his genius was being thwarted because all the shops are shut—or at least the fancy ones are that sell the funny things he needs. I wish he'd go back to painting.' She had hung one of his offerings in their entrance.

'I wish he'd stick to his job.'

'You always said you couldn't complain about him in that respect.'

'I'm not complaining. But he's . . .'

'What?'

'I don't know. Unpredictable. That's what he is, unpredictable. I never know what to say to him.'

'That's because he's artistic and you're not.'

'Hmph.'

'And whatever you say, I'm fond of the lad. He's so cheerful, so full of enthusiasm for life.'

'I didn't say I wasn't fond of him,' grumbled the Marshal, 'he's just a bit of a handful, that's all.'

'Well, in a few months he'll be gone. I'll get the cake.'

The storm had been over for some time and given way to such a brilliant sunset that the rooms were filled with the pink glow of it as if with some artificial light.

'We'll sleep better tonight,' the Marshal's wife remarked when she was clearing away the supper things. 'That storm's cleared the air beautifully.'

It was true that they fell asleep more easily than they had done for some time but, even so, the Marshal's sleep was troubled and at one point he found himself struggling with what he felt was a very nasty situation, though he wasn't sure exactly what it was. One thing he was sure about was that he didn't want to answer the telephone because he knew that the Prosecutor was on the other end of the line boiling with rage. The worst of it was that, even without picking up the phone, he was getting the full blast.

'Have you seen her clothes? Look at them, man, look at them!'

And the Marshal went through Clementina's pitiful selection of clothes again and saw, to his horror, that all the buttons on them were bright blue. What's more, there was still a button missing from her only cotton dress and as he picked it up, Linda Rossi said in his ear, 'You see, I told you.'

How could he have failed to notice the bright blue buttons before? He thought he'd looked through everything so carefully. He began to sweat with embarrassment at his stupidity and the doctor looked at him sadly and said:

'We can't move the body, you know.'

The Marshal sweated even more. That the body had remained in the flat all this time because of his failure to notice the buttons . . . and in this heat, too, though there had been the storm . . .

'She'll sleep better,' his wife said.

Clementina was in her bed. He was relieved that she was only asleep and not dead. The important thing now was to keep her alive or he stood to lose his job.

The phone went on ringing so there was a telephone in her flat, after all, but he refused to answer it until all those boxes of clothes had been removed.

'Will you sew the other buttons on her frock? I have to sit here with her or she'll die. She's very frightened.' He was pleading with Linda Rossi and the German girl but they didn't understand him. The girl went on crying and Linda Rossi only stared at him and said: 'Why don't you answer the phone?'

'I can't.'

'The phone,' she insisted, grasping his arm.

'I can't!'

'Salva!'

He opened his eyes, wide awake.

'The phone, Salva. Do you want me to answer?' She had already switched the bedside light on.

'No, no.' He reached out and picked up the receiver, glancing at the alarm clock. It was a quarter to three in the morning.

CHAPTER 8

'Guarnaccia.' His head was still so full of his dream that he was both surprised and relieved to hear young Bruno on the other end of the line and not the Prosecutor.

'There's a call for you, Marshal. Says his name's Franco and that it's urgent—he says you gave him this number and that—'

'Put him through.'

'Marshal? It's me. I think you'd better come round here right away.' The big barman's voice was as soft and calm as ever, despite the urgency of his message.

'What's happened?'

'There's a man trying to get into Clementina's flat—he's probably got in by now. I saw him climbing up the scaffolding and since they've been and taken those seals away—'

'I'll be right there.'

'What do you want me to do?'

'Just keep out of sight and watch.'

'Right. And if he tries to leave I'll stop him.'

What was the use of saying the man could be dangerous? Franco had been running things round there in his own way for years and there wasn't time to argue with him now. The Marshal hung up and struggled quickly into some clothes.

'Where are you going?' His wife was alarmed.

'Out. Don't worry.'

When he stopped at his office to pick up his holster, Bruno was there, fully dressed, and he had woken Di Nuccio who was on his way down from the dormitory, cursing sleepily.

'You can't go by yourself, Marshal,' said Bruno earnestly, as though it were the Marshal who was only eighteen years old, not himself. 'I thought I should wake Di Nuccio, too.'

'Mph. Let's go.'

Unpredictable as ever, but the boy was right. They took the van.

'Turn into any side street before you get too near the square,' ordered the Marshal.

They did the last brief stretch on foot and it was difficult to prevent their footsteps from echoing so that they had to slow down as they neared Clementina's house.

Whoever had climbed up the scaffolding was still in there. They saw a pale flash of torchlight pass across the window and vanish. Then Franco's bulky frame emerged from the shadows.

'He's still up there,' he whispered.

'Go back home.'

'But, Marshal—'

'Go back home, and quietly.' There was no need to add that. Franco retreated as silently as a big cat in the jungle.

'Shall I start climbing up?' whispered Bruno.

'No.' The last thing he wanted was a National Service boy getting hurt. But what was he going to do? Thanks to the Prosecutor, he no longer had the keys to the flat, and while they could catch their man easily enough by waiting down there in the shadows, he wanted, more than anything, to know just what he was doing up there where there was nothing to steal and where the evidence, such as it was, had already been collected. He was hardly the ideal person himself to be swinging around on scaffolding. Before he could decide, the street door opened and he whipped round to grasp the arm that came round it.

'It's me.' Young Rossi's face appeared bleached white in the shadows. 'There's someone up there. I just called your number but they told me—'

'Be quiet. Go back up to your flat and stay there—and don't make a noise on the stairs.'

But Rossi had felt slippers on and vanished as silently as Franco had done, leaving the street door ajar. The Marshal began to fear that, sooner or later, some little noise would bring the whole neighbourhood out to collect under Clementina's window once again, and any confusion would make it that much easier for the man to get away. As if to confirm his fears, a light went on in Pippo's flat, opposite. He made a sign to the boys to keep still and silent, hoping they were invisible in the shadows under the scaffolding. They watched the lighted window but no face appeared there. They heard a bout of coughing, a flush of water and the light went out.

The Marshal touched Di Nuccio's arm and pointed upwards.

'But try and surprise him,' he murmured, 'I want to know what he's doing.'

Di Nuccio began to climb and a shower of raindrops was released from the torn netting. The Marshal watched him anxiously, knowing it must all be wet and slippery, but Di Nuccio was careful and avoided the soaked planking which would otherwise have made his climb easier. He made no noise.

The Marshal could feel Bruno's disappointment, though his face was barely discernible. He sent the boy round the corner at the end of the building to wait out of sight in case the intruder slipped through their fingers. Then he stood himself inside the street door and waited, hoping that Di Nuccio wouldn't have occasion to fire a shot and wake up all the neighbours.

The wait seemed inordinately long. The streets were so silent that he heard a train whistle and screech as it pulled into the central station on the other side of the river. Then nothing except the sound of his own breathing. He peered up through the blackness of the staircase. After what seemed half an hour but couldn't have been more than three or four minutes, the lights came on and he heard Di Nuccio's voice two floors above. So there had been no struggle, no drama. Di Nuccio had managed to surprise him, just the sort of job he would enjoy. Once he heard their steps begin to descend he started to breathe more easily and began climbing the stairs. They were so steep that he made slow progress—but why were the others coming down even more slowly? Much too slowly. He heard Di Nuccio mutter something angrily and a sound of protest from the captive. He paused to listen and realized at once that their slowness and the dragging noise of one pair of footsteps meant that they'd caught the blackmailer with the limp. But a second realization, that he was exaggerating his slowness on purpose, didn't come quickly enough. Before they came into view, the automatic timer controlling the dim stair lights clicked off, and as the Marshal felt about on the flaking plaster of the wall for a switch he heard a thud followed by a gunshot, of deafening loudness in that confined space.

'Marshal!'

He was already thudding up the stairs, having found a lightswitch.

Di Nuccio was getting slowly to his feet, holding one shoulder with a bloody hand.

'The window . . .' His face was greyish.

The Marshal passed him, sliding the Beretta from his holster as he reached Clementina's flat. But the man was already out on the scaffolding. Lights were going on in every house in the street and people were banging shutters open to hang out and call to each other, 'What's happened?'

'Damn!' He could start shooting in the darkness at the risk of hitting a by-stander. The man was swinging down towards the platform of planks below to his right.

'Bruno!' It all depended on him. He was a well-set-up lad and could defend himself, but the man swinging down on the scaffolding looked more like a gorilla than anything human. He couldn't see Bruno because of the planks and the netting but he heard his running steps and the fugitive heard them, too. He set off at a limping run along the platform and it wasn't his limp that stopped him but the rainwater left by the storm. He skidded and fell heavily on his hip. His head hit a joint in the metal poles with a crack that would have broken any normal skull but he wasn't even stunned. As his impetus took him over the edge of the platform he called out, trying to the last to save himself, but his clutching hand slid off the edge of the slimy wood and he fell, sending the hanging net swinging outwards and crushing the upturned face of Bruno who had just arrived below.

The Marshal was sitting with his hands planted firmly on his knees, staring with big, troubled eyes at the white wall in front of him. His hat was on the formica chair beside him. The other chairs in the corridor were all empty except one at the far end where a grey-haired woman sat crying silently, every now and then dabbing her cheeks with a rolled-up handkerchief. The lights in the corridor were dimmed and the occasional loud remark of some invisible nurse sounded incongruous in such a hushed atmosphere. At the end of the corridor there were double doors with two round windows labelled 'Operating Theatre. No Admittance to Unauthorized Persons'.

Was that where Bruno was? He had no idea. He had been alive when the ambulance came, but he had lain so still in the road beneath the blanket that Pippo's wife had brought down that it didn't seem as though he would ever move again.

Franco had stood there looking down at the huddled form

and said, 'Poor kid. He looks bad.' And then with typical insouciance he'd added, 'Hadn't you better call in reinforcements to take your customer away? You'll be wanting to go to the hospital with this lad.'

'He got away,' the Marshal had growled.

'Like hell he got away,' said Franco calmly, 'I've locked him in the lavatory at the back of the bar and two of my regulars are standing guard. Oh, don't worry, he's not armed, I checked. But I thought you'd want to dispose of him before the ambulance arrived.'

A nurse came hurrying along the corridor and the Marshal got to his feet. But she walked straight past him and spoke to the silently weeping woman who stood up and followed her. Even in her grief she was visibly embarrassed because she hadn't had time to dress herself properly. The Marshal saw that she wore no stockings and was pulling her cardigan over her chest to hide what was perhaps a none too clean old frock in which she did the housework. Had her husband had a heart attack? Probably. And now maybe he was dead. The nurse had led her into a small, brightly lighted room and closed the door, but he heard some low murmurs of explanation broken into by the woman's wail of grief and fear. Then things quietened down and the corridor was silent again. Once, he thought he heard the squeak of a trolley and half rose to his feet, but no trolley appeared.

They had given Bruno oxygen in the ambulance. What did that mean? Someone had said, 'Don't worry. I've seen people come through worse than this.' It was a funny thing that ambulance men, while looking so sound and reliable, always had a cheerful air about them. Why should that be? It seemed unlikely that they were chosen for it. Perhaps it was something about the job itself, but it was odd. Postmen were a bit like that, too, but that wasn't the same sort of job at all . . .

The Marshal's head gave a sudden jerk. Had he been falling asleep? Di Nuccio was coming along the corridor with his arm in a sling. He was still extremely pale but, apart from that, he looked fit enough.

'How are you feeling?'

'Fine. It was only a flesh wound. Could have been worse, the way that gorilla smashed me when the lights went off. Even so, it's not going to be much fun admitting that he made me shoot myself in the shoulder, whatever the circumstances were. How's Bruno doing?'

'I don't know.'

Di Nuccio sat down next to the Marshal.

'What are you doing? Get a taxi and get yourself to bed.'

'I can't leave till we know about Bruno.'

'You'd be better off in bed. It could be all night.' But he let Di Nuccio go on sitting there because otherwise he would be sitting there alone, waiting for the nurse to come for him as she had come for the weeping woman to say . . . No! Bruno was young and healthy and full of life. He would pull through.

'Bruno'll make it,' Di Nuccio said, as though reading the Marshal's thoughts. 'He's as fit as a fiddle. He lent me those dumb-bells of his when he was going through his muscle-building phase and I couldn't do a tenth of what he could do.'

But the Marshal thought to himself: What good are muscles if your brain's damaged? He didn't speak, only went on staring at the wall in front of him. There were a lot of things going through his head but he was dumb. The effort of speaking grated on his nerves. He wanted Di Nuccio to go on talking to fill the silence, but not about Bruno. He wished, not for the first time during this case, that Lorenzini were with him. Young Brigadier Lorenzini was only the same age as Di Nuccio but there was something more solid about him, somehow.

'Do you think there's somewhere we could get a coffee?' Di Nuccio asked.

'What . . .?'

'A coffee. Or even a glass of water. I'm feeling a bit off.'

The Marshal turned to look at him and was filled with remorse. The boy was on his last legs. Even if it was only a flesh wound, he'd lost a fair amount of blood and should have been in bed resting, instead of which he was sitting here waiting for news of Bruno and keeping the Marshal company. And the Marshal had only wished Lorenzini had been there instead.

'Stay where you are,' he said. 'There's some sort of vending machine in the waiting-room along there. I'll get you a drink.'

'I'll go.'

'Sit still.'

After the artificial gloom of the windowless corridor it was a shock to find that dawn had broken. The glass-fronted waiting-room was filled with a pale pink light that made the rows of empty chairs look squalid in contrast. Because of yesterday's storm the sky seemed much higher and purer.

The Marshal fished for coins in his pocket. The machine offered a choice of coffee or hot chocolate and he had a feeling that in his condition Di Nuccio would be better off with hot chocolate, well sweetened. He also had a feeling that Di Nuccio wouldn't thank him for it so he pushed the button for coffee.

Coming back along the corridor, he saw that Di Nuccio was slumped back in his chair as if he were asleep, but when he reached him he saw that the boy's eyes were open.

'Here, drink this.' He gave him a small paper cup and took a sip from his own. It was only then that he thought to ask, 'What was he doing when you climbed into the flat? Did you manage to surprise him?'

'Our friend the gorilla? I did, but I should have got there two minutes earlier, even a minute would have done it.'

'What was he doing?'

'Burning something.'

'Burning what?'

'Paper. And it's no use asking me what paper because there's no hope of finding out. He was in the kitchen when I climbed in at the bedroom window which he'd forced and left open, and I smelled burning right away. But whatever it was he'd already burnt it in the kitchen sink and turned the tap on it. It was probably only because the tap was running that he didn't hear me come in. I looked in the sink and there was nothing left of whatever it was except a little blackened water.'

'So how do you know it was paper?'

'The smell of the smoke, like when you light a fire with newspaper. The smoke was still hanging in the air in the kitchen—and I don't know what else he could have burnt so easily and completely.'

'I suppose you're right. But what papers? I didn't find a thing.'

'Well it must have been something well hidden because look at the amount of time he was up there. We had plenty of time to get there and catch him at it, so he must have had to search.'

'He didn't say anything?'

'Not a word. After the first shock of feeling my Beretta in his ribs he gave a quick look about him like a trapped animal and then grinned at me as if to say, So what? There's not much you can do about it now.'

'We'll see about that.'

'He'll be done for breaking and entering but do you think a blackmail charge would stick?'

'I don't know. There's no letter, no real evidence. Only the Rossis' word against his. But from the way you say he reacted to being caught, I'm willing to bet that it's not the first time he's been arrested.'

Rapid footsteps were coming along an adjoining corridor. A nurse appeared at the turning and made straight for them. She recognized their uniforms.

With no preliminaries she snapped, 'Have this boy's

parents been informed?' She shot a vicious look at the coffee cups as though she'd caught them in the middle of a drinking orgy.

'I—they were seeing to it from Headquarters . . .'

'In that case, why aren't they here?'

Di Nuccio spoke up: 'They won't be able to find them. Bruno told me they've gone abroad on holiday, so . . .'

The nurse didn't answer him but looked at the Marshal, furious, 'This patient should be at home in bed!' It was clear that she held the Marshal responsible for the condition of both boys and, since he felt much the same way himself, it was with mumbling humility that he dared to ask:

'How's it . . . how is he?'

'There's no change. He's still unconscious. There's nothing you can do here. You'd better leave, both of you.'

She turned and marched away, her white shoes slapping on the tiled corridor. The Marshal stood where he was, looking after her uncertainly. It was Di Nuccio who had to decide.

'Let's go. We can come back in the morning.'

'It is morning.'

They walked side by side along the corridor. When they went through the door to the waiting-room their tired eyes were dazzled by the rays of the sun and the Marshal paused to put on his dark glasses.

'I'll call a taxi.'

On the way back to the Pitti Palace they were too exhausted and depressed to talk. They both had their heads back and their eyes closed so that the driver, when he pulled up, called out, 'We're here!' thinking they were asleep.

'Go straight to bed,' the Marshal said as they reached the top of the staircase and he unlocked the door. 'And stay there all day.'

'But we're so short—'

'Go to bed.'

He didn't intend to go to bed himself. It wasn't worth it

for a couple of hours or less. His first thought was to go to the kitchen and make himself a decent cup of coffee to wash away the taste of the weak and bitter hospital brew, or the taste of the hospital itself. He opened the shutters and the kitchen window and got the coffee on as quietly as he could. Even so, his wife appeared in the doorway in her cotton nightdress, her hair ruffled and her face pale with sleep.

'I didn't mean to wake you.'

'I wasn't properly asleep. I've been waking up every hour since you went out. What's been happening?' She got two coffee-cups out of the cupboard. 'You look dreadful.'

'Bruno's hurt.'

'Bruno . . . Oh no!'

'I'll tell you about it in a minute but let me drink this coffee first.'

'But at least tell me if it's serious.'

'Yes. At least, I think so.'

'And his parents?'

'Di Nuccio says they're abroad on holiday.'

When the coffee came bubbling up the warm air was filled with its scent and the birds were chirping on the grass outside so that it didn't seem possible that anything tragic had happened.

'Tell me about it, Salva.'

He told her. They didn't sit at the table but stood near the sink, looking out of the open window and sipping their coffee. The clear burning sun was soothing to the Marshal's tired face though it made his eyes water.

When he had finished telling her, she said, 'You should try and get some sleep.'

'No, no. By this time . . . I think I'll ring the hospital in an hour.'

'Is there no way of tracing his parents?'

'They're abroad. I've no idea where, so until Bruno comes round . . .'

'Has he any other injuries besides his head?'

'I don't know.' Why hadn't he asked? He should have insisted on seeing the doctor in charge instead of letting himself be bullied by an ill-tempered nurse. When he telephoned he would demand some detailed information.

But when he telephoned, the doctor who'd been on nights was no longer there. He was told that Bruno was in an intensive care unit and that there was no change. He was still unconscious.

And somehow the day had to be got through.

At least his numbed and trance-like state caused by lack of sleep took the edge off having to deal with the Prosecutor. He would have been informed already, of course, by Headquarters, after they'd taken the man with a limp away. Perhaps he was already on his way to question him in the cells over there. The Marshal decided to let things take their course and wait for the Prosecutor to call him, meanwhile writing out his report. He settled down at his desk, glancing every now and then at the telephone. Dead on nine o'clock it rang. So soon? He took a couple of deep breaths before picking up the receiver.

'Is that Marshal Guarnaccia?'

'Speaking.'

'I shouldn't be disturbing you but . . .'

'Who is it?'

'Linda Rossi.'

'Ah. Good morning.'

'Good morning. I hope I'm not . . . How is that poor boy?'

'Not too good, I'm afraid. Still unconscious. What can I do for you?'

'I just wanted . . . Is it true? About Clementina?'

'Yes, it's true. I'm afraid I couldn't tell you sooner—but don't let it upset you too much. The man who broke in last night is in custody. There's no danger to you.'

'It was a shock when I opened the paper. You'll think me awful, disturbing you like this when you've got so much on, but . . . We called you last night, you know, at least, my husband did, but you'd already left. Franco said—'

'Yes. I know.'

'We were trying to help.'

'I'm very grateful to you.' If he didn't open the way for her they might go on like this for hours. 'Is something wrong? Do you need my help?'

'Oh, you don't know how grateful we'd be if—my husband—We only heard yesterday when we went to the Tenants' Association. The date of the hearing's been confirmed. It's unbelievable what some people will do to get you out—there was a couple whose case was heard yesterday, their flat was falling apart, literally falling apart, and they'd been begging for years for it to be fixed. A huge chunk of plaster had fallen on their little boy's head and the floors weren't safe—and do you know what the owner's lawyer claimed? That they'd repeatedly sent workmen round there and the tenants had refused to let them in. Bare-faced lies, just like that! And they were so surprised by such an unexpected and outlandish accusation that they were too shocked to defend themselves. If you're honest yourself you can't imagine anyone being capable of pulling a trick like that. And of course, owners are always richer and more influential than their tenants. They have friends in high places. You're just helpless. And what the lawyers are saying about us is a pack of lies but unless we can—'

'Just a minute,' interrupted the Marshal. 'What are they saying?'

'That's just it. If they'd brought up about my getting married and having a baby in the house we were ready for them. But obviously they've decided that the baby could make things drag on longer since we'd have been given more time to find other accommodation. So they've made up this story, saying I've been sub-letting, having paying guests. It's completely untrue but how can we prove it?'

'How can they prove it?'

'They claim they have a witness, but even if their witness is lying, what can we do? It's our word against theirs. I promise you it's not true! We've never even had so much as a friend to stay overnight. There isn't room!'

'I believe you. But what do you want me to do?'

'You're our only hope. The woman at the Tenants' Association asked us if we could produce a witness, somebody official, not a friend or neighbour, somebody who'd be believed.'

'I see. But what can I have witnessed, exactly?'

'We told her what had happened—about Clementina—and it was she who suggested it, otherwise I wouldn't . . . You've called on us, you see, a couple of times, unexpectedly, so if you would say that you had seen no sign of anyone camping out here, as it were . . .'

'I see,' said the Marshal again. 'Well, I'll probably be able to do that.'

'I have to give your name,' Linda Rossi insisted anxiously, 'I'm supposed to go round there today and give in a list of witnesses who will be appearing . . .'

'All right. Put my name down.'

'I'm afraid you'll have to—I don't know your name. We just know you as "the Marshal" . . .'

'Guarnaccia. Salvatore Guarnaccia.'

'Thank you. Oh, Marshal, I'm so grateful to you. And bothering you at a time like this when you must be so worried about that boy.'

That boy . . . The Marshal had hung up but his hand stayed on the receiver. Was it too soon to ring the hospital again? That boy . . . How often had he said those words, shaking his head?

'He's unpredictable . . . that's what he is . . .'

He couldn't remember exactly how long it was since he'd last phoned. More than an hour, surely? Anything could happen in an hour. Or nothing. No change. Sometimes people stayed in a coma for years. But they hadn't said precisely that he was in a coma, they'd said unconscious and that's not the same thing. He didn't know enough about these things to know what questions to ask and he just let them palm him off with non-information. Well, they couldn't stop him telephoning, even if it annoyed them.

But the phone began ringing under his hand. He'd all but forgotten the Prosecutor. Well, the sooner that was over, the better.

'Guarnaccia?'

'Speaking.'

'Good morning. I've got news for you—I just hope you don't think I've been too long about getting it.'

It certainly wasn't the Prosecutor, but it took the Marshal some seconds to realize that it was Spicuzza from the San Giovanni Commissariat. Bruno's accident had wiped this train of thought from his mind. Fortunately, Spicuzza carried on chattering, pleased as he was with himself, and there was time for the Marshal to recover his wits.

'Bad news first—if you could call it that. I can't find any record of a crime which might have involved this woman's husband and child—I see the story's out in the morning's paper, by the way.'

And of course the Marshal hadn't. If only he weren't so slow! The Prosecutor wasn't so far wrong in his judgement, he had to admit.

'Anyway,' Spicuzza went on, 'nothing for you in that line but I've got her Dangerous Persons certificate. It was made out here on December 28th, 1966.'

'Then you have her address of the time?'

'Yes, she lived in the Santa Croce Quarter—don't worry, there's a photocopy of the certificate on its way to you by hand. You'll have it any minute. But there's something else—'

'Wait—does it say who applied for the certificate?'

'The hospital authorities, I'm afraid. That's not much of a help to you, is it? It looks like she was already in hospital when she went loony. In fact, there's a note attached to this certificate—just a slip of paper, written by hand, to the effect that, despite the Dangerous Persons certificate, she was to remain where she was until her physical condition improved enough for her to be transferred to the psychiatric ward of the same hospital, Santa Maria Nuova, for observation.

'Her physical condition?'

'That's right. And the note's signed illegibly but by a consultant dermatologist. It took me a while to make it out but that's what it says, all right. Did you see her body? Were there any burns, skin grafts? I said it might be an accident, if you remember.'

'There wasn't a mark on her that I could see, and nothing of that sort in the pathologist's report, either.'

'Maybe the hospital could help you.'

'That's true, though it's twenty years ago. I think I'm more interested in that address for the moment. Thanks, anyway, for being so helpful.'

'You're welcome. Goodness knows there's nothing doing here. We got a pickpocket this morning—in the cathedral, if you please. Excitement of the week. Been doing the round of churches and museums with the tourists. Cultural type.'

'Oh, *that* pickpocket.'

'Done the Pitti Palace, as well, has he? Silly twit—he'd dressed himself up in holiday clothes and was carrying a camera and guidebook, nicked, of course, but you can't fake that three-day city sunburn and the dazed look they get from an overdose of museums. Once we knew he was operating it didn't take long to find him, and catch him in the act.'

'My compliments,' the Marshal offered, 'and thanks again.'

Di Nuccio tapped and came in. 'Marshal?'

'Why aren't you in bed?'

'I feel all right, honestly. And don't you remember, you told me to ring the registry to see if I could trace the madwoman's sister? Not much use, though. Without the first name and her address the computer won't produce.'

'Surely there's some way of doing it! If I knew her first name and her address I wouldn't be asking.'

'That's what I said but I was told pretty sharply that they're not a police records department. I still think there must be a way of getting at the information but since the head clerk's away on his holidays—'

'We'll have to wait till September 1st. Don't tell me.'

'I'm afraid so. Is there any news?'

'Nothing. He was still unconscious last time I rang.'

'How long ago?'

'It must be an hour.'

'Couldn't you try again?'

'I'm going to.'

'Call me if there's anything—oh, I almost forgot what I came in for. This came for you, by hand.'

Ten minutes later the Marshal took his hat and jacket from behind the door. He stopped in at the duty room before leaving.

'How's your shoulder?'

'All right. I'd rather stay up, Marshal, really—'

'Can you do a bit of typing with one hand?'

'I suppose so. It just means one finger instead of two.'

'Well, if you can't, get one of the other lads to type for you and finish typing up the notes of the report that's on my desk. I've already done the bulk of it and I'll look through it when I get back.' He didn't say that he was incapable of sitting still and concentrating. Any excuse was good enough to get out of the office and walk to shake off the dread that was gripping him.

'Did you call—'

'There's no change.'

'But don't they say anything else?'

'Yes. They say there's a clot lodged in his brain and that they'll probably operate today.'

'Jesus . . . Marshal, I found this on his locker.'

It was a postcard from Bruno's parents. They were in Vienna and going on to Amsterdam. The message ended: 'See you Sept. 1st. Love.'

'Should I inform Headquarters? You never know, they might be able to—'

'Yes. Call them.'

'You're going out?'

'I'll be back by lunch-time. If not I'll telephone.'

He walked. He felt that if he walked far enough and with enough determination he might somehow ease the weight on his chest and breathe properly again. He walked steadily, looking neither right nor left, seeing only a dark-tinted blur of colours and hearing only a deadened buzz of meaningless noises, like someone half asleep on a train. Sometimes he bumped into groups of tourists who walked uncertainly, gazing up at the high buildings and blocking his way. He was aware of their stopping to stare after him but he never turned to apologize. His dark glasses cut him off from them and their world. He crossed the river and walked up the embankment on the other side.

There were times, in his more lucid moments, when he would get angry with himself during a difficult case for his lack of brains and efficiency. He'd even been known to make lists and plans and draw diagrams which he would then stare at for hours without their suggesting anything to him other than his own stupidity. Then, at a certain point, he would forget all about them and go his way, absorbed, inexorable, following his instinct. It had happened with almost every case he'd been involved in and he had never stopped to think about it afterwards because he found his own behaviour a bit embarrassing and preferred to forget the whole business as soon as it was over.

This time there was no deceiving himself with lists, no futile efforts at putting his limited intelligence to work on a lot of contradictory facts. This time, probably because of Bruno, there was none of that. There was only pity for a poor old woman attacked in her bed whom he had thought to keep alive in his dream by sitting with her.

'Will you sit with me?'

It was Angelo who had first aroused that pity. Angelo, whose face lit up at the sight of a bird.

And Bruno. He couldn't keep Bruno alive by sitting with him, though, God knows, he'd have been only too willing to sit there night and day. They wouldn't even let him in. Would they shave his head? And his parents were enjoying their holiday, little knowing what was waiting for them when they got back. His own two boys . . . He'd always taken it for granted that they'd do their National Service with the Carabinieri . . .

'Look out!'

A crocodile procession of Japanese tourists had jostled him off the narrow pavement into the path of a taxi. The driver had just braked in time and was glaring at him. The Marshal shrugged and stepped back. He must pull himself together. He'd already walked a little too far along the embankment and he crossed over and went back a few yards. Heaven knew how far he would have walked if it hadn't been for that taxi. He made his way to the church of Santa Croce and stopped in front of its marble façade to fish out the address from his pocket. The street he was looking for was a tiny one, just off the square, and when he got there he found the road up and planks laid over gaping holes, though no one was working. The shops all had their metal shutters down except for what looked like a fishmonger's where some alterations were going on. A grey-haired man with a big moustache was standing in the doorway with a brush in his hand. Seeing the Marshal hesitate, looking at the door numbers, he smiled at him:

'Nice mess, this,' he said.

The Marshal looked beyond him into the shop. They

seemed to be re-doing the place while it was shut for the holidays.

'I mean the road,' the man went on, 'and God knows when they'll be done. New gas pipes. A few more storms like yesterday's and we'll be baling out like in '66.'

'Were you here then?' the Marshal asked, waking up at the thought that he might have found somebody who'd known Clementina.

'Where would I have been? See this counter?' It was an elaborate affair of marble with coloured inlay. 'You won't see many like it these days, but all this part in front used to be closed in with glass. Smashed to bits. And two world wars it had gone through without so much as a chip! And the cellar! Where all my stock was! We had to use gas masks to go down there and clean it out. I hope I'll never have to go through the like again.'

'No . . . I wonder if you could help me. If you were here all that long ago, perhaps you knew a woman—she'd be in her thirties—who lived over there at No. 5.'

'What name?'

'Clementina was how she was usually known.'

'Clementina, Clementina, doesn't ring a bell. What was her surname?'

'Franci. Anna Clementina Franci. Her husband was Chiari.'

'Say no more! I'm with you now. It was the Clementina that baffled me, never knew she was called that. Anna Chiari's the woman you mean.'

How odd it sounded. She had become a real person. Anna Chiari, not crazy Clementina.

'Did you know her?'

'Of course I knew her. Chiari had a leather shop right there on the ground floor and she was a customer of mine, poor soul. She never came back after they took her away.'

'Dino!' called a voice from the back of the shop.

'Just a minute! What did you want her for?'

'Didn't you see in the paper that she's dead?'

'Dead?'

'Dino!'

'I'm coming! Well, I didn't, but then I'm not much of a one for reading the paper, I watch the news on television. She recovered then? I'm not so much surprised she's dead as surprised to hear she was still alive. They said she was very bad—'

'Dino! The van's waiting and he's blocking the street!'

'I'll have to go.'

'Wait! What happened to her? I need to know.'

'Dino!'

'I'll have to go, but ask anybody round here—ask Signora Santoli, No. 5, first floor. It's a long story but she's always glad of company—All right, all right! I'm coming!'

He dropped his brush and dived into the back of the shop leaving the Marshal to stare across at No. 5.

CHAPTER 9

'Who is it?'

'Carabinieri.' There was a spyhole in the door and the Marshal had no doubt that an eye was peering out at him, checking on his uniform. He stood back a little so she could see him better and then waited as a number of bolts and a chain were undone. The door opened and a woman looked at him inquiringly. Although she was well past middle age she was robust and very upright and so neatly dressed that she might have been expecting a visitor.

'Marshal Guarnaccia. I apologize for disturbing you but I'd like to talk to you for a moment.' Seeing a shade of anxiety cross her face, he added, 'Please don't worry, there's nothing wrong. Just a bit of information you could give that might help me with an inquiry.'

'I see. I just wondered because sometimes my mother-in-law . . .' She glanced over her shoulder and then beyond him at the opposite door. 'You'd better come in. The neighbours will think . . .'

He followed her into the entrance hall, which was small but gleaming with cleanliness.

'Come into the sitting-room where we can be comfortable.'

The sitting-room was as clean and polished as the hall but it was anything but comfortable. The shining bare floor and symmetrically arranged chairs gave it the air of a well-to-do dentist's waiting-room. There was even a neat stack of magazines on a low, carved table.

'Please sit down.'

At least it was cool and the Marshal was glad enough to sit himself down in one of the chilly leather armchairs, placing his hat with his sunglasses inside it carefully on his knee. The woman sat bolt upright on a hard chair facing him and waited for him to begin.

'It's about a woman who used to live in this building. It's a long time ago now, but perhaps you remember her. Her name was Anna Clementina Franci. Her husband was Chiari and I believe he had a leather shop in the ground floor here.'

'Anna—?' Her face became more animated. 'But . . . I read in the paper this morning . . .'

'That she was murdered. Yes. I'm trying to find out something about her past and since you were her neighbour . . .'

'I see. But it's a long time ago, as you say. I understood from the article that it was burglars. At least, that was the impression it gave, so I don't quite see . . . Forgive me, you know your job best I'm sure. I'm just a bit surprised, that's all.'

'Murders happen,' the Marshal said, 'and sometimes they happen to people you know.'

'It's not that. I know what you mean, but, frankly, what surprised me when I saw the article was not that she was dead but that she'd lived on all this time, though I gather she wasn't her normal self.'

'No, she wasn't normal. She was in San Salvi for quite a number of years until most of the patients there were discharged.'

'Oh, I knew she'd gone into San Salvi.'

'You did?'

'Certainly. I went to see her there.'

'Really? You were close friends, then?' He couldn't imagine this kindly but rather prim lady among the inmates of San Salvi. Nevertheless, she looked like a strong character, the sort to do calmly what she saw as her duty, however unpleasant it might be.

'I wouldn't say close friends exactly—but I'm being neglectful, I do beg your pardon. On such a hot day you must be in need of refreshment.' Her eyes glanced off his sweated uniform and the Marshal became conscious of what he must look like after a long and agitated walk in the heat. This woman looked the sort who would remain cool and composed no matter what the temperature, and no matter what her feelings. She went across the room now to open a heavy, dark cupboard. There were three or four bottles in it and a neat row of small glasses, but the Marshal had visions of long-opened, sticky vin santo. This wasn't a house that saw many visitors, he was sure.

'You're very kind,' he said quickly, 'but what I'd like most would be just a glass of water.'

She straightened up. 'Of course. I'll get you one.'

While she was gone, a tiny, ancient woman with a walking-stick came into the doorway and stopped there, staring at the Marshal in that unselfconscious way of small children when they stare at a stranger.

'Good morning.' The Marshal started to get to his feet but the old lady, hearing footsteps approaching behind her, vanished. He heard a voice say very quietly, 'Go to your room.'

'I want my breakfast.'

'You've had it already. Did you forget? Go to your room, now.'

A door closed. Signora Santoli came back with a glass of water in her hand. The Marshal was still on his feet.

'Do sit down. You mustn't mind my mother-in-law. Did she come in here?'

'Just as far as the door. I suppose she was curious to know who was here.'

'Please don't mind her. She's become more or less a child.'

'A stroke?'

'No, arteriosclerosis. I can't complain, since she's docile enough. The only thing is I can never go out, because even though I double lock the door, she's often managed to open it and then she wanders off and has no idea where she is or how to get back home, poor thing. It was easier when my husband was alive, though of course she wasn't nearly so bad seven years ago as she is now.'

Seven years. Seven years trapped in this house, keeping up appearances in spite of a life that must be almost totally devoid of even the smallest pleasures. Some women were saints.

As if she could read his thoughts, Signora Santoli went on: 'Fortunately, I'm very fond of music and I've treated myself to a stereo set, not a very good one but it's adequate.' Her eyes strayed across to where an obviously new stereo set was set up in one corner, the only modern note in what was a rather gloomy, old-fashioned room. 'I enjoy watching television, too, and my mother-in-law goes to bed early. Her health is otherwise very good, you know, one must be thankful for that. And I have a neighbour who comes in for an hour on Saturday mornings so that I can do a little shopping for myself instead of having everything sent in. It makes a nice change.'

'Though I imagine,' the Marshal said, 'that your neighbour is on holiday now.'

'She is, but August will soon be over, won't it?'

'Yes,' said the Marshal with feeling, 'it will, thank goodness.'

He sipped the water. It was cool, so it must have been in the fridge, but it was tap water and unpleasant. He was pretty sure that there wasn't much money to spare in the household and that buying the stereo set had been a very big event in this woman's life. No doubt she'd agonized over the decision for months beforehand before taking the plunge. Seven years . . . With a start he remembered the Prosecutor's words about the way he let people involve him in their 'little problems'. But the Prosecutor never saw these people except in his office where their 'little problems' were not in evidence. Out of pure defiance he sat there and let Signora Santoli carry on talking.

'Although my husband was Italian,' she was saying, 'I'm Swiss, myself. We met when I was working as a children's governess here. Unfortunately, we had no children ourselves, which was a great disappointment to both of us, especially to me as I'd been used to having children around me because of my job. Well, we must take the rough with the smooth, don't you think so? And if I'm not too old when my mother-in-law goes, I intend to register myself as a child-minder. Few people can afford nannies and governesses, these days, but so many young mothers are obliged to carry on working that I'm sure I can make myself useful.'

'I'm sure you can.'

'Would you like me to get you another glass of water.'

'No. No, thank you.'

'Then perhaps you should tell me what you'd like to know about Anna. I shouldn't be wasting your time talking about myself.'

'I want to know anything at all you can tell me. You see, I know nothing about her life before she went into San Salvi except that she had a husband and child.'

'Ah, little Elena. What a lovely little girl she was, and so full of life. Many's the hour she spent up here with me—it was through little Elena that I came to know Anna and her husband. Before that, although we'd been neighbours for so long, it never went further than a few polite words if we met downstairs. They lived on the ground floor behind the husband's workshop. He made leather bags and belts and so on, and I think he did quite well. I only went in their house twice, but though it was small and on the ground floor, she'd made it very pretty and put a few plants out in the tiny courtyard behind so that they could sit outside on hot nights.'

'But weren't they rather cramped, living behind the workshop with a child? If he was doing well . . .'

'In fact, they'd started building. One of those cooperative building schemes. Very sensible of them, really, to stick it out here until they could afford something of their own.'

'I see there's no longer a shop on the ground floor.'

'No, indeed. It was completely restructured and now it's an elegant little flat which I'm sure costs the earth. It's always rented by foreigners. Things have changed so much in this Quarter since the flood. When I first came here, Florence was the sleepiest little city I'd ever seen. Now it's all tourism and fast food. The old ways are gone and everyone wants to make too much money too quickly. There's still some fine craftsmanship here but it's a luxury now.'

'That's true.'

'Anna's husband was one of the old-style craftsmen. Poor man, he was barely forty when he died. I didn't know him well but I think he was a very hardworking, respectable sort of man. It was little Elena I was fond of. She must have been about six months old when Anna came knocking at my door one evening. She was in a panic because the baby was sick, and as the doctor had already been and left some medicine, saying it was nothing serious, she hadn't the courage to call him again. Although we didn't know each other well she'd heard I'd looked after children so she came to ask my advice. Couples with their first child easily get into a panic like that, with the result that the baby gets hysterical. When I got down there she'd been screaming for hours and they were beside themselves, especially Anna, who, as I found out on knowing her better, got hysterical when the slightest thing went wrong. I only discovered the reason much later. Anyway, needless to say, the baby soon settled when she felt the presence of somebody calm, and after that Anna would come to me whenever she needed help. It wasn't long before I started having little Elena up here when Anna was helping her husband in the shop. It was a great pleasure for me to have her and I missed her terribly when she died. It's strange to think she'd have been a young woman by now.'

'Was she killed along with her father?'

'They died within minutes of each other. He was trying to save her, you see. You didn't even know about that?'

'Nothing at all. I wasn't here all those years ago. I'm not from Florence.'

'Ah. I'm afraid that even after all these years in Italy I'm not very good at distinguishing accents. I'd have thought that a tragedy like that would have been in the national papers, even so. Though it's true that so many terrible things happened, so many people burned—and that poor man whose body was hanging from the roof for twenty-four hours. It's not something you ever forget.'

For a moment, the Marshal had the impression that she must be talking about the war and that she was a bit confused. That was forty years ago, not twenty. But before his embarrassment at her confusion could make itself felt he remembered the words of the fishmonger who had sent him up here: *'A few more storms like yesterday's and we'll be baling out like in '66.'*

The flood . . . But she'd talked of people being burned . . .

'Did they die in the flood, the husband and child?'

'Both of them, poor things. And the miracle was that Anna didn't die, too. In a way you could say that she did die, since she was never the same person afterwards. Living on the ground floor as they did . . . They were asleep, of course, when the banks burst, with it being so early in the morning. The water rose so quickly that by the time they awoke their doors wouldn't open. It was the strangest thing, I often think of it still, but that night I had a dream about water running down the stairs of this building, like the terraces of one of those big fountains. It wasn't a dream about the building being flooded, just this cascade of water on the stairs.'

'Perhaps you heard the rain in your sleep.'

'That could be. It had rained and rained for days. But it may have been because we'd seen a film called *The Bible* the evening before. We'd gone out that evening because the fourth was a holiday and, like everyone else, we'd planned on having a lie-in. Little did we know. At any rate, when I woke up it was as if I were still dreaming. I'm not sure what woke me, whether the explosions had already started or whether it was the roar of the floodwater and Anna's husband screaming for help from the window below. They'd tried at first to get out into their little courtyard because the flood had broken the door which wasn't very strong, but all that happened was that more water rushed in. Of course, if they'd managed to get out of the building at that point they'd all three have been killed at once because the water was travelling at 60 kilometres an hour and hurling tree-trunks and cars and all sorts of debris along these narrow streets. Nobody could have survived in that.

'I don't know whether they realized it, but at any rate they were perched on the windowsill with the water rushing by them, screaming. We hadn't even a bit of rope in the house but my husband thought of tying some bed sheets together. He was shouting down to Signor Chiari to tie little Elena on to the end of the sheet. It looked terribly risky, of course, but what else could we do? The water roaring past was getting higher every second, they'd have been swept away. He couldn't make himself heard. It wasn't just the water but the explosions which had started by then, plus the fact that Anna was completely hysterical and making things more difficult by screaming continually. Every time there was an explosion we saw great columns of water going up. It was the sewers exploding and gas pipes and boilers, but just then it seemed like the end of the world, especially as it had broken into our sleep and we were too dazed to understand. Signor Chiari, whether he could hear us or not, began trying to tie the sheet round little Elena, under her arms. I suppose it sounds simple. It's the sort of thing you see on television all the time, isn't it? But in reality it was impossible. The current was tearing at their feet and he was clinging to the child with one arm and the shutter with the other. How could he hope to tie the sheet round her? Every time he grabbed at it he had to let go and clutch at the shutter again, and Anna just screamed and screamed instead of trying to help him. We felt so helpless up here watching him and I think we knew even then it was hopeless, though we didn't know what else to do except to go on dangling that useless sheet.

'Then there was a terrible blast—it was the boiler in the cellar next door going up and it shattered that window there, where we were hanging out, cutting us all badly. I remember falling back on the floor. When we looked out again little Elena had gone. Anna was still screaming and I don't know if she had even realized the child was gone as her face was pressed against the wall beside the window. We saw her husband throw himself into the water, shouting for Elena. He disappeared immediately but then we saw him come up further down the street near a table which had become lodged between the wall and a lamp-post. We saw his arm reach out and try to cling to it. It might have saved his life, but then the floodwater brought an overturned bus rolling along the street, filling it completely. When it had passed, the lamp-post, the table and Signor Chiari were all gone.

'It was only then that we brought our eyes back to the window below. Anna had gone, too. It seemed certain that the bus had dashed her from the windowledge as it passed, but we went on calling to her for some time on the faint chance that she might have got back into the house. After a time we gave up, because if she had gone back in, the water was now up to their ceiling and not far from our own windowsills. We had to begin thinking about ourselves.

'We dressed our cuts as best we could and went up to the top floor, taking as much food as we could carry along with a few valuables and important papers. More than anything, we were terrified of the explosions. There's a terrace garden on top of the building and everyone collected up there. It was a shocking sight. Plumes of black smoke were going up everywhere as well as great sprays of water as the sewers went on exploding. It was still raining, of course, and we stayed up there huddled under umbrellas and wrapped in blankets, thinking it was safer than inside in case our cellar, too, went up. Hour after hour we sat there, shivering, waiting for help that didn't come. We saw other people on roofs like us, or staring out of top-floor windows, stunned. I suppose we must have been soaked and frozen, sitting out there in November like that, but I can't remember feeling it. It's difficult to explain now, but it was as if everything was somehow suspended. We barely even spoke among ourselves. We just waited. Waited for help. Waited for somebody to tell us something, to explain. Then the car horns started sounding, hundreds of them, like a great wail of sorrow and anger going up all over the city. For a while it cheered us because it gave the impression that there were people out there, cars, action, and we thought then it was only this Quarter that was flooded and that all this noise meant help was on its way. But the noise went on and on, not intermittent but continuous, and we began to realize there was something odd about so many people leaning on their horns like that. We had no way of guessing that the whole city was going under and that the hundreds of cars whose horns were wailing were driverless, tumbling along in the water that had activated their electrical circuits . . .

'We went in at some point, to eat something and try to get dry. Our hunger must have got the better of our fear. There was no gas or electricity or water and the phones had stopped working. We went back on the roof and waited. Late in the afternoon we heard helicopters, though we couldn't see them, and we started hoping again. The helicopters never came near us. Afterwards we found out how badly they'd been needed out in the country areas where people were trapped on the roofs of low farmhouses that were soon submerged. That was where most people drowned. We were much luckier in the city because of the buildings being so high.

'Once the current slowed down we saw thick black oil floating on the yellow water and our fear of fire got worse. If the building had set on fire what could we have done? Then it started to go dark. Can you imagine what it's like when darkness falls on a city and not a single light goes on? It wasn't just frightening it was eerie, desolate. A darkness that civilized people aren't accustomed to. It was then, as we stood watching and waiting and hoping for something, anything, to happen that we realized how bad things must be. Not a single light, Marshal. And in the darkness dogs were howling. It had stopped raining and the stars were brighter than you ever see them over a city because there were no lights. Not knowing what else to do, we went to bed. Nobody slept. We were all in the top flat, most of us having arranged ourselves as best we could with rugs and chairs.

'The water went down in the night leaving a foul-smelling mud behind it, and when it was light enough to see we came down here to see if there was much damage. My first thought was Anna, wondering if she was down below buried in all that filth.'

'And was she?'

'Yes, but we didn't find her, not then. My husband went down right away—not that we had any idea of finding her alive, he only hoped to recover her body if it hadn't been washed away. In any case, he wasn't able to get in since the outgoing water had left shelving and other furniture blocking the broken window and the door was swollen and wouldn't budge. From the street he could see the black oily tidemark showing the level which the water had risen to. It was higher than the Chiaris' workshop ceiling. There was a tank out there in the road and some soldiers called to my husband to come and help them. Injured people were being brought out of the building where the explosion had been and the soldiers were starting to shore it up in front. No one had been killed—luckily there was nobody living on the ground floor there because it had caved in completely. My husband was out there working with the soldiers most of the day. The rest of us in here tried to clear some of the mud out with buckets. It was a hopeless task but we went on with it, not knowing what else to do. All along the street people were doing the same, all with the same dazed expression. Nobody spoke much and nobody let out one word of complaint. When my husband came back, late in the afternoon, he brought some men with him. They weren't experts or anything, just the people from a bar on the corner of the square who'd been out distributing mineral water. I must say people were wonderful—it wasn't at all easy to get about the streets, you know. Half a million tons of mud, the papers said, a ton for each person, and all of it contaminated with petrol and sewage and the dead bodies of animals . . .

'Anna was down there alive. At first it appeared to be a

miracle. We'd seen how high the water was. But after they'd taken her away, we found the place . . . Like many of these high, old buildings there were false ceilings, you know the sort, made of straw and plaster. She'd climbed on top of a high old-fashioned wardrobe, which fortunately stayed upright because the water had rammed the bed up against it, and when the water reached her even there she'd clawed a hole . . . It was only just big enough to let her head through, and there she'd stood with the water right up to her mouth. Had it risen another inch or so she would have drowned standing there. She must have known that, as she stood there waiting while we stood waiting on the roof. And if it was so terrible for us when darkness fell and no one came, just think of Anna. Just think of her . . .'

'But in the morning, didn't she climb down? Didn't she call for help? She must have heard people moving about, your husband trying to get in.'

'She climbed down but she didn't call for help. I mentioned that we were all too dazed to speak that first morning. My most vivid memory of that day is of the other women who, like me, were uselessly shovelling at all that mud. Every so often one of them would pause to examine a piece of furniture buried out there in the street in case it should be hers. If it wasn't, they just carried on shovelling without a word passing their lips or even an expression crossing their faces. No, Anna didn't call for help. For all I know she never spoke again. It was only by chance that they found her when they did.

'I didn't understand at first why my husband insisted on checking whether her body was in there before he did anything else when there must have been so many people still alive who urgently needed help. Most of us were in such a state of shock that apart from the immediate danger of fire we didn't think of other dangers, like infection. But he realized right away that the greatest danger in those first few days was of an outbreak of typhoid. No one knew for sure how many people were missing and every so often they uncovered a body when they were shifting debris, but there were so many animals drowned, dogs and cats in the city and herds of cattle washed in from the country, not to mention all the meat and fish in the basement of the central market. They were still clearing that days later, men with gas masks. It must have been the most terrible job because anyone who had to walk anywhere near it had to cover their faces and some of them couldn't help retching. So it was because of typhoid that my husband insisted, and thank God he did or she might have been in there for a week until the pumps arrived to shift the mud.

'There was so much stuff blocking the window that they decided to break the door down with an axe. I was here in our flat then, trying to cover the broken window before it went dark. It was raining again. I heard the noise of them breaking down the door but I didn't know what they were doing until my husband came up for me.

'*"Can you come down a minute? It's Anna. I've called an ambulance but I'd rather you came down . . ."*

'*"You surely don't mean she's alive?"*

'*"She's alive, but . . . Come down with me, will you?"*

'When we got there, the men who had helped him were still standing looking, not knowing what to do. Anna was there in her little kitchen which had had to serve them as dining- and sitting-room too. The place was more than knee-deep in mud and the furniture was all overturned in it. When I got past the men and saw Anna she was bending over to fish something out of the mess. It was a piece of broken cup with the handle still attached. When she straightened up I saw that she was covered in mud herself, even her hair, and she was almost unrecognizable. She had a mud-soaked rag in her other hand and I saw her begin very slowly and carefully wiping the bit of cup with the air of somebody doing a perfectly normal bit of washing up. Then she set the piece on a shelf attached to the wall, balancing it very carefully so that it didn't fall off.

'"*Anna.*'

'She didn't answer me, and I soon realized that she was quite oblivious of our presence. She just went on picking up bits of debris, wiping them, and setting them on any surface that was still more or less horizontal. Her face was quite expressionless but I saw that her eyes were unnaturally bright as though she had fever.

'"*Try and get her to speak*," my husband whispered to me.

'I did go on trying but it was quite hopeless. I never heard her speak again.

'When the ambulance men arrived she was sweeping very slowly at the surface of the mud with an equally muddy sweeping brush. Despite our fears to the contrary, she went with them without protest, neither knowing nor caring why she was being taken away in a tank along with other injured people.'

'Did they take her to Santa Maria Nuova?'

'I think so. At least, that's where she was when I next saw her, but there was so much confusion in those first days that she might well have been taken somewhere else first. The hospitals were so overcrowded. That was the reason why I put off going there myself for some days, but then I decided I'd better because the worst of the cuts from that window there was looking rather bad. It ought to have been stitched and it was looking a bit septic. It's left me with quite a scar, as you can see.' She turned up her elbow to show him the broad white mark.

'I can't say for sure what day I finally went to the First Aid department at Santa Maria Nuova. It may have been the Sunday or the Monday but those first few days all run into each other in my memory, I'm afraid.'

'I understand. The day isn't important. Did you see Anna?'

It was strange to be calling her that, but they seemed to

be talking about quite a separate person who hadn't yet become Clementina.

'I saw her, but only for a moment. Once my arm had been dressed—they said it was too late to stitch it—I made inquiries and was told that she was there on the women's medical ward. I went up there and spoke to the sister in charge but I only got a brief glimpse of Anna. I'd been right about the fever. She had pneumonia and was in an oxygen tent. Nevertheless, the sister said she thought she'd pull through.'

It only needed the mention of the hospital. Would they say that of Bruno? 'He'll pull through . . .' They might have operated by now . . .

Perhaps Signora Santoli had noticed his attention wandering and misunderstood.

'I'm afraid I'm not telling you the sort of thing you want to know but I'm just telling you what I remember as I remember it.'

'No, no. Please go on. These are exactly the things I want to know. I'm already beginning to understand a lot about Clementina's strangeness.'

'How funny you should call her that. I didn't even know she had another name.'

'I imagine that if she didn't speak for so long, the people in the asylum took to calling her that rather than Anna.'

'I suppose that's the explanation but it makes her sound like another person.'

'She was another person, in many ways, by then.'

'Well, it's no wonder, is it? She lost everything, husband, child, income, property, even the beginnings of the place they were building. All washed away. That was what I was thinking as I came away from the hospital that day, of what she would have to face when she came round from her illness.'

'She never did face it.'

'I don't wonder. After all, you have to have something,

any one little thing to hang on to, to make you keep going. She had nothing at all. Not even her broken bits of belongings and ruined clothes that were all sucked away with the mud. That was what I was thinking as I walked back through what was left of the city that day. All around me people were trying to put their lives back together. It looked hopeless but they were trying. I remember all the shopkeepers trying to salvage clothes, pictures, furniture, from under all that mud and sewage and oil, working away by themselves without complaint. It was still difficult even to walk—I was looking for the place they'd told me to go to at the hospital, where a pharmacy had been set up outdoors and where I had to buy antibiotics and more bandages. I remember some soldiers heaving the carcase of a cow on to the back of a truck with ropes and a man tramping through the mud carrying a statue in his arms as though it were a dead person, and I was still thinking about Anna. What could she salvage? I decided then that when I got home I'd go into her flat and see if there wasn't some little thing left there that I could take to her—up to then we'd been too busy working in the cellar trying to free the boiler. I suppose I was hoping to retrieve some keepsake, something to take to her in the hospital. It was a foolish enough idea but I didn't know what else to do for her.'

'It wasn't a foolish idea at all. Tell me, did you hope to find anything in particular?'

'I thought perhaps a photo of little Elena.'

'Ah . . .' said the Marshal, satisfied, 'exactly. But you didn't find one?'

'No. And unfortunately I didn't have a photo of her myself, which I regretted very much then and do now. I'm afraid I didn't find anything and the whole thing turned out very embarrassing because I was in there searching about when who should walk in but Anna's sister. You can picture my embarrassment, knowing how it must look . . . Still, she must have accepted my explanation since she came up to my flat and stayed some time confiding in me. It was she who told me that little Elena's body had been found in the cellar of a house two streets away. She'd just been to identify her.'

'And the husband?'

'It was some days more before they recovered his body which had been carried much further away. I didn't mention him since I couldn't be sure how much she knew and she was already very upset. I soon realized that it was Anna she was most upset about rather than the child, whose death she seemed to accept philosophically. Of course she wasn't so close to the child even as I was. She didn't visit all that often. Anna once mentioned to me that she had a very difficult life with her husband and that they didn't see each other as often as they would have liked because of him. It seems the sister was quite the business woman. According to Anna, she took after their father. I could well imagine it was true. That day was the first time I'd seen her and despite what she'd gone through, I still got the impression of a very strong character who knew what she wanted. Not a bit like Anna who was very delicate. She was well dressed, too—like everyone else in those days she'd had to come through the streets in wellingtons but she had a very good fur coat on. I can't afford good clothes myself but I have an eye for them. She was a very well-bred woman, not the sort to confide in people too easily, but no doubt she was glad of a friendly stranger to unburden herself to that day.

'"If there's one thing I've always been terrified of," she told me, "it was something like this happening to Anna. I'm a very different character and goodness knows my life hasn't been easy, but I can take it. I don't know how well you knew her but, believe me, the smallest mishap was enough to unbalance her."

'I said I'd realized that.

'"But you perhaps don't know the cause of it. My sister and I were born into a very comfortably-off family but we had an unfortunate childhood. My mother died when we were quite small. I was nine and Anna was only five. That in itself is enough to cause insecurity in any child, of course, though no one really considered such things in those days as they do now. But, unfortunately, Anna was alone in the room with her mother when it happened. A heart attack, quite sudden. We don't know whether Anna called for help but we do know that she stayed there, standing beside her mother's body until my father arrived home and walked into the room. Anna wasn't crying, she was just standing there very white and still. Of course, it may be that she had called for help, because as it happened there was no servant within hearing distance. It was only the day after that I was informed of my mother's death. We were kept apart, we children. I suppose somebody thought it best. Since there was no female relative available or willing to take on the responsibility of two small girls we were sent to a convent. Because I was the elder, Anna relied on me as she would on a mother, though I still wasn't ten years old. In my opinion, she never really recovered. Perhaps she should have had professional help but it wasn't the fashion then and the nuns were more strict than kind. From that day to this I've always feared for Anna, always known she couldn't face even the smallest of life's crises. When she met Chiari and wanted to marry him my father was very much against it. An artisan, you can imagine . . . I was the one who convinced him. Chiari was such a steady, calm person, just what Anna needed. With the problems she had, that was all that mattered in my opinion, and I never regretted having supported her. Now this . . . she'll never recover from this. But whatever happens, she'll always have me. As long as I'm alive she'll never be alone and she'll never want for anything, I swear that before God."

'I never saw her again.'

'And Anna?'

'It was a very long time before I saw Anna. Very shortly

after that I was obliged to go to Switzerland where my father had been taken seriously ill. I stayed there for some months until he died. When I got back life had returned to normal here. It was wonderful the way help poured in from all over the world. Nevertheless, it was the fact that life was normal again that made me feel the loss of little Elena, that was when it really hit me for the first time. I suppose that was because there had been too much turmoil before. It was a small thing that brought it home to me. I was queuing in the fish shop downstairs one Friday morning and one of the women was recounting the story of some terrible tragedy, I think it was in Wales. I didn't hear the whole story so I don't know the details but apparently all the children in a village were killed. It must have happened around the time of the flood because this woman was saying that the parents had sent all their now unwanted toys over here for the children of Florence. I was on the point of opening my mouth to say "Then perhaps little Elena . . ." I stopped and said to myself "She's dead."

'That night, I confess, I had a little weep. The next day I made inquiries about Anna.'

'Had she been transferred by then?'

'Yes, she had. It seems she'd recovered her health but, as her sister had feared, not her senses. I asked for her at Santa Maria Nuova. They said she'd never spoken but that on a number of occasions she had tried to throw herself from a window, always just as it was going dark. It had been decided that she should be transferred to San Salvi, but her transfer had been delayed for some time because she still needed hospital treatment.'

'To her skin, by any chance?'

'Yes. You knew that? It all came off, you see, because of her being in that contaminated water for so many hours. There were all sorts of chemicals in it. They said her skin came off in ribbons but that it grew again quite satisfactorily without any lasting ill-effects. Then they transferred her.'

'And so you went to see her in San Salvi?'

'Only twice, I'm afraid. She didn't seem to recognize me and she never spoke. One of the nuns told me she'd taken to sweeping the place all day long. There had been more attempts to throw herself from the window towards dusk. I didn't have the courage to go a third time, besides which, not long after my second visit, my mother-in-law began to sicken and she moved in here with us.

'The last time I had news of Anna was on the second anniversary of the flood. Seeing the old news reels on TV, I got to thinking about her and I called San Salvi. They told me very kindly that it was pointless my feeling guilty about not going to see her since she recognized no one, not even her sister. It seems she'd begun to speak again but that her language was aggressive and obscene, especially to the nuns. I thought I could understand that, though I said nothing. I wondered how the sister was taking it. I'm sure that if she hadn't had problems with her husband she'd have had Anna at home, no matter what her behaviour. Well, I suppose she must have recovered to some extent if they eventually let her out. I wonder what happened to the sister? It said in the paper Anna was living alone when she died.'

'Alone, yes. And in great poverty.'

'In poverty? I'm surprised at that, after what her sister said to me that day.'

'In view of what you've just told me, it is surprising. She may have had money hidden that we haven't been able to find.'

The Marshal got to his feet. All of a sudden he'd had enough of sitting in this dark, tidy room. He wanted to telephone the hospital and he felt a need to be on his own and think over all that Signora Santoli had just told him. Even with all his other preoccupations, he was aware that this dignified and lonely woman was sorry to see him ready to leave.

'If you don't mind my asking,' she said, 'when is the funeral to be?'

'I don't know, to be honest, but I can telephone you when I do, if you like.'

'Thank you.' They went out into the hall and she wrote her number for him on the neat, empty pad by the telephone.

'I'd appreciate it very much,' she said as he buttoned the slip of paper into his top pocket. 'I'd like to go to the funeral. After all, she was once part of my life. One clings to small things as time goes on.'

'Yes,' the Marshal said, 'you're right. I think that's why it struck me so forcibly when I didn't find a single snapshot or memento in her flat, what you tried to find for her after the disaster and couldn't.'

'It's true, her whole past had been wiped out. She did have one thing, though; you've reminded me of it, though she may not have kept it. The second time I went to San Salvi I took her the article from the paper that told her story. I thought it might shock her into speaking. After all, how can we ever be quite sure that the mind is wandering in darkness all the time? It's what I feel about my mother-in-law. How do I know that at some fleeting moment she isn't aware, aware of what's happening to her and aware that I'm here and caring for her? It's often only that that keeps me going. It had no immediate effect on Anna, that page from the paper, but I left it with her because you never know.'

'Did it have the sister's name and address on it, by any chance?'

'I'm certain it did, but I can't remember it, I'm sorry.'

'That's all right. I can get it from the newspaper's archives. I don't think Anna did throw it away,' he added, 'but it's gone now.'

'I'm afraid I haven't been much help to you.'

'You've been a great deal of help. I'll let you know about the funeral.'

When she had shut the door after him he heard her saying very gently, 'All right. It's all right. I'll come and sit with you for a while now.'

He walked down the stairs and out into the heat. He had an idea now who the man he was looking for might be and it wasn't a man with a limp. The only thing that still puzzled him was how had Clementina found out?

CHAPTER 10

It was dark in Clementina's tiny kitchen. Perhaps there was going to be another storm. The room was so close after being shut up so long in the heat that the Marshal opened the small window, letting in some damp air and the smell of approaching rain. That didn't make it much lighter and pressing the light switch produced nothing. They must already have sent someone from the electricity board to disconnect the power until the next tenant signed on. The Marshal wondered who the next tenant would be. They could hardly expect to rent the flat out in its present condition. The gloom was a nuisance, though he had little enough to do. He opened the table drawer which had once puzzled him and now puzzled him no longer. He opened it to its fullest extent but he didn't touch anything. The sheet of newspaper from the back had gone, as he expected. Why she had kept it there all those years was not so clear. On that question turned the point of just how crazy she really was. Had she, as Linda Rossi had said and Signora Santoli suspected, had periods of lucidity when she remembered her past and could compare it with her present? It was more comfortable to think of her as completely crazy, and so oblivious. Perhaps it had been more comfortable for her, too, to let herself sink into madness during her years in the asylum so that it became a habit. Nevertheless, she had kept that page from the newspaper for twenty years almost. That and the photo of her in her madness, brandishing her sweeping brush for a young reporter. Somebody had taken away the wrong cutting after killing her, removing her present instead of her past by mistake. A mistake that hadn't much mattered as long as her death was reported as a suicide.

Anna Franci and crazy Clementina . . . He'd phoned Galli as soon as he'd got back from Santa Croce to ask for the page from the archives.

'I'll see to it for you. I know just where to lay my hands on it because I dug it out the night I wrote that first piece on her.'

'I wish you'd told me about it.'

'I wish you told me she'd been murdered! But seriously, I'd have told you if you'd rung back when I was in. I forgot about it after that because I never did write it up. Some character from San Salvi called me and convinced me to write about her being a patient there. All the same to me, as I told him. Neither story was much cop for this season. A nice juicy scandal with a spot of sex and violence is what sells the paper in the holiday period, that and the Bingo competition. And I suppose you think your job's depressing. I'll send you a copy over.'

The Marshal closed the drawer and walked slowly through the flat. The bedroom was even darker because the shutters were closed. He wasn't looking for anything now, just taking possession of the place for a moment. Up to now someone had always got there before him, as they had at the asylum, removing all trace of Anna Franci and her story. Someone sharper than himself who had always managed to be a step ahead. The murder story had only broken in this morning's paper and yet by then he had already taken the precaution of sending his gorilla-like henchman up here to get rid this time of the right bit of newspaper evidence. How had he known so soon? The Marshal couldn't believe it was a coincidence. It was true you could get the first edition of the paper shortly after midnight at the central station, but if that was how he managed then he must have been doing it every night to be sure. He had a lot at stake but it still seemed far-fetched . . .

'In any case,' said the Marshal quietly in the silence of the dark little bedroom, 'I'll find him.' He took a last look around and then let himself out, locking the door. At any other time, in any other mood, he might have paused to wonder why the keys had been returned to him by the Prosecutor. They had been on his desk when he got back from Santa Croce, a wordless message of recapitulation. But he didn't pause to wonder about that or anything else. He was no longer assailed by doubts or by anger at his own lack of intelligence. He was conscious of Bruno, still and silent in his white hospital bed, of Clementina, once Anna Franci, now shut in a refrigerated drawer, and of a respectable-looking grey-haired man whom he intended to track down by the end of the day. That was all. That was if you could call it 'conscious'. His wife, after sitting opposite his silent bulk all through lunch, had tentatively said, 'I'm sure that by this evening Bruno will have come round from his operation. You'll see.' He hadn't even answered.

He stopped on the stairs and rang the bell of the Rossis' flat. No one opened the door and he went on down to the street to cross the square and go into Franco's bar. Franco was behind the counter and the smile with which he had begun to greet the Marshal faded from his face.

'What's the matter, Marshal? You look a bit strange—has something else happened?'

'I want to know the name of the owner of that house.'

'Clementina's flat? I couldn't tell you. I think it's all dealt with through an agency. The Rossis—'

'They're out.'

'*Has* something happened?'

'No.'

The Marshal turned and went out again. He was vaguely aware of having produced an odd impression. He liked and respected Franco, who had been a big help to him, and he wouldn't have liked him to think he was being funny with him because of the midnight gambling business. He could have gone back and explained, but he was plodding onwards and these vague thoughts weren't enough to stop him. Nothing would stop him now until he'd done what had to be done.

He heard the thunder begin as he climbed the stairs to his Station and unlocked the door. Di Nuccio appeared immediately.

'I just telephoned the hospital. They've operated and they said it all went as planned.'

'Is he conscious?'

'No. Not yet . . . There was a call for you—just a minute.' He disappeared into the duty room and returned with a slip of paper. 'The Tenants' Association, it came from. A woman. She said it was important.'

'Hm.'

'Shall I get the number for you?'

'No.'

'They said—'

'It doesn't matter.' He couldn't deal with the Rossi problem now but he would call the Tenants' Association after he had been to visit the man in the cells over at Headquarters. They could probably even tell him who the owner of those flats was. Everything in good time. He couldn't let them delay him now and they'd surely try to. He'd already promised to appear at the hearing and that would have to suffice for the moment.

'I have to go out again,' he told Di Nuccio.

'What time will you be back?'

'I don't know.'

'Because there was a girl here wanting to see you and she said it was very urgent.'

For the Marshal only one thing was urgent: catching up with a respectable grey-haired man who was always one step ahead of him.

'Tell her to come tomorrow morning early.'

'I'm sorry, Marshal, but I didn't know—I've already told her to come back today towards six. I thought you'd be in.'

'Well, I might be.' He looked at his watch. It was 4.10. 'I might be . . .' He walked into his office and sat down at the desk, pulling his battered typewriter towards him. Di Nuccio hovered in the doorway.

'What is it now?' He slid a sheet of paper into the machine and tugged at it because it was crooked.

'That girl. Well, she wouldn't tell me what she wanted, insisted on seeing you. She said you knew her. All I want to say is that I believed her when she said it was urgent. She was crying buckets—I've never seen anyone cry like that.'

'Oh, *that* girl . . .' The Marshal began to type and Di Nuccio stared at him, puzzled, then went out and shut the door. He would have stared even harder if he could have seen that the Marshal, with two plump fingers, was typing his own name and address straight across the page, time after time, sometimes varying it with a line of random letters and numbers. When he'd filled five pages he stamped them all here and there with various rubber stamps from his drawer and then pushed them into a large envelope, satisfied.

'The Prosecutor's on his way over here to question him, if you want to wait.'

'No. I'll go straight down.'

The officer called in a young Carabiniere. 'Show the Marshal down to the cells.'

'Yessir.'

The Marshal followed the boy in silence, watched him as

he unlocked the door and stood back beside it, keys in hand, to wait. He stepped inside and heard the door lock behind him.

The man was lying on the narrow bed, smoking. He didn't bother to move, only watched the Marshal with narrowed eyes through a skein of smoke. His shirt was open to the waist and the thick mat of hair on his chest glistened with sweat.

The Marshal's big, bulging eyes were equally watchful and wary. He couldn't afford to make a mistake, even less so than his opponent who was now grinning at him confidently. There was one small hard chair in the cell and the Marshal sat down on it after placing it as far away from the bed as possible. He didn't speak, just went on staring at the gorilla-like man on the bed, sizing him up. It wasn't difficult. They'd shown him the man's record upstairs, but even without it there was no mistaking that he had spent more time in prison than out of it and that crime was his way of life rather than his profession. He had never gained anything much from it and never would, but it was the only life he knew. His only defence would be to deny everything and no amount of clever questioning would budge him, as it might someone more intelligent who'd try to balance possible gains and losses and follow some lawyer's advice in the hope of a lighter sentence. He was brutal and probably touchy. Brutal enough to stand his ground against all the odds and touchy enough to be unnerved already by the Marshal's unexpected silence so that he was the first to break it.

'I've got nothing to say to you.'

'Keep quiet, then.' The Marshal went on staring.

'I've said all I'm going to say. I broke into that flat because I knew it was empty and since I didn't steal anything—'

'I'm not interested.'

'So what are you here for?'

'I've got something to tell you.' But he didn't tell it.

The man, whose name was Bruti, dragged at the last half-inch of his cigarette and rolled sideways to stub it out on the floor.

'Got any fags you can give me?'

'No.'

He rolled on his back and stared at the ceiling. A fly settled on his chest and he slapped at it. It circled above him and settled there again.

'You could suffocate in this bleeding hole. When are they going to transfer me to Sollicciano?'

'I don't know.'

He would be happier once he was settled back in prison with plenty of old friends around him and the familiar routine. He'd only been out eight months.

'Bastards!' The remark was aimed at nobody in particular but probably included all policemen and flies.

'Is that where you met him? In Sollicciano?' asked the Marshal.

'I thought you weren't interested.'

'That's right. It doesn't much matter. I can find out, anyway.'

'Find out, then.'

'I will, I should have asked him but I didn't think of it at the time . . .'

There was no reaction from Bruti. Probably it was wishful thinking on the Marshal's part that made the glistening chest muscles appear to tense up.

'Funny,' he went on, 'I wouldn't have thought that you'd be the sort to let yourself be pushed about that easily.'

'Nobody ever pushed me about.'

'He's clever, that's the trouble. People like you should stick to their own kind. You know where you are with them. Get yourself involved with somebody too smart for you and you're bound to end up taking the rap.'

'For what?'

'In this case for murder, to name but one charge—I

suppose you've had a judicial communication for Clementina's murder?

'That means nothing.'

'No. At least, it didn't mean much at the time when there was no real evidence against you, but now they'll charge you. I thought I should tell you that. What you do about it is up to you, but it didn't seem right to me that he should get off scot-free while you spent the rest of your life inside.'

'I don't know who you think you're talking about.'

'Suit yourself. I just thought it fair to tell you. You'll be charged before the day's out.'

'Charged with what? You've nothing on me except that I broke into an empty flat and stole nothing because you interrupted me.'

'So we did, but then, there was nothing in there to steal, was there?'

He didn't answer.

'Well, as I say, suit yourself. If you want to stick to your story, that's your business. It's true that as long as there was no evidence, no motive and no witnesses, it was the best thing you could do. The only trouble is, as I said before, the chap's got brains and you haven't.' The Marshal flicked at the large envelope which he was holding on his knee. 'He even went so far as to say you were mentally deficient—I suppose he was still annoyed because you took the wrong newspaper cutting the first time. Is it true that you can't read?'

An accusation of murder had had no effect but this question made Bruti's face darken and his eyes glitter dangerously.

'Nobody said that!'

'That you're mentally deficient? He said it all right. I'm not saying I altogether believed him but you did take the wrong cutting and I know you can't read, anyway. It's in your file. I wouldn't worry about it much, if I were you. It's nothing compared to some other things he said. I'll be honest with you: I didn't believe much more than half of it, but that's only my opinion. It doesn't help you much because he's bound to have some fancy lawyer who'll have no trouble convincing the judge. It's plausible enough, what he says, and with your record . . . Well, he'll be sitting pretty once you're behind bars. He'll have not only got what he wanted, he won't even have had to pay you for the job. He hasn't paid you, has he? What you don't seem to understand is that he was never going to. I may have given you the wrong impression. Perhaps you're thinking that something went wrong and that he turned on you to defend himself. That's not the way it was. He was the one who came to us with this story.' He flicked the envelope again. 'That was the way he planned it, haven't you understood yet? You were the ideal mug, with a record as long as your arm. Once you'd done the job for him, all he had to do was come and tell us all about it.' He began sliding the five typewritten and much stamped sheets out of the envelope, frowning. 'He's a clever customer all right . . .'

The effect was gratifying but dangerous. Not for nothing had the Marshal sat as far away as possible and even now he was more than glad that the man couldn't read, for he shot bolt upright and made a grab for the papers which the Marshal thrust back into the envelope so fast as to crumple them badly.

Bruti flung himself back on the bed with such a volley of foul language that the young Carabiniere outside opened the grille to find out what was up.

'It's all right.' The Marshal waved him away and the grille slid back. 'Well, that's what I came to tell you, for what it's worth. If you want to defend yourself, you ought to know what he's accusing you of. According to him, he sent you round to see Clementina on some business, quite innocent business, to do with the flat, and when you saw a half-crazy woman living alone, knowing how much money she had stashed away, you went back there one night and—'

'That's rubbish. He can't get away with that! The old bag hadn't a penny!'

'You mean you had a good look round after you'd done it and didn't find any? But that won't save you because she did have money, plenty of it, so who's going to believe you weren't hoping to find it? You've been taken for a ride, Bruti, so you'd better get it into your head and start getting a better story together. You see, he says you told him what you'd done, told him in detail, and some of those details he could only have got from you. They weren't in the paper. You see what I mean. You've no hope of getting off with him as a witness against you, and all you're doing by keeping your mouth shut is making sure that he comes out of it as an innocent man who's been good enough to help us with our inquiries. You've been made a fool of, but I suppose it's no more than you deserve, when all's said and done. How did you bring yourself to do it? You've got a record of violence, I know that, but this was different. You killed a defenceless old woman in cold blood—and, as far as you knew, it was just because he needed to sell the house and couldn't get her out.'

'I was supposed to get paid, wasn't I? What he wanted was his business. In any case she was too soft in the head to know any different—he hadn't even paid her her full pension for years. Gave her some cock-and-bull story about a new law and that they'd put her away if she complained. She thought he was doing her a favour letting her have half of it, the crazy old bag! People like that *should* be locked up—she even hit me in the face with a brush when I went round there. I'm glad I did for her and I'll do the same for him if he tries to do me down with his fancy lawyers! Never mind that crazy old bag, what about me? Eh? What about number one?'

'That's right,' the Marshal said, 'you get thinking about

number one, because the Prosecutor's on his way here.'

'Well, tell him! Tell him it's all lies. Tell him *he* sent me round there to threaten the old biddy and try and get money from that couple with the kid to pay for the work on the façade that he couldn't find the wherewithal for! Tell him—'

'Tell him yourself,' the Marshal said, 'I'm not interested.' And this time he was telling the truth. The only thing he wanted to know now was the man's name and where to find him. And that, after the trick he'd just pulled, he couldn't ask.

He met the Prosecutor at the top of the stairs.

'Ah . . . So you've talked to him. I'm afraid we'll get nothing out of him. I've made out a warrant for breaking and entering which will at least keep him with us for the moment.'

'You can make out another,' the Marshal said, 'for murder.'

'For . . .?'

'He's confessed, more or less. But you'd best leave it until tomorrow. And I'll need another warrant.'

He wasn't conscious of the fact that he was virtually giving the Prosecutor orders. If the Prosecutor himself was aware of it he made no protest. The man who had once complained at the 'blank incomprehension of the man' now only stared uncertainly at the Marshal, who said, 'I might need it tonight, that other warrant . . .' as though to himself.

'I see. In whose name?'

'I don't know.'

'You don't—'

'I could find out tomorrow when the Registry reopens but he always gets one step ahead of me, and this time I have to be one step ahead of him or he'll slip through my fingers. I have to find him tonight. Leave Bruti until tomorrow. I'll be in touch . . .' And he went plodding slowly away, breathing a bit heavily after the stairs. The expression on the

Prosecutor's face remained fixed in his mind as something connected with the return of the keys but he didn't think about it. And when the Prosecutor called after him, 'How is that boy . . .?' he didn't even hear but turned the corner and went on his way. If anyone had been capable of breaking in on his mood and demanding to know where he was going and just what he intended to do about putting his hands on a nameless man of unknown whereabouts, he wouldn't have had an answer. But nobody was capable of breaking his mood, not even when he found himself, for no clearly defined reason, back at his Station and discovered the weeping girl plying her handkerchief in the waiting-room. He showed her into his office and sat down, prepared to listen patiently, his big eyes staring at her without really seeing her.

'In another two weeks it would have been all right—at least I'd have had time to look round for something but Laura says I ought to get out right away and not be involved and, in any case, he'll sack me now, for sure. Laura's left already. The minute she got back from her holidays this morning she emptied her desk drawers and went, but she's got a husband so it's all very well, she doesn't need a permit —but if I get involved in all this, even though it's not my fault, they'll never give me one. If only it could have happened in another two weeks! Laura's husband's in the trade, that's how he guessed what was going on and he made her leave, but what am I supposed to do?'

Slowly and with great impatience, the Marshal began to untangle this knot of garbled information. As usual, no sobs interrupted the girl's flowing lament but huge tears rolled down her cheeks as she talked and the handkerchief rolled up in her hand was soaked. He gave her his, which was soon reduced to the same condition.

'Why in two weeks?'

'Because my two-month trial period would have been up and he'd have had to take me on permanently.'

'But you don't like it there.'

'I know, but then I could have left.'

'You want to be taken on permanently so you can leave?'

'Yes. And now what am I going to do? How can I manage now?'

He went through his pockets looking for another handkerchief. There wasn't one but he found a packet of paper tissues in a drawer and pushed the lot across the desk to her.

'Thank you. You're the only person who can help me. I don't know where else to turn.'

By this time he'd worked it out. 'Is it your police permit that's the trouble?'

'Of course. That's what I'm saying. If he takes me on—'

'I see. To get a five-year permit to stay in the country you need to prove you've got a permanent job and can support yourself.'

'My temporary one's going to run out—they gave it to me to cover my trial period and then I'm supposed to take a letter to the Questura from *him* saying I'm employed—'

'All right. Well, that's not the end of the world. You'll just have to get another job and another temporary permit and start all over again.'

'But they won't give me any sort of permit when all this comes out! And even if I do what Laura says and walk out now the police will still catch up with me, won't they? They'll think I'm involved although I didn't know anything about it until Laura's husband—'

'This Laura—I take it she's someone in your office—just what did she tell you?'

'About what he's up to! When I told her how he'd screamed at me about the labels. She told her husband and *he* knew right away what was going on and said he's not the only one doing it by a long way and that he's heard people are after him for payment and if it comes to a head then the whole thing will come out. To think he's been taking it all out on me, that's what's so awful! How could I have known about those stupid buttons? I had an order for three thousand pieces to—'

'Signorina, will you explain what exactly you think he's "up to"?'

'It's the labels.'

'Not the buttons?'

'The buttons have to be changed, that's the whole point! I've felt ill all day just thinking about it. The doctor's given me antibiotics and he says it could be a virus but he doesn't know what I'm going through.'

'Would you like a cup of coffee?'

'No. Yes. I could do with smoking a cigarette if you wouldn't mind.'

'Go ahead.'

He got up and asked Di Nuccio to bring some coffee and then let her ramble on until it arrived before trying again.

'What exactly is the problem with these labels?'

'They say "Made in Italy" and they're not.'

'The labels?'

'The clothes. They're made in Taiwan or some such place. I don't know where. It's fraud, Laura's husband says. There's a law against it.'

'There is.'

'So it's true, then. And he thinks he can get away with it by having the clothes finished off in Italy, so he gets the buttons sewn on here. Only this time the manufacturers made a mistake and sent the stuff with buttons already on and I didn't know it was serious, how could I? The order was late so—'

'All right. Drink your coffee, it's getting cold.'

'Now I've got his wretched buttons changed and the order's so late the buyers rang up from Germany this morning and refused to take it. He'll sack me.'

'Well, for the moment he's away, isn't he?'

'He rings up every day. And he's been back I don't know how many times, rushing in and screaming abuse at me and then dashing back to his bitch of a wife at the seaside. If you ask me, she's the cause of all the trouble. After all, the business is in her name. Women like that make me sick. They never do a stroke of work themselves, they always find somebody else to slave for them. Anyway, the way things are going she'll have to find some other mug because that cancelled order will be the last straw. Laura does the accounts, or she did, and she says so. If he goes bankrupt, what will happen to me?

'Nothing, Signorina.'

'If I leave, like Laura says, before the crash, it might look as if I'm running away because I'm involved in the fraud, but if I wait till he sacks me it'll be that much more difficult to get another job, so what shall I do?'

'Nothing.'

'How can I do nothing?'

'Go home and get a good night's sleep. Then go on with your work as best you can and start looking for another job. Nothing will happen within two weeks even if he is going to go bankrupt. If you then get your full permit, well and good. If not, then I'll write you a letter for the Questura which will help you get another temporary one until things get sorted out.'

'But he could still sack me because of this order.'

'Well, if that happens—'

'I'll come and tell you right away.'

'All right . . . you come and tell me. Now you must excuse me.' He got to his feet.

'I'll tell you right away. I'll go back to the office now and see how things are. He may have turned up.'

'All right.'

'And then I'll ring you.'

He managed to get her out of the door and she went on her way still weeping.

'Di Nuccio!'

'Marshal?'

'Get me those people who telephoned earlier . . . the Tenants' Association.'

'Right away.'

More people's problems. And yet, all the time, in the back of his mind was the one thought: By the end of the day I have to find him.

He picked up the phone as it started to ring.

'That number for you, Marshal. It's a Signora Betti.'

'Hello? Am I speaking to Marshal Guarnaccia?'

'Yes. Can I help you?'

'I rang earlier but you were out.'

'I know. I've already told Signora Rossi that I'm willing—'

'Oh, it's not about the Rossis—I'm more than grateful to you, of course, they're good people and deserve help—but I wouldn't be disturbing you for that. Didn't they tell you? I left a message saying it was urgent.'

'Yes, they told me.' Didn't she know that everyone who called here said it was urgent, be it a murder or a missing cat?

'It's about Signora Franci.'

'Clementina?'

'Yes, Clementina, as they called her. When I saw in the paper this morning that she'd been murdered it was a terrible shock. They said it was suicide before and knowing what newspapers are—well, first of all, is it true?'

'That she was murdered? Yes, it's true.'

'Then I did right to call you. I think I can help.'

'The owner of the house?'

'Exactly! Then you already know.'

'I'd very much like to hear what you know, beginning with his name.'

'Fantechi. Carlo Fantechi.'

'Thank you. And his address?'

'That I don't know, I'm afraid. We've been dealing through the agents who let the flats. They'll be closed at this time but if you get in touch with them in the morning they'll be able to tell you.'

But still the Marshal was convinced that he hadn't that much time to waste.

'What I'm really concerned about,' Signora Betti went on, 'is that I may be indirectly to blame for what happened.'

'You?'

'Yes. That's if my suspicions are justified. The trouble was that when she came to see me I couldn't make up my mind about her. She was very strange—well, I saw in the paper after it happened that she'd been in San Salvi but I didn't know that when I met her. I didn't know what to make of her, and that's the truth. There were moments when she seemed quite crazy, which made me wonder if she was telling me the truth, and yet every now and then she would give me such a sharp-eyed glance that I was at a loss. I don't know if I'm making sense to you.'

'You are.'

'Well, you probably know more about her than I do. She could have been making the whole thing up or it could have been true and she was exaggerating her own eccentricity. In the end I decided not to act until she produced some evidence. Judging by what happened to her, I'm afraid that was a terrible mistake. However, the story was a complicated one and I'm not sure, even now, what I should have done. I'll explain as briefly as I can. In the first place she came to me because, like the Rossi couple, she'd been threatened with eviction. When I asked her the terms of her rental contract she said she didn't have one. She said she didn't pay rent and had a right to the house for as long as she lived.'

'Did she say the house belonged to her sister?'

'Yes. It was true then? It's such an outlandish tale that I'm more than relieved you already know something of it. Yes, the house had been her sister's she said, but the sister's now dead, so it's the property of her brother-in-law though she had the right to live in it for her lifetime. That, as far as it went, seemed normal enough, but what came after it was less credible. If she'd told me outright she'd been in San Salvi the whole thing would have made sense, but she didn't. What she told me was that this man was virtually terrorizing her, threatening to have her locked up unless she got out so he could sell the flat. When she still didn't leave she said he threatened to stop her pension.

'"They'll put me away. If I can't prove I've got a house and a job they'll put me away. But I won't go!"

'She was quite clearly terrified but what she was saying made no sense at all. This man must have been trying to make her believe she'd have to go back into the asylum. If only she'd told me about San Salvi I'd have made inquiries there. If she'd been in there all those years it may well be true that she no longer had control of her own money, even her pension. I'm afraid I just didn't believe her, at least, not sufficiently.'

'What did you do?'

'I told her that if, as she claimed, she had the right to reside in the flat under the terms of her sister's will, then she should get hold of a copy of the will and bring it to me. If it were true, then in no circumstances could she be evicted and we would defend her. That was the last I saw of her. Oh—another thing she said was that he'd tried to trick her out of leaving the house once before by offering to send her on holiday, on a cruise, of all things.

'"But I'm up to all his tricks! My sister was a fool all her life to go on putting up with him, but I'm no fool! He won't get me locked up!"

'Is it surprising that I didn't believe her?'

'Not a bit.'

'If only she'd told me the whole truth. Well, what's done is done. But now I'm pretty sure that man was not only threatening her but cheating her, I mean if he was legally responsible for her . . .'

'Yes. I think he may well have cheated her out of a large inheritance.'

'And I sent her to ask for a copy of the will! We're supposed to be here to help people, but I've been thinking about it all afternoon, ever since I first tried to call you. If it hadn't been for me, he might have pushed her out of her flat but she'd still be alive today.'

'Helping people isn't easy. She didn't tell you the truth. People never do.' He didn't, even so, tell her the Rossis had tried to hide their baby from him. After all, he hadn't told them the truth either, had he?

'But in this case the consequences . . . I told her, you see, that we have a lawyer here who would look into the matter. She must have threatened him with that. When I heard she was dead—even when they said it was suicide—I felt terribly guilty for not quite believing her. When it turned out to be murder—do you think her brother-in-law did it?'

'Yes and no. He got somebody else to do it.'

'There must have been a great deal of money involved for him to have taken such a risk.'

'I doubt if it was as simple as that. I don't imagine he's a professional criminal, just a desperate man. He's probably already spent her money.'

'Perhaps you're right. Whatever the reason, I doubt if I'll ever quite forgive myself, though I feel slightly better for having told you.'

'I'm more than grateful to you.'

'It's the least I could do. I'll be honest with you, though. I had my doubts about involving myself, but Linda Rossi turned the scale. With all this on your hands you found time to help them. I couldn't for shame go about my business and not help you with this. When you need me as a witness I'm ready.'

She rang off.

So now he knew how Clementina found out, or tried to.

'*I won't go!*' She had said that same thing to someone else, too, hadn't she? The memory had barely time to come to the surface of his mind before the phone rang again. If he hadn't been so absorbed by the idea that was forming he might have prevented Di Nuccio from putting the call through, but before he knew where he was, the tearful voice was in full lament, and this time she was even sobbing. He hadn't a hope of interrupting and didn't try.

'He's not here but the driver hasn't even turned up and now I've no idea where that order's finished up. And that's not all!'

The memory surfaced and the images fell into place. He waited for a gap that would allow him to make himself heard.

'Laura just phoned me to say she's heard a rumour he's in prison—that's why he didn't turn up—not *him*, our driver! What if the police come here? You're the only person who can help me—I promise you I didn't know, I didn't know anything! The fact that I didn't change those buttons is proof, isn't it? Well, isn't it?'

'Signorina, please stop crying and calm down. It's all over.'

'But what shall I do?'

'Nothing. At least, carry on going to the office every day for now.'

'But if the police come?'

'The Carabinieri will come. I'll come. And nobody, at this stage, will be bothering you. Do you understand?'

The only answer was a sob, but it was a quieter one.

'Now, listen carefully: the business card you gave me had the name—' he fished it out of his pocket—'the name Antonella Masolini.'

'I told you, it's in her name—'

'That's right. Her maiden name, I imagine. Is the husband's name Fantechi?'

'Yes. Carlo Fantechi. Do you know him, then? Does that mean he's already been in prison?'

'Not necessarily, but I think he may well have been and that that's where he met up with your driver.'

'It wouldn't surprise me at all to hear that Bruti's been in prison, he's such a nasty bit of goods.'

'Can you tell me how long your boss has been married to this Antonella Masolini?'

'I don't know for sure but not all that long. Maybe about four or five years.'

'Give me their address, will you?'

'Here or at the seaside?'

'Both, if you like. Where is he now?'

'I think he's at home. He telephoned from there before I came to see you and he said he'd be coming in first thing tomorrow morning, so I suppose he's still here.'

'And did he call you every day?'

'Every morning, even when he was at the seaside.'

'You told him, then, that I'd been to see you?'

'You said I should tell him, that you'd be coming back . . .'

'That's all right. I remember what I said. Try to remember now exactly what you said—I mean about Clementina. Did you tell him I said she'd been murdered?'

'I think so . . . I suppose I must have done—but what's that got to do with—'

'Give me those addresses.'

He wrote them down. He'd got what he wanted without waiting until tomorrow. But he still had to collect that warrant and, for all he knew, the respectable grey-haired man who now had a name but who was always one step ahead could be driving towards the nearest border.

CHAPTER 11

'Not bad . . .' Di Nuccio couldn't help commenting as he followed the Marshal into the spacious entrance hall. In front of them was a broad marble staircase with a red carpet running up the centre and a group of tall potted plants on the first landing. 'It looks more like a hotel . . .'

'Can I help you?'

The window of the porter's lodge was on their left and a thin face was peering out at them over the top of a newspaper. The Marshal walked over and said: 'Fantechi.'

'They're away.'

Ignoring this, the Marshal asked, 'They own their flat, don't they?'

'They all do in this condominium. It belonged to his first wife.' He gave a sign to Di Nuccio and they both stepped inside the lodge, out of sight.

'How long have you been here?'

'Me? Fifteen years . . .' He folded the newspaper and looked from the Marshal's blank face to Di Nuccio's belligerent one. 'Is something up?'

'Yes,' said the Marshal, without bothering to tell him what. 'Which floor?'

'They're away, I tell you.' He tailed off as the Marshal's blank stare was suddenly replaced by a dangerous one. 'It's the third floor—listen, I'm not getting myself into trouble for anybody. It was him told me not to—in any case, it's true there's nobody up there.'

'Where's he gone?'

'Only to get cigarettes. He rang down and asked me to go but I can't leave the place unattended, my wife's not here. So you see it was true when I said there was nobody—'

'We'll wait. What's his wife like, the second one?'

'His wife? Listen, I can't—'

'You can't what?'

'Nothing. I'm just saying . . . I don't think I should be giving information without people's permission.'

'No? I didn't ask you for any information, I asked for your opinion. What's she like?'

'Well . . . young.'

'How young?'

'No spring chicken but I bet she's more than twenty years younger than him. I'd give her thirty-five or thirty-six, and flashy with it, you know what I mean?'

'No.'

'Well, he's careful not to let her out of his sight much and I don't blame him.'

'No? But he has let her out of his sight. She's at the seaside and he's here, even though he told you to say he wasn't and not to let anybody up. If I were you I wouldn't get on the wrong side of the law for him.'

'What's he done?'

'Who said he'd done anything?'

'No need to, is there, if you're here?' He hadn't said a word against Fantechi but the Marshal, observing his sharp face and steady eye, reckoned he had every one of the residents summed up and didn't much care for this one.

'You're married, you said?'

'Who, me?'

'Yes, you. You said your wife wasn't here.'

'What's that got to do with Fantechi? All right, I'm married. Satisfied?'

'Where's your wife? Does she go out to work?'

'She works here. There's the stairs to clean, for a start. That's not a man's job.'

'Plenty of porters do it.

'Not me.' A man's job was evidently sitting for hours behind the lodge window, reading the paper, listening to the radio, and keeping a sharp eye on the comings and goings in the building.

'I imagine she works for some of the residents, then, as well.'

'Two.'

'Including Fantechi?'

'Yes, if you want to know. Listen, what's he done? You're not saying but I'm nobody's fool and I've heard things, too. Nobody pulls the wool over my eyes.'

'What sort of things?'

'Eh?'

'What have you heard?'

'I'm not one to poke my nose into other people's business when there's no call, but if you really want to know I've heard he's been inside. His story was he'd been abroad on business, but the way I heard it he was away doing his little bit of time after a fraudulent bankruptcy. Once his first wife died—and she was a real lady, not like—Good evening, madam.'

The Marshal turned to see a smallish, elderly woman, thickly plastered with make-up, very expensively dressed, pulling a miniature dog on a leash. Her response to the porter's greeting was a very faint inclination of the head. Even so, he got up hurriedly and went across to push the lift button for her. She stood waiting without acknowledging this little service. When he came back he looked rather shamefaced and shrugged his shoulders. 'Top floor right, that one. Well, what should I care? She gives me a fat tip every month. It's all show. Comes from some old aristocratic family but most of the money's gone. Even so, you can take it from me, it's not money they can't do without, it's being kowtowed to. They can't stand being ignored or treated like ordinary human beings. I'm pretty sure she can't really afford the tip she gives me but she'd be willing to go without food if she had to so long as she's treated better than the rest of them in the building. You can imagine what she thinks of Fantechi's tarty wife, looks straight through her.'

'You don't think much of any of them, do you?'

'Why should I? If you knew what my wife has to put up with. Dressing up in a fancy apron and cap to serve tea and cheap biscuits to the silly old bag's friends every Thursday afternoon, not to mention putting up with the Fantechi woman who puts on all the airs and graces of a countess though she's nobody and like as not no better than she should be either. That sort can always get somebody to foot the bill as long as they have their looks, but she'd better watch out for herself when she loses them. Who'll put up with her then?' That was surely a remark from his wife's repertoire. 'As it is, they fight like cat and dog. The night before they left for the seaside they were at it. He'd been out on some jaunt with his business friends and they all came back here after midnight and carried the party on. When my wife went up in the morning there were plates and glasses strewn all over the shop and her ladyship was screaming the place down. He was doing his best to keep his end up.

'*"What do we have a cleaner for? Let her see to it!"*

'*"It's not my maid's job to clear up after your disgusting friends!"*

'"My maid"! And who paid for her maid, as she calls the wife? Not to mention the four fur coats and the fancy new villa at the seaside. The minute she didn't get what she wanted she'd threaten to leave him, and, between you and me, he'd be better off—Here he is. That's him.' The porter leaned forward a little as if to call out, but the Marshal put a heavy hand on his shoulder and quietened him.

Fantechi crossed the entrance hall without raising his eyes. He was wearing a white silk suit but it was as crumpled as if he'd slept in it. His grey hair was brushed but he hadn't shaved that day and his eyes were dazed. He pushed the button for the lift and stood with his back to the lodge waiting for it, his shoulders tense, his hands clenching and unclenching.

The Marshal and Di Nuccio emerged.

'Signor Fantechi?'

The Marshal had been sure he would make for the exit where he surely had a car parked, so that when Fantechi flung himself towards the staircase without even a glance at them, both he and Di Nuccio were surprised enough to allow him a head start. They recovered and ran after him, their footsteps almost soundless on the thick staircarpet. Di Nuccio went ahead of the Marshal, who was soon panting but not unduly worried. The man was unlikely to be armed and where could he go to earth except in his own flat, even if Di Nuccio didn't reach him first. Di Nuccio didn't reach him. Apart from the start he'd had, Fantechi had fear to help him. When the Marshal reached the third floor left Di Nuccio had his finger on the bell and was holding it there.

A dog began to bark and then to howl. A very large dog by the sound of it. They heard it crash against the inside of the door. The bell seemed as loud as a fire alarm but that and the howling of the dog brought no one out on the landing or stairs to see what was amiss. Apart from the old lady on the top floor, the building must have been empty. They were all on holiday. Di Nuccio stopped ringing and began hammering. They heard a window or a glass door slam and break inside the flat and the dog went pounding away still bellowing. The lift doors opened and the porter appeared.

'Open this door,' the Marshal told him.

'I shouldn't—'

'You've got the keys. Open it.' It looked a good deal too solid for the Marshal to want to try breaking it down.

'It's your responsibility . . .' But he produced his bunch of keys and let them in.

The dog came bounding out of the darkness in the shuttered flat and leapt at the Marshal's shoulders, almost bowling him over.

'Giulio! Down, boy! Giulio! Don't worry, he knows me.'

The porter grabbed the great beast by the collar. 'Calm down, boy, calm down. It's all right, I've been feeding him and taking him out while they're away, so . . . quiet, Giulio! Good dog.'

But the other two had left him, striding forward to where one shaft of light sliced the darkness. It came from a bedroom on the left of a broad corridor. A french window was open. Broken glass lay on the floor around it and a muslin curtain was moving very slightly in the air.

They walked out on to the balcony overlooking a courtyard with a palm tree growing in the centre of it. Fantechi lay face down on the flags below with one arm trapped beneath his body and the other flung out as though to ward people away from his crushed head. But no one came near the body and the pool of blood around the head spread undisturbed in the evening light.

'I'll call an ambulance,' Di Nuccio said.

The Marshal didn't move. After a moment a faint click distracted him and he looked upwards to see the white powdered face of the old lady looking down from the highest window on the right. She was clutching the little dog close to her and when she saw what was below she retreated quickly and closed her shutters. The Marshal went on staring out. The porter appeared below near the body and, after bending over it, looked up and made a negative sign to indicate there was nothing to be done, but the Marshal didn't respond. He was staring down but without really seeing the body on the flags. He saw Clementina, not lying dead but dancing round and round in the square, her face red with food and wine, happy on the last night of her unhappy life. He saw Bruno, at times, too, bouncing to attention with a click of his well-polished heels.

'For God's sake, Bruno, don't do that behind my back! You'll give me a heart attack!'

'Sorry, sir.'

'And don't call me sir!'

Then another image came into his head, of someone he'd never seen at all. A woman lying, not face down like the man down there but on her back, her smoothly oiled and tanned body catching the last rays of the sun before it sank beyond the sea's horizon.

'Ah, Marshal! Good morning!'

'Look who's here!'

'Lovely day, isn't it?'

'Nice to see you again, Marshal. What will you have?'

The Marshal faced Franco across the bar. He hadn't expected such a welcome. Even people he'd never seen before were smiling in his direction over their breakfasts. Perhaps the grateful coolness of the misty September morning had something to do with the general cheerfulness. The city had begun to bustle again as if set going by clockwork, and the passing traffic added its noise and smells to those of the teeming bar. The butcher came in, fat and smiling in his white apron, having left his wife in charge while he grabbed a quick coffee, and he, too, greeted the Marshal and laid a big red hand on his shoulder.

'I hope your wife's not going to desert us completely now her own shops are open again.'

'I don't think she will. She enjoyed coming here. It's just that lately she's been spending all her spare time at the hospital.'

'With that youngster? Did he never come round?'

'Not yet.' And today his parents would arrive. As soon as the doctors had decided it might help if someone were there talking to him, in spite of his lack of response, the Marshal's wife had spent hours by his bedside. He knew she was glad to do it and felt better for no longer being at a loose end without her own boys. It's an ill wind . . .

'You must tell her,' the butcher said, 'that we'll always be glad to see her. I like a customer who understands what she's buying. Will you have a coffee with me?'

'Whatever the Marshal has is on me,' interrupted Franco, smiling and nodding his large head. 'Nobody's paying for his coffee—what about a drop of something in it?'

'No, no,' the Marshal said, 'just a coffee.'

When it came it tasted better than any coffee had for months.

The sky seemed higher and the filtered light was alive and shimmering. He could breathe better and the traffic, which everyone complained about all year round, was as cheerful as a brass band in the sunshine. Bruno must get better; it couldn't be otherwise.

'Something to chew?' suggested Franco, who was busy making toast.

'No, no. I'm fine as I am.'

His idea in calling here had been to give Franco a gentle hint about his after-hours activities being known about, but now he was here he didn't feel like striking a sour note that would spoil the atmosphere. He could always call some other time. Whether his wife would still come and shop down here he couldn't say, but he himself would surely drop in for a coffee at Franco's whenever he found himself in the neighbourhood. He liked these people, Franco and his big placid wife especially.

'Just fancy,' Franco was saying, 'you finding out about Clementina losing her husband and child in the flood and all these years she never said a word.'

The Marshal became aware of being surrounded by curious and expectant faces and realized what was expected of him in return for his coffee. He told them as much as he could, enough to make them feel they were in the know without touching on matters that were *sub judice*.

'It was quite something,' he finished up, 'learning what the flood really meant. I was still down in Sicily then—of course we saw it on the news but it didn't mean so much from a distance.'

'Just as well for you you weren't here,' the butcher said,

laughing, 'though you'd have been all right where you are. The Pitti Palace was never under water because of having that slope up to it.'

'That's right,' piped up a tiny, paint-splashed man, 'we got our bread given out there. You'd have been all right.'

'Even so,' the Marshal said, 'it's amazing to me how you managed.'

'We hadn't much choice,' Franco said, 'and anyway it'd take more than half a million tons of mud to get this lot down.'

'It got Dino down!' the butcher said and everybody laughed.

'Who's Dino?'

'You haven't met him,' Franco explained, 'he was shut in August. He has the take-away roasting place just further down on the left.'

'I've never seen him cry before or since,' said the butcher, 'but he cried that day when he dug out that whole loin of beef—a beauty it was, I sold it to him myself and he'd already paid me, that was what was the killer! He had it in his arms like it was his only child. "Not a slice off it," he kept saying, wading round with it in his wellingtons. "Not a slice off it and roasted to perfection." In the end he flung it back in the mud and held his arms up to the sky, roaring at the Almighty, "I'll never forgive You for this!"'

They pulled out many similar anecdotes for his entertainment and the Marshal kept the sadder details of Clementina's story to himself, leaving them at last, reluctantly, to their noisy breakfast.

He had other calls to make. He'd already done the first job of the day by calling on Linda Rossi who was more astonished than pleased at their good fortune, coming as it did in the wake of so much tragedy.

'Then we don't have to leave? You're sure?'

'Quite sure. Nothing will happen for the time being. It'll take quite a long time for the Finance Police to untangle

Fantechi's affairs. After that there'll be a lot of debts to be paid off and most, if not all of his property will be sold. As sitting tenants you'll have first refusal, so if you can possibly manage it . . . The price won't be high, they'll want a quick sale.'

'Perhaps my mother can help us . . . I can't thank you enough. I felt so guilty about bothering you with our problems when you had so much on your mind. I hope you'll forgive us, we were desperate.'

'You did quite right. It's part of my job.'

And he'd said that with some satisfaction because it *was* part of his job, and if a certain prosecutor didn't see it that way he'd do better to work with the police. He'd be no loss to the Carabinieri. The police only had crime to worry about and wouldn't waste time on 'other people's little problems'.

Not that there'd been any more remarks of that sort. The man had been positively subdued at their last meeting. He'd asked after Bruno. There was no getting away from the fact that if the Marshal had been allowed to go about things the way they should have been gone about he'd have had the keys in his pocket that night. He must have realized, too, that but for the Marshal's attention to people's little problems the case wouldn't have been concluded and he himself free to leave for his holidays on schedule. 'The best of luck to him,' muttered the Marshal, 'and let's hope he comes back a reformed character.' He was walking back towards the Pitti, his car now being under repair. Thank God it was September.

The rest of his morning was spent on paperwork to do with Clementina's case. Its conclusion was a visit to the hospital. And if Bruno's parents had arrived, then that too would have to be faced.

He found his wife sitting on a hard chair outside the door of Bruno's room. That could mean only one thing.

'They're here?'

'Go in. They're waiting for you.' Why should she look at

him so oddly? Had they already said something? He wondered whether it wouldn't be better to wait here until they came out. It didn't seem proper, somehow, to talk to them with the boy lying there. But his wife said again, 'Go in.'

He opened the door.

Three pairs of eyes turned to look at him and he stopped dead on the threshold. A man and woman were seated on either side of the bed, and in between them Bruno sat bolt upright, grinning.

'Marshal!'

He walked slowly forward and held out his hand.

'So I've decided,' announced Bruno after a quarter of an hour during which no one else had managed to get a word in edgeways.

Even now, all the Marshal could manage to get out was, 'Well . . .'

'They'll send me to Rome first, won't they?'

'I . . .'

'You'll be able to give me a reference. What will they think about this scrape, though, that's what I've been wondering? I can't make up my mind whether it'll go against me or whether they'll give me a medal. What do you think?'

'I . . .'

'I wouldn't mind getting a medal. Anyway I was thinking about it all this morning while they were tapping and testing and telling me I was a phenomenon and I've made up my mind. No university for me. As soon as I'm back on my feet I'll apply for a commission!'

The two parents looked helplessly at the Marshal but, as usual, Bruno had left him speechless.

The Marshal's next call was the last of the day. The last of the case. The rest was more paperwork.

'And how I'll get through it all I don't know . . .' The passenger sitting beside him in the van made no answer. He took up a good deal of room but he created no disturbance, sitting bolt upright and staring out at the traffic ahead, and the low sun. They turned in at the gates of the asylum and followed the signs to the administration block.

'Out you get,' the Marshal said, 'we're here.'

Mannucci seemed pleased to see the Marshal again and pushed aside a mountain of old files by way of welcome. He did give a puzzled glance at the Marshal's companion but made no comment.

'Sit down and tell me all.'

'There isn't much to tell that you won't already have seen in the papers. I must say, though, I was a bit surprised . . .' He tailed off, embarrassed at himself.

'Surprised at what?'

'Well, I suppose I should have thought of it myself but I wondered at your not thinking, given the dates, of the flood having put Clementina in here. You're the expert . . .'

'That's right, I'm the expert. I wasn't here then, Marshal, but I have all the figures for the period if you're interested in seeing them. We've never had fewer admissions here than during the period following the flood. You don't believe me? I can show you.'

'No, no, if you say so . . .'

'I do say so, and I also say that our Clementina was already severely unbalanced to have reacted like she did, though I can't prove that to you, I'm just surmising.'

'You're right,' the Marshal said. 'I happen to know she was.'

'There's nothing like a physical disaster to bring people to their senses. There was a doctor used to work here who always said, "Drop any one of these patients in the middle of a desert or a jungle and leave them to it and they'll come to their senses within minutes and start fighting to stay alive." He was talking about short-term patients, of course, not the sort of people who are left in here now. No, it would never have crossed my mind to connect her with the flood once somebody had been good enough to remove the evidence. What I should have thought of was her legal rights—but not knowing there was any money to speak of . . . That sister of hers was a foolish woman to trust her husband like that, by the sound of it.'

'I don't know. I somehow think he was more weak than evil. He did Clementina no harm until this new wife came on the scene. That's a hard one.'

'You've talked to her? It said in the papers she's made herself scarce.'

'So she has. That's how I came to collect my friend here . . .' And his big eyes strayed to his companion who was now crouched on the floor by his side, his equally large eyes looking from the Marshal to Mannucci and back. 'That's what I came for, to bring him.'

Mannucci laughed and then stared. 'He looks sane enough to me—and even if he's not, we don't admit patients here now.'

'You're admitting this one.'

'You're not serious, are you?'

'I was never more serious in my life. His name's Giulio. And before you say anything else, just think of what the Press will make of it. You said you could never get much attention from them and you never will, either, unless you start thinking like they think. You'll never get them to care about the poor creatures you look after here.'

'But—'

'Giulio has just witnessed the suicide of his master and been abandoned by his mistress. His master was responsible for the murder of one of your ex-patients and would you believe, just by chance, Giulio's turned up here. Can't you see the headlines? "Dog Seeks Asylum!" There's murder, suicide, a money scandal and lots of sentimental interest with the dog. What's more, Giulio's not going to be a patient, he's going to work here, so I hope you're ready with your facts and figures on how short-staffed you are.'

'I'm ready, all right. No problem there, but—'

'You'd better come with me.'

The sun was very low. The tops of the trees were already darkening against the sky but the lawn was still touched with a rosy golden light and Angelo's bare feet below his too-short trousers were curled in the last warmth of the grass. His head was down on his knees but turned to one side so that he could look up at them, and his eyes were alight with pleasure.

Giulio shifted along the bench and put his big head down to lick Angelo's face.

'Stroke him,' suggested the Marshal.

'Can I? Can I stroke him? Can . . .' He rocked upwards and then down again, burying his face. Then he sat bolt upright and put his arm round the huge dog without looking at him. Giulio squashed right up against him, panting happily.

Angelo kept his shining eyes fixed on the Marshal.

'Is he sitting with me? Is he . . .'

'Yes. He'll sit with you all the time if you feed him. Will you remember to feed him? We'll tell the sister to give you food for him but you must give it to him yourself. You can take him for walks, as well. I'll leave you his lead.'

'I . . . I . . . I just want him to sit with me, to sit—is he frightened?'

'No, no. He's a big dog. He's not frightened of anything.'

'He's not frightened.'

The dog put a heavy paw on Angelo's knee.

'Look! Look . . . he . . .'

Angelo could no longer speak. The Marshal thought he might be going to cry, his eyes were so bright. He turned and walked away to where Mannucci stood waiting for him in the long shadow of a cypress tree.

THE END